Laura,
Your friendship is
amazing, Thank You!
love,
Susanne
and
Tobie

GRANOLA, MN

by Susanne Aspley

Books by Susanne Aspley
Ladyboy and the Volunteer

Bilingual children's books:
I Know How to Hola
I Know How to Ni Hao
I Know How to Bon Jour

www.aspleywrites.com

Dedicated to
SGT Karry Jean Lenon

CHAPTER ONE

What begins as an ordinary day, the way most days do in Granola, veers a little off course when the first customer, a young black man, walks into the hardware store.

Don't see them around our Wonder bread town much, if at all. Maybe he took a wrong turn off the interstate and is just in need of directions. But he doesn't look lost.

"Good morning, ma'am. I need a new furnace filter," he says quietly, walking toward the counter.

"Uh," I answer.

Looking at a small scrap of paper in his hand, he adds, "A size 20 by 25 by 1, please. Something that's good with allergens because we have two kitty cats at home."

"Sure. I'll show you where they are," I answer, skirting out from behind the counter.

I lead him to the side of the store where the filters are lined up neatly like beloved, library books. After pulling the correct filter off the shelf, I turn around and bash him across the face with it.

"Owie!" I scream.

"Why are you the one saying owie? *You're* the one that hit *me*," he asks, stumbling backwards.

"I meant to say sorry! Gosh, I didn't mean to do that. Dang it, sorry. Are you okay?"

"It's all good," he answers, rubbing his nose. He then casually checks his fingers for any blood. "And yes, that looks like the filter we use," he adds.

"Do you need anything else?" I ask, flustered.

We stand in silence for a few seconds, both staring at each other in guarded fascination. He has the darkest of eyes, opening into an unfamiliar world.

He gently puts his hand on the filter, but I don't let go. Clutching it so hard, I leave fingerprint indentions on the cardboard sides.

"No, this is all," he says.

He tugs. I tug back. He tugs again.

"Alrighty then," I sigh, finally thrusting the filter towards him. I then quickly scoot back to the register, wanting the safety of the counter between us.

I ring it up.

"$11.49, please," I mumble.

He pulls a crumpled twenty dollar bill from his Levi's, smoothing it out before handing it to me. It's still warm from being in his pocket. After tucking the bill into the register, I quickly flick the drawer shut.

"You can keep the change if you want," he says, eyebrows raised toward the register.

"I don't want to keep your change."

"You just did."

A hot and heavy blush flushes over my face.

I open the register again and push the change slowly across the counter towards him. Looking up, I notice he doesn't really blink. It's more like both of his eyes wink at the same time. But slightly off.

Then, I flat out stare at him because I want to figure out which eye actually starts the blink first.

He does it again. It's the left one. Definitely the left one. A slight smile slides across his lips.

I smile back, then flinch as if caught gazing directly into the burning, high noon sun.

"I just moved here. My name's Toby. What's yours?"

Pointing to my name tag, I answer, "Allison. Allison Couch. Welcome to Whitehead's Hardware store."

"Nice to meet you," he says. And just like that, walks out the door with his bent and dented furnace filter.

I'm left twirling, like a kindergarten girl in a new Disney princess dress. I hurry back to Mr. Whitehead's office to ask if he knows who this guy might be.

"Toby? Toby Davenport?" Mr. Whitehead answers excitedly, pushing back from his computer. "Why didn't you tell me he was here, damn it?"

"I just did."

"He must've just got out of the Army. That young man is a national treasure. Was awarded the Silver Star. He saved a lot of lives over in Afghanistan. Very proud of him. He's a real war hero, I'll tell you that much," he answers.

I shove my hands in my red apron as he continues, "Hell yeah. Everyone at the American Legion has been talking about this fellow moving here. I believe he's home living with his mom now."

"Wait, is his mother Mrs. D, the new principal over at Grimoire High School?"

"Yep, that's her. Real nice lady. She bought the dutch colonial over on Chestnut Street. Nobody sees her much because she's always busy at the school."

Nodding my head, I shut his office door and go start the popcorn. Best get back to work, as I'm sure I had my excitement for the day.

Last year, I told Mr. Whitehead we should buy a movie theater style popcorn maker and keep it in the rear of the store. People would then have to walk all the way to the back to get the popcorn. Maybe on their way, they'd see the ice scrapers or ugly garden gnomes, remembering they need a few more. Minnesotans can never have too many ice scrapers or ugly garden gnomes.

Mr. Whitehead thought it was a great idea and bought the machine the next day. The buttery scent mixes in nicely with the distinct hardware store scent of fertilizer, metal tools and fresh lumber. Plus, it masks the stink of paint thinner that someone accidentally kicked over awhile ago.

The second customer of the morning is Jungle Jim. He shuffles in every day as if he's wearing cement shoes, and every day Mr. Whitehead emerges from the back to argue with him.

See, Mr. Whitehead served in Vietnam. And even though Jimmy was drafted about the same time, he never ended up in the war. Yet, he likes to imagine he did.

Jimmy smells like a bag of old pennies. In the summer, he wears wrinkled, Hawaiian shirts along with mismatched tube socks and flip flops. In the winter, he slogs through the snow in an olive drab army parka and duct tape-wrapped moon boots. His hair is limp spaghetti.

Crumbs from his breakfast, or maybe supper the night before, dangle from the ends of his sticky mustache.

"Morning, Allison," he says.

"Good morning, Jimmy."

After wandering back to get some popcorn, he picks up a box of heavy duty garbage bags and waves them in the air toward me.

"Hey, Allison. Did I ever tell you about the body bags over in 'Nam?"

Mr. Whitehead barges out of his office, grumbling, "Jimmy, you need to knock that 'Nam nonsense off."

"But I was there!" he answers.

"No, you were not there, for cryin' out loud. What is wrong with you? I'll tell you what's wrong with you. You drink too much, that's what's wrong with you."

"I was on Meatball Hill! Gooks had us surrounded!"

"No, you weren't. The Army stationed you in Thailand to help run a government approved whorehouse for all the G.I.s on R & R. You drank mekong whiskey with ladyboys on the beach all day."

"That's not true. I was in the shit."

Mr. Whitehead takes a deep, annoyed breath and says, "You weren't in the shit. You weren't anywhere near the shit. You were so far from the shit, you probably couldn't even smell the shit."

"How would you know?"

"Because I was there. You weren't."

"Whatever," Jimmy mutters. He drops his shoulders and slinks out the door like a scolded dog.

Mr. Whitehead shakes his head, says "God Bless 'murica," under his breath, then returns to his office.

Granola, with a population of almost 2,000, is located just up the road from the county seat of Grimoire, and further over from the city of St. Cloud.

Once a small farm town with just the basic services, it's now being developed by slick men from the Twin Cities buying up corn fields and cow pastures. Huge, slapped-together homes are popping up on elaborate culdesacs. Young parents, hoping to raise wholesomely spoiled children in the country but still commute to St. Cloud, are snatching them up.

Whitehead's Hardware is the only remaining stand-alone building with it's own parking lot, next to the new, corporately owned strip mall. The developers are constantly calling to buy his building. They want to raze it in order to add on a Bigbucks Coffee shop.

But Mr. Whitehead is not selling. He refuses with not just a 'No', but a "Over my dead body no!' reply every time Mr. Clancy, Granola's building inspector, comes in to negotiate with him.

Mr. Clancy is as shady as the Amazon jungle. He invested tons of money into the strip mall and is on the board of the developer's corporation.

That's why he writes up all these violation notices about our roof, or the siding, or the handicapped space out front, or the height of the shelves, trying to get the building condemned. Then, Mr. Whitehead would be forced to sell the store to him.

However, the infractions never hold up in the Grimoire County Court. In fact, Judge Severson at the courthouse apologizes to Mr. Whitehead for having to deal with it all, dismissing the violations every time.

So, Whitehead's Hardware remains the last Alamo of Granola's original downtown stores. Or, as Mr. Clancy likes to put it, 'the last stubborn donkey standing in the way of progress.'

~~~

After lunch, Mr. Clancy wobbles in like a hard-boiled egg. His face reminds me of an unbuttered piece of toast with a jelly glob for a nose. He's looking for Mr. Whitehead.

"Mr. Clancy is here to see you," I call towards the rear of the store.

"Tell that sumbitch to get lost. I'm not selling," Mr. Whitehead yells back. I hear him kick his office door shut along with the click of the lock.

"Hmph," grunts Mr. Clancy. "I need to talk to him about the sidewalk out there. There's a two inch shift differential between some of the slabs, and that, Miss Couch, is against city code. It's a community safety issue. A public hazard. Someone might trip and fall. So tell that boss of yours when he's done locking himself in his room like an angst-ridden teen girl to call me. "

"The only one that trips and falls out there is Jungle Jim because he's an angst-ridden drunk!" Mr. Whitehead yells from his office.

"I repeat, tell your boss to call me," Mr. Clancy says, grimacing.

"I'll do that," I mumble, trying to sound believable.

"Thanks, dear. Public safety is my number one priority, you know," Mr. Clancy answers.

"I'm sure it is."

"Great," he says as he squints his eyes towards the ceiling, furrowing his fat brow. He's obviously snooping for another infraction to write us up about.

"Allison. Why is there a wet spot on the ceiling? Is that a leak? Did you have a water pipe break?"

"Nope. Not at all. What happened was I accidentally shook my pop and it spurted up there. It was a Sprite that got real fizzy when I opened it," I answer.

Mr. Clancy slams both hands on the counter and glowers at me. He's one of those people that would flip over the Monopoly board after being caught cheating with six hotels on Boardwalk, five on Marvin Gardens and even one on Reading Railroad.

"There you go again, Miss Couch. Lying to me."

"Not really," I mutter.

He swipes on his phone to take a photo of the ceiling, then says, "I always knew you were an odd bird from a strange flock. And don't even get me started on that grandma of yours. I'm an inch away from getting her hauled off to the cuckoo's nest where she belongs."

I refuse to answer, which makes him even more gaseous. His face turns wine red and the gin blossoms on his nose bubble to the surface.

"How does this dump even stay in business," he sneers more than asks.

He then whirls around and marches out the door like he has somewhere to go and something even more important to do.

As soon as he leaves, Mr. Whitehead clomps out of his office, sputtering, "Sumbitch."

We watch as Mr. Clancy backs his glistening white Mercedes out from the handicapped parking space.

"I can't stand that man," I say. "I feel like spraying myself with Lysol after talking to him."

"Don't listen to what that blowhard says about your grandma, Allison."

My parents died close together when I was a very young child. I still live with Grandma, who took me in so long ago. Now, it's my turn to take care of her ever since she was diagnosed with dementia and manic depression.

She's always been a bit on the wild side, plus the after effects of the bad, or what she would call, 'the good' drugs of the 60's, she's flown the coop to batshit crazy.

Grandma sometimes gets whacked up on her meds, so I have to dole them out to her carefully. If I forget to hide the pills, she'll take another one, and forget again, and take a few more during the day.

The only thing worse than Grandma taking too many or too few pills is when she walks down to Liquor Pig and buys a gigantic jug of Captain Morgan. Pirates and antidepressants are not a good mix for Grandma. Or for anyone, I imagine.

Apparently, Grandma knows when Porky's not around, and there's a new clerk in front. She walks in like nothing to it and gets her bottle. Then, she becomes drunk crazy, which is far, far worse than plain and simple crazy.

A few years ago, I told Mr. Whitehead that Grandma sneaks down to Liquor Pig and buys booze. He went over there and told Porky O'Brien, the owner, "Don't sell that old lady nothin'. And don't let her sweet talk you into doing it, either!"

Mr. Whitehead is pushing seventy years old. When I first met him, his eyes were blue, bright and clear. Now, they swirl with milky cataracts.

His wife, Betty, died about five years ago. His two grown sons and their families live in Grimoire, about ten miles away. One runs a McDonald's franchise there and the other works at the local TV station. But much to Mr. Whitehead's disappointment, neither want anything to do with hardware.

On my graduation day from high school, I walked down here to ask for a summer job. Mr. Whitehead told me to come in the next morning at 'oh nine hundred' to start work. Nearly eight years later, I'm still here and wouldn't dream of being anywhere else. I can't imagine his, mine, our hardware store being sold. Demolished. Turned into a Bigbucks, or take-and-bake pizza joint.

"I'm not selling this store to him. It's the darn principle of the thing. This town needs hardware. But you gotta know by now, this store is my life. My entire life," Mr. Whitehead says.

"I wish I could buy it from you, so when you die, I could carry on the business myself," I say. It's his life, but it's my life too.

He nods quietly. After a few seconds, he asks, "Do you mean that, dear?"

"Of course I do. I don't know how to make the keys yet, but I know everything else. Accounting, inventory, budgeting, customer service, you taught me everything, Mr. Whitehead. I don't want you to sell this place as much as you don't want to sell it."

"Well, I'll be a twisted sister. You really want to buy my store and run it for me? I know your parents left you a pile of money in the bank after they passed, but I wouldn't ask for much from you."

"Of course. But the problem is, you're not dead yet. And I don't want you to be dead yet either," I answer.

"No, I'm not. But you know, I can't take it with me."

"No, you can't."

"Have you ever seen a hearse pulling a U-Haul trailer to the cemetery?"

"No, but still…"

"Still what?"

"You still haven't shown me how to make the keys."

"Yep, you're right, I haven't yet. I will though, when I'm ready. That's all," he answers, walking back to his office and shutting the door softly behind him.

CHAPTER TWO

The next morning, I pedal my bike to work.

Passing by the fields, it's hard to believe this lush countryside turns into frozen tundra every winter, reaching sometimes thirty below zero. When Laura Ingalls Wilder and the rest of those pioneers built their little houses here, they must've settled at this sultry time, long before the yearly deep freeze. They were either very brave or incredibly foolish.

I lean my bike against the rear of Whitehead's Hardware and go in what he calls, 'the employee's entrance', even though it's just the back screen door and I'm the only employee.

"Good morning, Mr. Whitehead. Are you gonna show me how to make the keys?" I ask, like I do every day.

Mr. Whitehead thumbs through receipts on his clipboard, then glances at me, smiling. His eyelids lower and raise with effort, like there's a whole New York Broadway team of stagehands hoisting them up and down.

"Not today, Allison. I have some deliveries coming in. This, that and whatnot. Would you mind staying in front?"

Like every day, of course I don't mind.

I sign my timecard which is kept in a metal file box nailed to the wall. It's the only time card in there, and the only one that's ever been.

Above the box is a plastic wall clock with a bulletin board next to it. Tacked on neatly is Mr. Whitehead's business license. There's also some crap he printed off the internet to remind his employees (me) to wash their hands after using the bathroom and how to call an 800 number about sexual harassment in the work place.

I tie on my red apron and start the popcorn, not noticing when he walks in. When I turn around, he's standing right in front of me. It's Toby.

"Good morning," he says, smiling cautiously.

He probably thinks I'm going to hit him in the face with something again.

"Uh, hi," I answer.

Nervously, I take a blue and white striped bag out from the bottom of the machine and fill it to the top.

"You want some?" I ask, squeezing the bag so hard that most of the kernels cascade onto the floor.

"Sure," he answers, taking what's left of the crinkled sack of popcorn.

"Sure," I parrot.

"My mom sent me back here today for some light bulbs," he says. "100 watt bulbs. And she doesn't want those energy saving curly ones. She says those are too dim and we can save the rainforest and the whales some other time. She wants the *real* light bulbs."

"That sounds like something my grandma would say," I nod, and quickly walk to aisle two.

He follows.

I hand him a box of four, 'real' light bulbs. He puts his hand on the box, but I don't let go quite yet. For some reason, I want to feel *his* energy. He pulls on the box a little harder, but I still don't let go.

Slowly, his mouth blooms into a beautiful smile. His lips are wide and plush. I wonder what it would be like to kiss him. But I never had much interest in boys.

And even less good luck.

One time in high school some jocks left a little Cornish game hen stuffed with used condoms on my porch just to be jerks. And then there was that horrible thing with Devin Clancy, Mr. Clancy's son. Not long after, I decided to stay away from all the assorted pricks in and around Granola.

Toby seems different though. Composed but warm, charming and curiously imperfect.

I let go of the lightbulbs.

"Anything else I can help you find?" I ask, shoving my hands in my red apron.

"Nope, that's it."

"Our Christmas stuff is fifty percent off in the summer. We still have NASCAR tree ornaments, Dale Earnhardt Jr. tree toppers and a few boxes of neon pink tinsel left."

"As tempting as all that sounds, I'm gonna have to pass," he answers.

"Well, if you change your mind, you know where to get them," I say, relaxing.

I lead him back to the register and ring him up. He gives me a ten dollar bill, and I remember to make the change this time.

"Thanks," he says. "I hope to see you again."

"I'm always here," I answer. "You know, if you ever want to see me again."

"That sounds like a deal, Ally."

No one has ever called me that. Ally. I like that name.

He walks out the door, crushed popcorn in one hand and the environmentally unfriendly bulbs in the other.

~~~

After work, I stop by Chub Grocery to get some milk and mac cheese for supper.

In the store, some humdrum lady stands in front of the dairy case for an eternity because she can't decide between strawberry or blueberry. She's someone you would only notice because she's in your way.

Finally, she grows determined.

She flings opens the door, a light puff of cold air drifts out. She slams it shut. This makes the inside of the door frost over and now she can't see anything.

Opening it again, the door knocks up against her shoulder. She starts touching just about every single yogurt cup. Turning them around in place, she squints at the ingredients, trying to decide the pleasures of full fat yogurt against the benefits of low calorie or the hedonism of Whips. Maybe she's feeling exotic and will choose the Greek variety, even though it tastes like paste.

Empty handed, she shuts the door again. She melts, like she's going to dissolve into tears.

Maybe she isn't even thinking about yogurt. Maybe she had to put her fourteen-year-old dog to sleep this morning. Now, she's only staring at the display and thankful she has some other decision to make other than when to put her sweet yellow lab down, grateful to do something with her hands other than petting her best friend for the last time.

She finally grabs the largest tub of non-fat plain yogurt off the bottom shelf, throws it in her cart with no mercy left, and moves on.

Afterwards, instead of riding straight home, I decide to detour six blocks out of the way to ride past Toby's house.

It's 5:30. I have three boxes of mac cheese hanging from a Chub bag off my handle bars and a gallon of sweating milk in my lap.

His home, creamy yellow with elaborate white trim and a gambrel roof, perches on the corner of Chestnut. The sidewalk looks new, but ancient oaks with great, twisted trunks lift millions of green leaves well above the brick chimney.

Toby's outside. I slow down to see what he's doing. He's not doing much, seemingly only looking up at one of the majestic trees. There's a swirl of wind that wraps through the yard, ushering in fresh bluegrass, ripe twigs and moist dirt.

I pedal up his driveway and awkwardly stop.

"Hi," I say, balancing all the groceries.

He smiles at me. I smile back. I'm starting to like smiling at him, and seeing his own.

"Whatcha doing?" I ask.

Rubbing a hand over his short, neat hair, he answers, "Nothing. Nothing much, really. Just looking for this albino squirrel. It's a cool little guy with red eyes. I haven't seen it the last few days so I'm starting to get worried about it. Why, what are you doing?"

"Going home to make supper."

He takes a few steps closer to me and does that wink-blink with his eyes.

I continue, "You wanna come over for supper? Making mac cheese. Kraft. You like Kraft?"

"Absolutely, that's my favorite."

His mother comes out of the house, wearing a tailored skirt, silk floral blouse and fuzzy slippers. She must've just got home from a summer meeting at the school.

"Ally, this is my mom. Mom, this is Ally," Toby says, looking at me, then at her.

"Nice to meet you, ma'am," I say.

"Nice to meet you too, Ally."

Her black hair is graying at the roots, tightly curled and short. Folding her arms across her gigantic chest, she leans back against the porch railing. Her eyes narrow, and although she doesn't say anything out loud, says to me in no uncertain terms...'Treat my son right. He's been through enough.'

I give her a weak wave. She seems to relax, but only a little, still keeping her eyes on me.

"Okay, we better go," I say.

I swallow. What the heck am I suppose to do now? Tell him to get on my handlebars along with the Chub bag of mac cheese?

Instead, I bolt off on my bike towards home as fast as I can. I can't believe I just invited this guy over.

He falls into a jog behind me.

Catching up, he asks, "You want me to grab that milk bottle for you?"

I pass it off to him and peddle like a ADHD hamster. I doubt he can keep up. But he does, so I pedal faster. I'm pumping at full speed but Toby is right beside me, running and running.

Within a few minutes, we reach my house. I get off my bike like it's no big deal, but out of breath. He's not, and grabs the bag of mac cheese off the handle bars for me.

"I doubt you've met my grandma yet," I say, my hand hesitating on the door knob. "Or Bob."

"I don't think so. Why?" he asks,curiously.

"Well, you're going to meet them now."

I take a deep breath and we walk in. Bob has *Wheel of Fortune* blasting.

Bob is Grandma's long-loved boyfriend. He's a retired snow plow driver. After forty years of pushing through blizzards at all hours, he deserves to take it easy.

He comes over to the house every day and watches game shows. Sometimes he yells at *Family Feud* or whatever else is on. Sometimes he makes himself and Grandma a sandwich. Sometimes he falls asleep on the couch. Sometimes he falls asleep while eating a sandwich.

Like a permanent light fixture, he now just comes with the house.

Breezing through the living room, I say, "Hi ya, Bob. This here is Toby."

Bob glances up, back to the TV, then yanks his head toward us again. He waves the remote in the air like the grand ol' flag on a windy day.

"Hey, hello, Toby. Heard you moved to Granola. Thank you for your service, son."

"You're welcome, sir. Thanks for having me over for supper," Toby answers as he sits down at the dining room table, making himself comfortable.

Grandma stomps up from the basement.

"Sit down, Grandma," I say, and guide her into a chair opposite of Toby. "I'll go start the mac cheese."

She rubs her eyes, realizing Toby is here, hands folded neatly on the placemat in front of him.

"You brought a lad home," she calls over her shoulder as I get out the big pot to start the noodles. "About damn time, Allison. I was beginning to think you turned into a gay homo or something like that."

"No, Grandma, I'm not."

"I'd love you anyway, even if you were as queer as a cross-eyed unicorn wearing rainbow tights," she says.

"Thanks, Grandma. Now moving on, this is Toby. He's joining us tonight," I call from the kitchen.

"Make him some mac cheese, Allison. And don't say nothin' weird to scare him off."

"I'm making it now," I answer.

Grandma puts one hand on Toby's and asks, "Well, aren't you a humdinger handsome young man. Are you related to Denzel Washington?"

"No, ma'am. We aren't all related just because we're black," he answers, cringing in a polite sort of way.

"My cousin married our second cousin," she says.

"We don't need to hear about the Olson family, Grandma," I say.

"That's why Grettie Olson's three kids look like the Snap, Crackle and Pop midgets," she adds.

"Our guest is going to get up and run out of the house and I wouldn't blame him one bit," Bob yells from the couch. "Change the subject, please."

Grandma sits back, smirks, and asks, "Toby, do you like Rice Krispies?"

"Ethylon," Bob screams. "Change the subject!"

"You have good posture, Toby. Allison never sits up straight. She's got a nice figure but she's a sloucher."

"Thank you, ma'am. Yes, she does. And no, I'm not a big fan of Rice Krispies."

"You like mac cheese?" she asks.

"Sure do, ma'am."

"You got a menthol?"

"You don't smoke no more," I say.

Grandma then whispers to Toby, "Got any Mary Jane?"

"Who?" he asks, shaking his head.

"You know, some Scooby Doobie?" she adds.

"You don't smoke that anymore either," I say, setting four glasses of milk on the table. About five minutes later, I bring out four, steaming bowls of mac cheese.

"Are you kidding me? You can't get 'mango smoothie' when the clue is a tropical drink, and you've got all the Os and Ms?" Bob says, wiggling the remote toward the contestant on the game show.

He then clicks the TV off and joins us at the table.

Grandma throws down her napkin, glares at Bob, and says, "You watch too much television. All that TV is going to give you eye cancer. You know what happens when you watch too much TV? Your head turns into mush. Corn grits for brains."

Bob shakes his head and starts eating. Toby hunkers down over his bowl, but Grandma is on a roll. "Ya know what else? Even worse, if you're not careful, you end up stupid and vote for Trump."

"Who said I voted for Trump, for gawd sakes?" Bob asks.

"Don't lie to me. I know you did. He's like that sticky shit on your fingers after eating cheese balls," she says.

Toby rubs his face. For a second I think he *is* considering getting up and running out of the house.

"Just relax, Grandma. It's going to be okay," I say. "Let's enjoy a nice meal together with our new guest and not talk about politics."

"You working now, son?" Bob asks, in a man-to-man tone, stabbing his fork at Toby. "You tell me if you need anything. I got connections in this town, you know."

And for good measure, he shakes his fork a few more times. A noodle flies off, landing on Grandma's lap.

"You ain't got no connections, Bob," Grandma says, throwing the noodle back at him. "Connections my butt."

"I do so have connections. I bet I can get him a job with the state, plowing roads."

"Bob ain't got no connections. If you want connections, Toby, you come see me. I got the connections," Grandma says, winking at him.

Toby seems to be taking my family in a good natured, fearless sort of way. Which is the only way to take them.

"Well, you let me know if I can help you get settled here in Granola," Bob says.

"Thanks, sir. I'm taking some online classes right now, just to keep me out of trouble until I start college this fall over at St. Cloud. I'll just commute back and forth and stay here living with my mom."

"What do you want to study at college?" Bob asks.

"Elementary Education. I'd like to be a gym teacher. That's how my mom started out."

"Allison never been to college," Grandma says, taking a big swig of milk.

"I know that, Grandma," I snip.

"You know how to drive, Toby?" Grandma asks.

"Yes ma'am, I sure do."

"You got your license?"

"Yes, I do."

"Allison never got her license either. She only got her learner's permit. Why don't you teach her how to drive? I got that nice car in the garage," she says, stuffing mac cheese into her mouth.

"It's insured, current tabs, everything. She's a beauty, too. '79 Buick Regal, four door, V8. Spoked hubcaps and a grill like a shark. I keep her well maintained," Bob says proudly. "But Allison has no interest in her."

"Just never needed to drive anywhere," I answer, trying to shove as much mac cheese into my mouth as well so I don't have to talk about this.

"She's stubborn, that's what she is," Bob adds, now pointing his fork at me.

"I'm not stubborn," I answer.

"You are. And you're scared."

"No, I'm not. I'm neither, Bob."

"Allison Couch, you are both."

"Nope. I'm not. Neither. None."

"Prove it, then," Bob says.

I throw down my fork and wad my napkin in my fist.

Toby smiles at me and says, "Sure, Ally, I'll teach you how to drive. After we eat, let's go for our first lesson."

~~~

Grandma's pristine Regal Sedan has been parked in our little garage ever since she lost her license years ago.

Holding the key in my hand delicately, like a frail, baby bird, I gingerly pass it to Toby. He takes it, grins, and does that wink-blink with his eyes at me. I creak the passenger's door open and plunk down on the vinyl seat.

"I'll drive us over to the Price Wackers parking lot and we'll start there," he says.

He plugs the key into the ignition. It starts right up like a boss. A gold chain wearin', disco dancin' boss. He backs the swanky beast out of the garage.

We drive toward the abandoned Price Wackers store on the opposite edge of town. I look at him out of the corner of my eye, but my eyes start to hurt. So, I turn my head and just stare at the side of his face instead.

"What?" he asks, giving me a confused look.

"Nothing," I answer and try to tune in on the radio.

I remember listening to Casey Kasem when Grandma used to drive this car, with me standing in the passenger seat as a child, fiddling with the silver knobs.

The only seatbelt I had was Grandma's right arm smacking me against the seat like a pinball flipper. She'd laugh and scream, "Holy hell hang on!" as we bumped, ran into, or drove over something.

Toby and I drive in silence for a minute, then I ask, "Will you do me a huge favor?"

"Is it illegal or immoral?" he asks, snickering.

"A little illegal, I suppose."

I don't think he was expecting I'd answer so honestly.

"How is something *a little* illegal?"

"Okay. Maybe a lot, a little illegal. But not immoral at all. In fact, I think the moral part would cancel out the illegal part."

"What are you trying to tell me?"

"I need some bolt cutters."

"Okay…and why?"

"Will you go to Whitehead's Hardware tomorrow and buy a pair of bolt cutters for me?"

Toby pulls back his lips, and asks, "Ally, you work there. Why don't you just borrow one? Or buy one? Or ask Mr. Whitehead if he has one?"

"Can't. Don't want Mr. Whitehead to think I'm up to something fishy."

"Why the heck do you need bolt cutters? And just by saying it's not fishy, makes it very fishy."

"It's not fishy at all. It's more dog related."

"Yeah?" he answers slowly, his voice raising an octave in just that one word.

"See, there's this dog."

"So?"

"I need to cut the chain from around her neck."

"And?"

"The owner, Mr. Johnson, keeps her chained up."

"Yeah?"

"I mean, chained up all day, every day. Every night, all night. And not just for days or nights, but for years. He cropped her ears nearly all the way off with garden shears when she was a young puppy, then sewed them up with wire thread."

"That's not right," he answers.

"Mr. Johnson once told me her name is Megadeath. But I call her Maple because she's so dang sweet. Golden brown with icicle blue eyes. I stop over there every morning on my way to work with dog treats and pet her through the fence."

"Where is she?"

"Behind Johnson's creepy house on Elm, the one with the windowless white van parked in the driveway."

"What kinda dog is it?"

"A bull terrier mix."

Toby laughs, nods his head and says, "That's code word for pit bull."

"Mr. Johnson breeds her so he can sell the puppies in Minneapolis. I told Sheriff Goldberg they're probably sold for dog fighting, but he said there's nothing he can do about it. He said it's not illegal to breed puppies, and it's out of his jurisdiction what happens once they leave Granola. He also said there's no law on the books that people can't keep dogs on chains outside year-round, even in Minnesota," I answer. "All I know is I need to rescue her. And to do that, I gotta get the chain off her neck."

Without hesitating, he says, "Enough said. We'll get her out of there."

He takes a hard left and swings by his house. Running into his garage and out again, he throws a heavy pair of bolt cutters on the back seat, then off we go.

~~~

As we pass Chik-n-Frys, Steph, my best friend, is finishing her shift, walking to her car in the parking lot.

She sees me and starts jumping up and down in her brown and red uniform, boobs bouncing like a bad check.

I tell Toby to pull into the lot.

Steph has to work at Chik-n-Frys, she says, otherwise they'll kick her off welfare. But she still don't like it much. She has a two year old boy and baby girl, but doesn't know where the fathers are. I actually think she isn't quite sure *who* the fathers are.

Toby pulls in and Steph runs to my car window. She smells sweet and sticky, with deep fryer grease hula hooped around her. She's my age, however, Grandma once said she looks 'rode hard and put away wet.'

Steph plucked most of her eyebrows off, so cartoonishly colors them back in with a kohl makeup pencil. They remind me of skinny tadpoles sucking on her forehead. Her lips are outlined in dark purple, and she fills them in with copper frosted lipstick.

A little over five feet nothing, she has peroxide-blonde hair that reflects patina green in the sun. Her crooked teeth are bleached dazzling white, but she always has a cluster of zits clumped on that space below her bottom lip and above her chin.

It's like the deep valley of pimples. I call it the Acne Forest, only to myself though, not to her. She cleans it and puts all sorts of products she buys from the internet on her chin, which only makes it worse. And more red.

She scrubs so hard to get rid of the blemishes that they bleed, so she has about a dozen seeping, raised dots in that tiny space. And then she cakes makeup on it, foundation, then powder, and the blood or puss or whatever oozes and mutates with the makeup.

Her whole chin has become a calcified, crusty place of despair. Other than all that, she is very pretty.

"Hey ya, Allison," she says, leaning in my window, smiling and smacking her gum.

Bubblicious. I think she squirted on some Love's Baby Soft perfume before she left work to cover up the chicken nugget residue on her uniform.

"Hey, Steph," I answer, leaving her to do most of the talking. She loves to talk more than I, and I like listening to her more than listening to myself, so we get along great.

"Who's this? Your new boyfriend? Hey, isn't he that black guy? You know, from Afghanistan? Oh my God, that Army guy, right? He's gorgeous!"

"No, he's not my boyfriend. And yes, his name is Toby," I answer.

Toby grins at her and says, "Nice to meet you, Steph."

"I heard about you. My grandpa was in a war too, forget which one. I wanted to join the Air Force but I pissed hot on the drug test," she gushes. "Where are you love doves going?" she adds, shoving her hand through the window to shake his.

"Toby's gonna teach me how to drive, that's all."

"Baby you can drive my car!"

"Please, Steph."

"Really, Allison? You need to be doing more than that with this fine man. He sure has some nice biceps. Just look at those freakin' pipes," she says, pointing to Toby's arm. She then pretends to ride a motorcycle and squeals, "Vroom! Vroom!"

"He's sitting right here," I add.

"Hey, Toby. Everyone says Allison is the hottest girl in Grimoire county, but is a stick in the mud."

"I just think she's the prettiest girl I've ever seen," he answers.

"Can you imagine this chick in a wet tee shirt contest? She'd win for sure, but she never wants to do anything fun like that," she says.

"How exactly would that be fun, Steph?" I ask.

Ignoring me, she continues, "I bought Allison a raspberry jello shot one time. She choked and it spewed out her nose like gummy worms."

"Be quiet about that," I say.

"Last year, she took a toke on some good Minnesota ditch weed but didn't do anything but eat an entire loaf of bread and fall asleep hugging a roll of paper towels."

"Really, no one needs to hear this, Steph."

"A few months ago we went down to the Twin Cities and she had a few Bloody Marys at the Uptown Patio Cafe. She starts waving the pickle around when she sees a homeless lady. She ends up giving the lady all her cash plus the pickle and olives out of her drink. We barely made it back to Granola because we didn't have any frickin' money for gas."

"Steph, please."

"You should have seen her. She starts singing 'All the Single Pickles' by Beyonce. These cute guys came over with Bloody Marys, so she drinks a few more. But I couldn't get with none of the guys because she decides to puke in her purse."

Dying of embarrassment, I shake my head but she continues, "On the way home, Allison begins blubbering about homeless pickles. We stopped at Come-n-Pump so she could puke again. I had to shoplift a jar of pickles for her so she would quit bawling."

"Stop talking about this, Steph."

"Then, she felt bad about all the pickles crammed in the jar and wanted them to be free, so threw the entire jar out on the highway while singing Taylor Swift at the top of her lungs."

"Shut. up. now." I hiss, folding my arms tightly across my chest.

She swallows hard. Standing up straight, she backs off.

"Okay, whatever. But call me later," she says.

"Steph, I've told you a thousand times I don't have a cell phone," I answer, rolling up my window.

"You shouldn't go anywhere without looking down at a phone, Allison," she scolds. "People will think you are a deranged psychopath if you look around at the world instead of staring down at a phone."

Steph places both palms on my window, presses her mouth on it, leaving a smudged and sloppy lipstick kiss.

"And Toby!" she add. "If you have a brother, or a cousin, tell him to give me a jingle!"

"Nice to meet you," Toby calls as we pull away.

Steph cackles while doing the universal pelvic thrust in the parking lot, then busts out laughing. Thank gawd Toby doesn't see that as we get back on the road and drive towards Johnson's house.

"Uff da," I mutter, shaking my head.

"What does that mean, 'uff da'?"

"Ya know when somebody or something is really messed up? You say 'uff da'. I think it's an Up-North Minnesotan saying. Probably Norwegian."

"Never heard that before," he answers. "But I get it."

"What do you say in the Army when something is messed up, then?"

"That's fucked, or fucked up or fuck it. Anything with that as the root word. You know, it's versatile."

"I like that better, it's definitely more accurate."

"Yeah, but don't say it," he answers.

"You just said it."

"But you don't have to say it."

"Maybe 'uff da' is Norwegian for 'fuck it.'"

"Quite possibly," he nods, smiling. He then adds, "Hey, say the word *milk*."

"Why?" I ask, confused.

"Just do it once."

"Milk."

"White Minnesotans always pronounce it MEALK," he says, grinning, his eyes twinkling.

"Because that's how it's pronounced. What's so funny? about that?"

"Say 'silky milk'," he adds, smiling from ear to ear.

"Fuck no," I answer, smiling back.

He laughs, and then falls silent as we turn the corner. We're about a block from Mr. Johnson's house, so he pulls over to the curb and shuts off the car.

The street lights are tall, skinny aliens, analyzing the pavement like microscopes, in small, bright patches. Trees along the block arch over in a luscious canopy. The humid, thick air is trapped underneath, stuck at a heavy standstill.

As he creaks open the back door to get the bolt cutters, he begins humming the Mission Impossible theme song, "Do. Do. Do do, do do. Do do, do do."

I get out too and follow him.

CHAPTER THREE

With Toby by my side, I feel brave, invincible, running through the yards toward Johnson's house. Suddenly, he dives into the bushes.

We remains silent as a car turns the corner. It's a beige minivan driven by a woman chatting on her flip phone.

I stop. With my hands on my hips, I ask him what the heck he thinks he's doing.

Toby puts a finger to his mouth, shaking his head. Then he darts out, sprints to the next bush and dives in again. He continues doing this run, tuck and roll thing through several yards to move ahead.

Once I catch up again, I ask a little too loudly, "Why are you doing that?"

"Why am I doing what?" he whispers from the bushes.

"Jumping around like you're in a Fallujah fire fight?"

"Since you told me we have to steal a dog from private property? No one is going to call the cops on you if they see you, Ally. But they will if they see a black guy creepin' through their yard at night."

"Yeah, you're probably right."

I follow him to the next bush. We're almost there. He crawls out from the shrubs and dashes toward a wide oak tree. Peering around, he runs back and grabs me around the shoulder, trying to hunker me down low as we approach the house. We both plaster ourselves behind the next tree, like James Bond in Paris.

"That's it," I whisper, pointing at the shambling rambler kitty corner from us. "We have to sneak around to the back yard. The dog is tied up behind the house, inside a high, chain-link fence."

The floodlight attached to the garage shines up the driveway, but there's only quiet darkness inside the house.

"Come on," he says in a hushed tone, taking my hand.

We sprint through the neighboring yard, keeping close to the trees, and round the house. He pulls my hand harder and we fall down together.

"Is this what you did in the Army?"

"Yes," he whispers. "And we practiced sound and light discipline, too."

"What's that?"

"It means be quiet, please."

Out on the street, another car passes. Toby and I are laying on our stomachs, but I'm not being quiet enough.

Maple bursts alive, frightened, snarling with alarm.

"Hold on," I whisper, and crawl on my hands and knees toward the fence.

The poor animal is berserk, lunging in fear.

"Hey, Maple," I say softly.

She retreats about a foot, so the chain isn't strangling her anymore, but she's still madly trying to defend this horrible person's property.

I stick my fingers through the fence, wiggling them at her. "Maple. It's just me. Who's a good girl, Maple? Who's a good girl?" I say softly.

She sits, ears back, and cautiously wags her tail.

Toby runs up and catapults over the fence like Bruce Jenner before he became a Kardashian drag queen.

"You forgot the bolt cutters," I yell.

"Hush. I got them right here," he whispers.

Maple is beyond frightened. She stands up stiff and urinates on herself. Toby grabs her chain and yanks her towards him. In a second, he cuts through the collar and the chain falls to the ground in a sickening thud.

"Come on, girl," he says.

Maple scrunches up her butt and poops while trying to walk forward. She then whines, whimpers, confused, refusing to move.

"Let's go, Maple," I say, clinging to the fence. Then call at Toby to, "Just throw her over!"

I can hardly see Toby's face in the dark, but the whites of his eyes narrow into slits.

Okay. Throwing a terrified, seventy-pound pit bull over a high fence isn't the greatest suggestion.

Toby runs toward the gate by the house and snaps that lock off also. Maple erupts into pure happiness, finally realizing she is being set free. She rushes out behind Toby.

"Maple, let's go," I call and run towards the street, clapping my leg for her to follow.

We all dash back to the getaway car. Toby opens the door and Maple leaps in like Superdog.

Porch lights flick on. Tires squeal. Off we speed.

Mission Accomplished.

As we pull into the garage, I finally exhale and say, "Wow, thank you. We did it."

"Yep, we sure did," Toby answers, chuckling.

He walks me and Maple to the porch. Pulling a black bandana from his back pocket, he kneels down and ties it gently around her neck.

"Just a little swag, is all," he says to her. "No more chains for you, good little girl."

"Thanks again," I say, opening my front door.

"No problem, Ally" he answers, doing that wink-blink thing with his eyes. Smiling, he then turns and jogs on back home.

Maple rockets into the house and makes a beeline to the couch. She jumps up, lays next to Bob, and puts her big head in his lap, content and grateful.

"Isn't this Johnson's mutt?" he asks without moving his eyes from the TV.

"Not any more, Bob. She's mine now," I answer.

Grandma walks out of the kitchen and says, "Mr. Johnson is an asshole, always hated him. That sorry animal has been tied up behind his house for about fifty years. That ain't no way to treat a dog."

"That's why we're going to keep her," I say, sitting on the couch next to Bob and Maple.

Grandma grabs a fistful of venison jerky from the kitchen, sits down next to us, and starts feeding Maple.

Half an hour later, there's a knock on the front door.

Bob turns down the volume. Maple slowly slinks off the couch to go lay down in the kitchen. Grandma jumps up and screams, "It's the FBI! It's the CIA!"

"Grandma, it's okay," I answer as calmly as I can and walk toward the door.

"It's the coppers!" she adds, and runs upstairs, slamming her bedroom door behind her.

It's Sheriff Goldberg. Over the years, he's been here many times, trying to smooth things over with Grandma, or back in the day trying to smooth things over with my parents.

I creak open the door.

"Good evening, Allison. How are you tonight?" he asks in his formal cop voice.

"I'm doing well, sir."

"May I come in?"

"Actually, you're freaking Grandma out. She thinks you're going to arrest her for something. Unless you are, it's probably not a good idea. If you don't mind, sir."

"I *do* mind, dear. I need to come in, please," he insists.

"Okay, sure" I say and get out of his way.

Stepping into the hallway entrance, his head rotates around like a searchlight. He puts his hands on his black leather belt that's dangling with gadgets, guns, and cuffs.

"Who's here tonight?" he asks.

"Just me and Grandma."

I then point to Bob on the couch, who's clicking through the channels. He looks up, waves the remote at the Sheriff, then focuses back on the TV.

"And Bob. You know Bob?" I add.

"I know Bob. Everyone knows Bob. Hey there, Bob."

"Hey there, Gabe," Bob answers. "You doing your tomatoes this year?"

"No, only roots. Carrots and onions. Wife likes beets. I hate beets. Not doing much else 'cause the damn deer eat everything with vines."

"They do like their zucchini, I'll tell you that much."

"You betcha, Bob," Sheriff Goldberg says.

Turning back to me, he asks, "Say, Allison. You wouldn't happen to know about a lost dog, would you?"

I clench my teeth and don't move. Maple walks out of the kitchen and plops down on the carpet in front of the TV. Bob softly shakes his head.

"No, sir. I don't know about a lost dog," I answer with a straight face, because that's technically not a lie.

Maple licks her paws, then begins howling.

Bob throws her another stick of venison jerky. Catching it in midair, she trots off to the kitchen again.

Sheriff Goldberg purses his lips.

"Are you sure, Allison? Maybe not lost, but a 'found' dog then? Boxy head, muscular body, brown with blue eyes? Exactly like the one that was just over there in your living room? Maybe you've seen her chained up behind Mr. Johnson's house on the corner over on Elm street," he asks, eyebrows up.

"Yes. No. Sir. That's too bad Mr. Johnson lost his dog. But he was mean to that poor thing. Sending all her puppies down to Minneapolis to dog fight," I answer.

Sheriff Goldberg clears his throat.

"Believe me, Allison. I looked into charging Johnson for something, anything. Unfortunately, he isn't breaking any laws keeping her chained up outside. Or breeding her. Just the way our laws are written. I told you that before."

"That's still not right," I mutter.

"I'll tell you what I'm able to do within the law. I'll smooth this over with Mr. Johnson so he'll leave you and the dog alone," he says. "And I will strongly discourage him from getting another."

"Thank you, sir," I answer, staring down at the floor.

"And you will never do something like this again. Do you understand me? Am I being clear?"

"Yes, sir. And I appreciate it. I promise to take care of her the best I can."

"Good. I know you will. They're man's best friend. And now you have your own," he says. "But you will get her spayed and vaccinated as soon as possible."

"I'm going over to Grimoire next week or so, Gabe. We'll bring her in then," Bob calls from the couch.

"You do that," Sheriff Goldberg answers.

He then walks out of the house with his mouth on his walkie-talkie and says, "All clear."

I shut the door and snap the lock down.

I remember when Sheriff Goldberg came over one night, twenty years ago. I was almost six. My dad had died the year before, so my mom relied on Grandma for help.

Grandma was babysitting me. She got a phone call, made some phone calls, and this guy Bob came over a few minutes later. He brought a Sub Station sandwich for me, and turned on the Game Show channel. Grandma told me to 'sit tight', and left. I sat by Bob and we watched reruns of *The Dating Game* as I ate the turkey and Colby with extra mayo on white bread.

Later that night, Grandma slowly opened the front door, holding a big bottle, a gallon probably, of Captain Morgan rum. Her face was glowing, red and blotchy. Her eyes, rolling yellow and swollen. Bob was snoring on the couch and I was on the floor clicking through the channels with the remote.

She pulled me clumsily by the arm up to her bed and we slept like two spoons in a downy drawer.

The next morning, I went downstairs when I heard a knock on the front door. Bob had gone home and Grandma was still passed out. I opened it up and Sheriff Goldberg was on the porch.

"Good morning, dear. Is your grandma awake?"

I remember looking at this large man, in his black boots, pleated pants, thick belt, and pressed brown shirt, pinned with a shiny silver badge. I stood in awe, unaware of the tsunami about to tip my world over.

"I'm coming in, Allison, sweetie," he said, and pushed me carefully aside.

He walked through the main floor, room to room.

In the kitchen, he called upstairs to Grandma, then stood with his back against the sink. Squeezing his mouth so tight, I thought his head would burst like a child's only birthday balloon.

A few minutes later, Grandma stumbled downstairs, and dropped into a chair at the dining room table. Sheriff Goldberg took a can of Grape Shasta from the fridge, cracked it open, and handed it to her.

As he sat down, he gave her a stack of neatly stapled papers inside a thick, manila folder.

I walked over to the table and tried to grab the pop to take a drink. Grandma batted my hand down and pushed a day old, half glass of milk toward me instead.

She flipped through the papers, then angrily dropped the folder back on the table.

"Ethylon," he said quietly. "There will be more people by here today. To help you through all this. I just wanted you to see my initial report, so you can deal with it better and know what to expect. The final toxicology report will come in a few days, but I don't think it will be different than what we have now."

His face folded into a squished, origami ball. He added, "I'm so sorry about your daughter."

Grandma shook her head, and told me what happened.

Dipping my little hands in the cups of hers, she spoke in short, sad words, that my mother was dead.

She wanted to tell me last night but couldn't. She tried to drink enough courage, but it only made her sick.

We sat on the couch, with me crying and her singing,

'Monkeys go to heaven in little row boats. Bunnies go to heaven in yellow rain coats. Cats go to heaven in high heeled shoes, but dogs go to heaven weeping the blues...'

Soon, the church ladies came over. The neighbors came over. The entire town came over. And a lawyer. And the Child Protective Services people. Two pastors and a priest. And all these cops. With lasagna, and cookies, and crockpots of Swedish meatballs, and flowers, and cards, and stuffed animals.

By late afternoon, Grandma couldn't take it anymore. She told everyone to 'fuck off and go home', grabbed her bottle, then sat quietly on the couch with me and Bob.

Bob gave me some orange marshmallow circus peanuts because he's the only person on earth that actually buys those things. We watched *Jeopardy* reruns until I put my head on his forearm and my feet in Grandma's lap. I closed my eyes. There was only the scent of his old flannel shirt and sickening sweet marshmallows until I fell asleep.

Grandma became my blazing shield and I clung to her. Back then, she was radiant, mentally healthy, with rich mocha hair and sizzling green eyes.

Over the years, as I grew up, she grew down. It began pounding her, like a slow, persistent sledge hammer, what happened to her beloved daughter, my mother.

Grandma is left with me, as I am left with her, connected forever in familiar grief and obligated patience.

Sometimes it feels as if my parents were just two people I made up, like childhood imaginary friends. I don't remember much about them, I was so young. I make-believe now they were the most splendid and perfect parents ever. I miss what should have been.

CHAPTER FOUR

The next morning, Jungle Jim barrels into the store as soon as I flip over the OPEN sign. His face is burning brighter than a baboon's butt.

"I won! I won five tickets!" he says, slapping his hands on the counter. He then bounces up, spins around and slams his hands down again.

I take a step back, thinking he's going to tackle me.

"Congratulations, Jimmy. You won what?" I ask.

"I won five tickets to *Jeopardy*. Five tickets!"

"That's great," I say, not sure if I believe him.

Mr. Whitehead ambles out from the back, folds his arms across his fat chest and says, "You ain't won diddly squat, Jimmy," he says. "You're imagining again."

"I ain't imagining nothing. I won! I really did!"

"To what?"

"*Jeopardy.*"

"To a damn game show…"

"That's right, to a damn game show," Jimmy answers.

Pulling out five tickets from his coat pocket, he waves them in front of Mr. Whitehead's face.

Mr. Whitehead swishes them away with his hand and scrunches up his eyebrows.

"Are you trying to tell me that Alex Quebec or Pat Jackoff or whoever the heck is gonna fly you and four friends you don't have, all out to Hollywood?" Mr. Whitehead scoffs.

"No, it's going to be down in Minneapolis at the Convention Center. For the first time, they're taping a *Jeopardy, On the Road* edition. I called in to the Grimoire radio station giving them away, and I won five of them. It also means I get to try out to be a contestant."

Mr. Whitehead grabs the tickets, flips them over, squinting his eyes. After reading the fine print, he hands them back to Jimmy.

"I guess you ain't kidding," he says.

"No, I ain't," Jimmy answers.

"Well, congratulations, and good luck trying out…"

"Yeah, but I don't think I'd be a very good contestant. I'm more of a street smart guy, not so much a book smart sort of guy, if you know what I mean," he answers, tapping the side of his head.

"I *do* know what you mean," Mr Whitehead agrees.

"Bob would love to go with you, Jimmy. He'd be a great contestant," I say. "He's real smart at game shows. And if he won, I bet he would give you some of the prizes. He's nice like that."

Jimmy turns to me and asks, "Really? You think he'd help me out?"

"Of course he would. He'd love to go."

"Why don't you take Allison here with you," Mr. Whitehead suggests. "And Bob and her grandma."

"You, Bob, and Ethylon wanna come down to Minneapolis for this with me?" Jimmy asks.

"Sure, sounds like fun. When exactly is it?"

"Tomorrow."

"Jesus Christ, Jimmy. Tomorrow?" Mr. Whitehead says.

"Last minute, I know, but yeah, it's tomorrow."

"Tomorrow it is, then. Go ahead and take the day off, Allison. You deserve a little vacation."

"But who's going to drive us?" I ask.

They both look at each other in blank silence.

Mr. Whitehead walks to work because he only lives a block away. He has a bunch of restored Mustangs and a Gran Torino, but he doesn't drive them anywhere.

When he does drive to Grimoire, he takes his old Datsun truck that's going to break down any day now. Besides, he has to stay and run the store.

Jimmy once had an AMC Pacer but he lost his privilege to drive permanently after his fourth or fifth DWI. They took Grandma's license away years ago also.

Bob refuses to drive to the Cities. The furthest he ever goes is to Grimoire, and complains the whole way there and the whole way back. And I still don't have my license.

"Maybe we could ask Toby to drive," I say.

~~~

It's five a.m. the next morning.

We pile into the Regal Sedan, with Toby driving and Jimmy riding shotgun. I'm in the back stuck between Grandma and Bob.

The Buick gags, dry heaves rather, but quickly belches to life, so off we go toward Minneapolis.

"MinneNapolis," Grandma says.

"It's not MinneNapolis. It's Minneapolis," I say.

"MinneNapolis," she says louder.

"I should have brought my flack jacket," Jimmy says. "There're gangs down there in the Twin Cities. You know, the Bloods and the Crips."

"They'll take one look at your face, Jimmy, and run the other way," Grandma says.

"Hey, everyone relax. It'll be fine," Toby says.

"I have to go," Jimmy says.

"We're going," Toby answers.

"I have to go pee! And I have to go bad!"

"We just got on the interstate two minutes ago, buddy."

"Pull over! You want me to go in the car?"

"Sure, I mean no. I'll pull over at the next gas station."

"Now, please. I can't wait that long! Pull over now!"

We stop along the interstate right outside of Granola.

Jimmy gets out and whizzes on the shoulder.

"Ya happy now, Jimmy?" Grandma asks.

"I'm happy," Jimmy answers, zipping up his jeans as he climbs back into the car.

"I had a boyfriend who used to piss himself when he got horny," Grandma adds.

"Ethylon, we don't want to hear about it," Bob says.

"Grandma, please. Let's not talk about things like that, okay?" I say. "Here, take your medication. I got a bottle of water right here," I add, remembering I didn't give her the morning pills.

Toby looks in the rear view mirror.

"Fuck," he mutters under his breath.

We all turn around as a Minnesota state highway patrol officer pulls up behind us.

Toby slides out his wallet and takes out his license.

"The registration and all the insurance papers are in the glove compartment, Jimmy," Bob says, pointing from the back seat.

Jimmy pulls the glove compartment open and a half empty bottle of Southern Comfort rolls out onto his lap.

"Hells bells! That's where I hid it. I've been looking all over for that rebel juice," Grandma says.

Hardly moving his lips, Toby says, "Jimmy. Listen to me. Hand me the papers, close the glove compartment and pretend the bottle isn't there."

Jimmy does.

"Jimmy, perhaps I wasn't clear. Pick up the bottle of booze and put it back into the glove compartment, quickly and quietly, and *then* close it."

"You didn't tell me that part, Toby."

"Just do it now, please."

"Hide the damn bottle, dip shit!" Grandma screams.

"Shhh," Toby scolds.

"Jeezuz H. Christ. We left Granola three minutes ago and Jimmy's already getting us arrested for open bottle and indecent exposure," Bob grumbles.

Jimmy stuffs the bottle back in the glove compartment just in the nick of time.

The trooper approaches Toby's window. He peers in at Toby, puts his hand on his holster, then notices Jimmy.

"Why am I not surprised," he says, throwing his hands up instead. "I should've known that was you, Jungle Jim, urinating all over my highway."

"Morning, Trooper Fiske," Jimmy says. "Sorry about that. But when a man's gotta go, a man's gotta go."

"Hey, aren't you Frankie Lutefisk? Velma and Roger's youngest boy?" Grandma asks from the back seat.

The trooper leans into Grandma's window and says, "Miss Ethylon? Now isn't this my lucky day. I haven't seen you in ages. And you know dang well my last name is Fiske, not lutefisk. How've you been, ma'am?"

"Nice to see you finally cleaned up your act, Frankie. About damn time you did. I used to pick you up hitch hiking. You still owe me for all those packs of smokes I bought you when you were underage. Remember that day I picked you up and you had a black eye, a bag of gerbils, and smelled like soy sauce and bad choices?"

He laughs, tips back his hat and removes his aviator sunglasses. "I sure do, Miss Ethylon."

"And I gave you a cold can of Coors to put on that eye to bring the swelling down?"

"And in this very car! So, where ya'll headed?"

"We're trying to get to MinneNapolis for a game show audition, but had to pull over so Jimmy wouldn't wet his pants. Sorry about that, Frankie."

Grinning, he asks, "When are you coming by to meet my new wife?"

"You got married?"

"Sure did, last year."

Grandma pokes him in his big gut and says, "She must be a good cook. I can see she gives you plenty of lovin' from the oven."

Trooper Fisk stands up and sucks in his stomach.

"I hope you and your wife have been working on having some babies. I bet your kids would be cute just like you," she adds with a wink.

"Been working on that just fine, ma'am."

"Just don't be an asshole to your wife like you were to all your old girlfriends."

Trooper Fiske awkwardly clears his throat, snaps back to professional police officer mode and says, "Alrighty then. Always a pleasure talking with you, Miss Ethylon."

"You take care, Frankie. I want to see some little lutefisk babies around town."

"Better move along, then. Don't forget to stop at The Tasty Spork down the road for the cinnamon rolls. They're the most delicious cinnamon rolls in Minnesota."

"You betcha. Give my regards to your lucky bride," Grandma calls, rolling up her window, and off we go.

~~~

About an hour later, we get to The Tasty Spork.

It's the breakfast mecca right off the interstate about halfway toward the Twin Cities, with the best cinnamon rolls in the upper Midwest.

The waitress smacks her gum and rubs her tired eyes.

"Sorry. We're out of cinnamon rolls," she says in a bored monotone.

We're all crammed in a booth. Jimmy lights a cigarette, even though there is no smoking in the entire place.

He takes a puff and asks, "We just passed a hundred billboards advertising your cinnamon rolls, and you're trying to tell me you don't have any?"

Bob grabs the cigarette and shoves it into Jimmy's water glass.

The waitress answers, "I'm not *trying* to tell you. I *am* telling you. We had a couple bus loads of senior citizens come through this morning on their way to the Big Beaver casino. They ate up every single one of them."

"You got eggs? How about some eggs?" Jimmy asks.

"On the menu."

"You got bacon?"

"On the menu."

"Good. I would like to order eggs, over easy with bacon," he says. "And pancakes."

"Same here, please," I say.

"Same here, thank you ma'am," Toby says.

"Same here too," Bob adds.

"I want the house salad," says Grandma.

Bob points to his watch, shaking his head and says, "For the love of gawd, a salad? Ethylon, this is breakfast time. Every person in the entire restaurant is ordering breakfast. Because…it's breakfast time."

"Don't be such a drama queen, Bob. I said I wanted a salad. With blue cheese dressing and extra croutons," she answers, glaring at him.

Bob holds up his menu, like a bulwark, in front of his face, and bites his lips.

"Alrighty," the waitress says, taking a step back. Then she adds, "Coffee?"

Jimmy lights another cigarette, and stands up in the booth, but not actually standing up, sort of curled with his knees buckled and crunched between the booth and table.

"Yes, please. For all of us. And cream. And no fake, diet chemical sugar. Keep that off this table. I only want the real sugar," Jimmy answers, sucking down his cigarette.

"How many chemicals do you think are in that cigarette of yours, Jimmy?" I ask.

"We are NAWN smoking," the waitress says, pursing her lips, then trudges away to place our order.

Grandma grabs the cigarette and takes a deep puff. Bob grabs it from her and drops it into Jimmy's glass again.

A few minutes later, the waitress brings over a tray with five white mugs, plunking them on the table along with a copper-colored thermos of coffee.

After she waddles off, Jimmy grabs the thermos and starts to pour the coffee. Except, he doesn't know how to work the lifty lid on the pot, and the coffee gushes out too fast and spills on the table.

"Have mercy, Jimmy, let me do it," Bob snarls.

He grabs the pot from him, but he doesn't do any better. More coffee streams out all over the table. Luckily, most of it cascades to the floor instead of onto our laps.

Toby raises his hand like he's in kindergarten, and the waitress makes her way over to the table again.

"I'm sorry, ma'am, but may we have a different coffee pot?" Toby asks. "This one must have a leak."

"That's right, ma'am, a real big leak," Grandma adds.

The waitress scrunches up her face. She throws down a few hand towels along with another thermos of coffee, then stomps off.

"Allison? Did I ever tell you when I was in 'Nam, we didn't have hot water for our coffee, so we'd just eat the little Sanka packets? Chewed on them like gum. Then, washed them down with mekong whiskey," Jimmy says.

"Well, that's different," I answer.

"And you know what else?" he adds. "They gave us drugs. They laced our food to make us killing machines."

"You took your own damn drugs," Grandma pipes in.

"Look who's talking, Mrs. Jerry Garcia," he retorts.

"He wasn't even in Vietnam," Bob says. "He was in Thailand running a whorehouse with the USO."

"You're the one that didn't serve," Jimmy says to Bob.

"Why weren't you in Vietnam, Bob? I thought everyone got drafted back then," I ask.

"Because he was a duck monger," Jimmy says.

"A what?" I ask.

"What the heck is a duck monger?" Toby asks, screwing up his eyebrows.

"I think he means malingerer," Bob says. "But I wasn't no malingerer. They wouldn't let me serve because I had flat feet, that's all."

"Quack," Jimmy says.

Bob stares daggers at Jimmy, and asks, "How'd you like my flat, duck foot up your butt?"

"I had a boyfriend once who quacked like a duck when I tickled his…" Grandma begins to say.

"Gentlemen, Miss Ethylon, please," Toby interrupts. "It really doesn't matter who served and where. Why don't we move on and talk about something else."

Quieting down, we all mix up our coffees with sugar and cream, trying to act normal long enough until the other customers stop staring at us.

I throw my head back and look at the ceiling, stained yellow with nicotine of years gone by. Dust bunnies hunch in the corners. The wallpaper is avocado green, with burnt orange swirls running to the harvest gold carpet.

Toby grabs a toothpick. Twirling it between his teeth, he looks at Bob and asks, "So, what's your strategy?"

Bob takes a swig of his coffee, sits straight up and burps, "Huh?"

"How you gonna win?"

"Win what?"

"The game show!" we all yell.

Bob peers down into his coffee cup, like it's a crystal ball. Suddenly, his head shoots up and he blurts out, "I'm gonna get the right answers!"

"Sounds like a good plan," Toby says with a grin.

Jimmy sticks his nose into his cup and says, "I love the smell of coffee in the morning."

"Ya'll know what I love in the morning besides a double vodka orange juice? I love the smell of play dough," Grandma says.

"I used to eat play dough when I was a kid," Jimmy says. "I could eat a whole damn can with a spoon. Sometimes I still do."

"Don't doubt that at all," Bob mutters.

Finally, the waitress returns with four plates of breakfast balancing on her arms and holding a listless bowl of iceberg lettuce in her hand. The cherry tomato rolls off and plops to the carpet. Her thick, sensible shoe accidentally smashes it to smithereens...pop...smoosh.

"Here's the salad. And here's all of the eggs, bacon and pancakes," she says, unloading the heavy plates from her beefy arms.

We all dig in, except Grandma.

She takes the packet of Paul Bunyan blue cheese dressing off her salad, places it on the table, and slams down on it with her fist. It spews out in a pale, chunky blast onto the wall.

"That's not how you open it," Jimmy offers helpfully.

"Grandma, please," I beg. "Stop making a scene."

Toby puts down his knife, covers his hand over Grandma's fist and says, "It's okay, ma'am. It'll be fine, whatever it is. Just eat your salad, okay?"

She calms down and pushes the sad roughage around with her fork. She then asks Bob, "Can I try a piece of your bacon, sweetheart?"

"People don't *try* bacon, Ethylon. They *eat* bacon. For cryin' out loud, if you had wanted bacon, you should've ordered your own plate," he answers.

"I don't want a whole order. I just to try a piece."

"No."

"Why is it so hard for you to share?"

"You always do this," Bob answers, protectively moving his bacon closer to him.

"Remember we should avoid using 'always' and 'never' when talking about our relationship? Didn't I tell you that, Bob?"

"You never told me that."

"I saw it on *The View*. And if Whoopie Goldberg says it's true, it's true."

"Well then, why don't you call up your friend Whoopie and ask for her bacon?"

"What is your problem, mister?"

"*My* problem? *Your* problem is whenever we go somewhere to eat, you always want to 'try' my cheesecake, or 'try' some french fries. Then, you always end up eating half of what I order while you only order some goofy bowl of wimpy rabbit food."

She places her right hand on the table.

He pulls his plate closer.

She raises her hand slightly, with the fingertips still resting on the table.

He shifts uncomfortably in his seat.

Tapping her first finger, she narrows her eyes.

He leans forward and circles his plate with his arms like a ring of covered wagons. She thumps her fingers on the table, beating them like war drums.

"Give me a piece of that bacon, Bob," she enunciates through gritted teeth.

"No."

"Yes."

"No."

"Now."

Bob retreats, waving his white napkin in surrender as she snatches all four pieces of his bacon.

The waitress comes over after our plates are empty and piled high. She thwacks down the bill.

"Here's your check," she says, pushing it towards Bob.

Toby looks up at her and pulls the check in front of him. She glares back.

Flicking the check out from his fingers, she shoves it toward Bob again. With her other hand, she grabs Toby's silverware and shoves them into her short, maroon apron.

"I got the bill, ma'am," he says.

"I doubt that," she replies, and hurries away.

"She thinks you're gonna steal the silverware, Toby," Jimmy says.

"He's not stealing the silverware," Bob answers.

"We can buy you some silverware, Toby. You don't have to steal it," Grandma says, patting his hand.

"Jesus Christ, he's not stealing anything," Bob says.

"Toby, you don't want this nasty silverware anyway. Everyone from southern Minnesota on up to Canada have had their lips on these things," Grandma says.

"Will you please stop talking about him stealing the silverware?" I ask.

"In 'Nam, we didn't have silverware. We ate our food with bamboo twigs," Jimmy says.

"I'm gonna poke you in the eye with silverware if you don't shut up," Bob says, stabbing a spoon towards him.

Unable to get a word in edgewise, Toby leans back in the booth with his hands up.

"Toby couldn't steal a hotdog off a bun," Bob adds.

Looking at me, Toby winks and mouths, "Steal a dog?"

Trying not to laugh, I grab the bill and stand up. Toby takes it from me and lays a ten on the table for a tip. Jimmy grabs the tip and tries to shove it into his pocket. Bob wrestles the tip out of his clenched fist, and slams it back on the table. Grandma plucks the check from Toby, and scurries to the register to pay the bill.

Once we're back in the car, Grandma folds her arms across her scrawny chest and huffs, "That waitress in there was racist, Minnesota style. Sorry about that, Toby."

"Thanks, Miss Ethylon," he answers. "It does happen sometimes."

"Well, I'm not racist. Did I ever tell you about Leroy McGee?" she asks to no one in particular.

"No," I answer. "And please, don't tell us about him."

So she tells us about him.

"Back in the day, Leroy was a roadie with Sly and the Family Stone. He liked a little 'road side attraction,' if you know what I mean."

"I don't know what you mean," I say. "And I don't want to know what you mean."

"Leroy had all the groovy moves. My favorite position was the funky chicken but the big voodoo cajun-style was good too."

"Please, Grandma."

"Everyday People!" she bellows.

"Enough, please just be quiet now," I say, and we get back on the interstate again.

~~~

The morning's glory is rising over the Twin Cities as we drive down south. There's little traffic as the skyline of Minneapolis appears on the horizon.

The saucer-topped Cappella tower, the solid IDS building, and the shipwrecked monstrosity of the new Viking's football stadium come into view.

Toby seems to know where we're going and how to navigate to the Convention Center. We snake through the streets, winding through the waking city.

Grandma yells at us to roll up the windows and lock the doors, so the 'dirty hobos' won't get in. I look around and don't see any hobos. There's only a few teenagers waiting at a bus stop, a woman jogging across the street and two men in business suits.

It takes about an hour to park, check Bob in and find our seats in the audience.

Two hours later, we lumber out as sad as polar bears in a Chinese zoo. That certainly didn't go as planned.

"How did you not know how many sides are on an octagon?" Jimmy asks. "Even I know that."

Bob gets into the car and slams his door. He doesn't want to talk about it.

So, Jimmy keeps talking about it.

"Like an octopus. An octopus has eight legs. Octagon, octopus, eight, get it?"

"Don't take it so hard, Bob. It could be worse. And I still love you even though you choked like a chicken," Grandma says.

Bob chews on his lips and keeps staring straight ahead. He tells Toby to drive. Home. He wants to go home. Now.

"At least you got a nice consolation prize, Bob," I say, a little too cheerfully.

"What the heck is he going to do with that stupid thing?" Grandma says, leaning over me and pointing to Bob's crotch.

He's holding a Nutra Baby Bullit on his lap. It's some sort of gadget to puree baby food.

"If you don't like it, Bob, why don't you give it to Steph? I'm sure she'll probably have another baby one of these days," I say.

"Don't feel bad, Bob. You gave it a good try. At least you were on a game show. That's more than most people can say," Toby says, pulling out of the lot and driving back toward the interstate.

"I had one chance and I blew it," Bob answers softly, running his hand slowly over the Nutra Baby Bullit box. He then turns to gaze out the window.

"Screw them, Bob. That whole show was rigged from the get go," Jimmy says. "They only want beautiful people on the show for contestants. They don't want ugly people on TV. You're ugly as sin, that's why they rigged it so you wouldn't win."

"Bob's not ugly," Grandma says. "A little pudgy is all."

"I'm telling ya, it was a set up. They don't want ugly, pudgy people on TV," Jimmy adds.

"Is that suppose to make him feel better?" Toby asks.

"No. But this will," Jimmy answers, pulling the bottle of Southern Comfort out of the glove compartment.

He takes a big gulp before handing it back to Bob.

Bob chugs some down, then holds it toward me. I shake my head no, so he gives it back to Jimmy.

"Give me some of that," Grandma screams, reaching for the bottle. "I'm the one that bought it!"

"Dang it, Ethylon. I'm not going to listen to your drunk mouth all the way up north," Bob says, holding the bottle away from her. "When you get sloshed, you get all hormotional like women do."

"That's not even a word, Bob. No wonder you got kicked off that game show," she says.

Grabbing the bottle, she drinks as much as she can before I scuttle it away from her and stick it under my seat.

Once on the interstate, Toby turns on the radio and we all silently watch the scenery whiz by, lost in our own thoughts, until we arrive back home to Granola.

CHAPTER FIVE

The next morning at work, I quietly sign my time card and mumble a 'hello' to Mr. Whitehead.

"How'd it go yesterday, Allison?" he asks. "With Bob and the game show and all?'

"It could've been better. Bob froze like a deer in headlights. Or I should say, in studio lights."

Mr. Whitehead nods his head and agrees, "Yep. Well, I'd probably do the same. But there's always next time."

"Always next time," I answer, and tie on my red apron and go start the popcorn.

A few minutes later, Steph bursts through the door and runs to the counter.

"You aren't going to believe it," she says, blowing a pink bubble inches from my face.

"I'm sure I will. Try me," I answer.

"I got it!" she gushes. "I got the Welfare-to-Work grant I applied for last year. Now I can go to LPN school. I'm going to be a licensed practical nurse! How cool is that?"

I lean over the counter and give her a big hug. It's about time she gets a good break in life.

"Wow, really? When do you start?" I ask.

"OMG," she squeals, but not 'Oh My God'. She says the letters, 'O M G'.

"I start next month at Grimoire Community College!"

At some point, Jimmy must have walked in while we were talking. He steps out from behind the hammer display after overhearing our conversation.

"I'll tell you what, Steph. Don't get a job at no nursing home. You'll end up wiping old men's butts. Get a job at a doctor's clinic, trust me. You don't want to wipe old men's butts," he says. "I know all about this because I lived over at the St. Cloud Vet's home for a year after I had my episode. All these nice LPNs worked there but I felt sorry for them because all they did was wipe shitty butts."

"Sure, Jimmy. Thanks for the advice," Steph says, rolling her eyes.

"How long is the school?" I ask.

"It's two years, but I gotta get my general diploma first. I didn't graduate from high school, remember? But that won't take me much time. I only need to study up on stupid stuff like math and English. And science. Yeah, and whatever else there is, basically everything."

"I know you can do it," I say, proud of my best friend.

"Why don't you apply, too? Why don't you go to school with me? It'll be fun."

"I graduated from high school, remember?"

"I know that, silly. I mean nursing school. Don't you want to be a LPN like me? I might go on to be a registered nurse after that. You know, a RN. Then, I'll be a doctor. I'll have so much money I won't know what to do with it all."

Shaking my head, I say, "You do it. You'll be excellent at it too because you take such good care of your kids."

"You sure, Allison? You could do it too, you know."

"Naw, I like my job here just fine. Mr. Whitehead is going to show me how to make the keys tomorrow, so, anyway, I'm going to be busy with that," I answer.

"You always say he's going to show you how to make the keys. But then he never does."

Defensively, I shove my hands in my red apron and say, "Tomorrow. He said maybe tomorrow."

"What you need to do is just buy this store from him, Allison. I know you could run it yourself," Steph says, pulling out her pack of Bubblicious.

She offers me a chunk and gives one to Jimmy.

"Why hasn't anyone invented chocolate bubble gum?" he asks, sticking the piece in his mouth. "That's what I'm going to do. I'd make a million bucks. I'd call it Jimmy's Blow a Big Wad bubble gum."

Steph and I both turn to glare at him.

Mr. Whitehead walks out of the back room.

"What the hell are you talking about, Jungle Jim? Did you come in here to harass my employees and customers or get some popcorn or buy something?"

Jimmy flips his hands in the air and marches out the door, trying to slam it, but it doesn't slam. It's one of those doors that slowly shuts on it's hydraulic hinges.

Mr Whitehead shuffles back to his office.

Steph clears her throat, then whispers, "So, dish it, girlfriend. Tell me about your hot date with Toby. He's a cutie pie, for real. Get him to come into Chik-n-Frys today so I can check out his ass. I only saw him sitting down."

"Steph, please."

"Well…did you make out with him?"

"No. We just stole Mr. Johnson's dog, is all."

Without missing a beat, she says, "Good. It's about time someone did. That poor doggie was always chained up outside looking so depressed. Pit bulls get treated like garbage. Whenever I see Mr. Johnson I flip him off."

"You need to come over and meet her. She's the sweetest dog. I named her Maple."

"I can't wait to meet Maple in person," she says, then quickly shifts gears. "Oh my gawd, I forgot to tell you. My son Jason's father got arrested with a huge bag of pot so is going to prison for a while since it's his third offense."

Trying to keep up with Steph's drama is like trying to bathe ten cats at once. Impossible.

"Sorry about that, but I know you're too good for that guy," I say. "He's been nothing but trouble for you."

"Besides, his mother hates me, which is fine because I hate her too. I went over there last week looking for diaper money for Jason. And grandma-from-hell comes out of the house and says Jason isn't her grandson in the first place. She's screeching that he's too scrawny and weird lookin' to be related to her and stuff," she says. "What a witch, always talking that way about her own grandson."

"I'd stay away from both Jason's father and his grandmother. Don't listen to them. Jason is a sweet boy. He's a little on the skinny side but not weird lookin' at all."

"Thanks, girlfriend. Well, gotta go. Text me or stop by my work later," Steph says, hurrying out the door.

I want to tell her for the thousandth time I don't have a phone. Instead, I answer, "I'll stop by when I get off work. And congratulations, Steph. You'll be an awesome nurse."

At noon, Mr. Whitehead emerges from the back room again and says, "It's half-price foot long sandwiches over at Sub Station today, Allison."

He hands me a twenty dollar bill and continues, "Why don't you go get me a meatball sub, and something for you too. I'll watch the front for a bit."

"Sounds good," I answer, taking off my apron.

Sub Station is down about a block in the strip mall. I order his sub to-go but sit down in the store to eat mine.

In walks Pastor Dan.

He's bald with a strawberry blonde goatee and a tapioca complexion. Wearing a tie-dye tee shirt and yellow rubber clogs, he tries to be hip but it's not happenin'.

"Allison Couch! I haven't seen you and Miss Ethylon at church in years. When are you coming back to our Young Christian Warriors group? Jesus misses you and so do I," he says like the phony he is.

I stopped going to church when I was a junior in high school, after I went on a weekend summer retreat to western Wisconsin with the Young Christian Warriors.

Devin Clancy snuck into the girls' cabin when I was the only one in there. He pushed me down on my bunk and pulled my shorts off.

I smacked him across the face with my King James bible, and his glasses flew across the room and broke. He went and told Pastor Dan I broke his glasses on purpose, forgetting the part where he got on top of me and tried to stick his dick in me.

Pastor Dan barely asked me anything, but talked to all of Devin's friends, the counselors, and the other girls in my cabin. Then, he talked to Devin again. He finally told me I need to stop imagining things and should be more 'mindful' of the way I dressed, even though I was wearing gym shorts and a tee shirt like everyone else.

The next day, all the boys called me a lying whore and a slut. The other girls were too scared to defend me because they would have been called horrible names too.

Later, I overheard Pastor Dan say, 'Allison Couch isn't the quickest bunny in the forest, but God loves all his creatures, even the slow ones.'

To make matters worse, when we got home from camp, him and Mr. Clancy came over to Grandma's. They insisted she give them money for a new pair of glasses for Devin and that I owed him an apology.

Grandma told them to take a flying fuck off her porch or she'd break their glasses, too.

"I hate church and I still hate Devin Clancy," I say, sipping on my diet Dew, anger buzzing through every single vein, muscle and bone I have.

His fake smile doesn't waver. It just hitches for a second. He answers, "Let bygones be bygones, Allison. Jesus forgives all our sins."

"That's great. Jesus can forgive rapists all he wants. That's his job, but it ain't mine."

Pastor Dan takes a step back, his plastic smile melting, and says, "I'll pray for you and your grandma."

Disgusted, I look down at my sandwich, not moving until he orders his food and leaves the restaurant.

CHAPTER SIX

Later in the afternoon, Mr. Whitehead goes over to the American Legion for his weekly meeting.

The new American Legion, built two years ago, is only a few blocks away. Seven flags wave outside, all the branches of service plus the Minnesota state flag and Old Glory, which they keep lit up every night.

Most Granola vets go there every day for strong coffee in the morning and cold Budweiser starting about noon. Tuesdays they serve hot meatloaf sandwiches with cups of thick, chicken noodle soup. Fridays is All-You-Can-Eat-Walleye. Saturday is Build-Your-Own Burger and tap beer specials. Sunday is no day of rest, as they put on the biggest and best brunch in Grimoire county.

The WWII men are dying off. The Korean vets are dwindling. The Vietnam guys are getting older and crazier. The Gulf War and Bosnia vets are now stepping up to help run the show. At night, when the old geezers go home, they start the pull tabs, meat raffles, and local country western garage bands. The Iraq and Afghanistan guys still haven't come around yet.

When Mr. Whitehead returns from his meeting, he lurches through the front door and proudly proclaims,

"We decided to put Toby on the float."

"What do you mean put him on the float?" I ask.

"For the Granola Independence Day parade. He's the young hero around here. So, we elected to have him represent us on our American Legion float this year."

"Does he know about this?" I ask, taking a step back.

"No. We just decided today at our meeting."

"Quite honestly, Mr. Whitehead, Toby doesn't seem like the parade float kinda guy," I say.

"And we also decided *you* are going to tell him."

"Oh," I say, amused that all of a sudden the entire town thinks me and Toby are an item.

"Why don't you ride along with him? It would be fun, Allison. Have you ever been in the parade before?"

"No. And I don't want to, either," I answer.

"Would you rather be the giant foam hammer?" he asks, now trying to manipulate me into asking Toby.

Every year for the past decade, Mr. Whitehead makes Jimmy put on this giant foam hammer costume, walk in the parade to represent the hardware store and pass out candy to the children.

The giant foam head has a little face hole to see out of. There are two holes for the arms, but the handle part of the costume is tight around the legs, so it's hard to walk in. And that's never gone well with Jimmy.

Last year, he fell down drunk and got a bloody nose. So, blood and snot was dripping down the front of the costume and all the children were terrorized.

The year before that, there was some confusion at the hardware store. He ended up grabbing a bag of sample packets of Ice-Free windshield washer fluid instead of the candy he was suppose to take. Parents complained because the children were sucking on the samples, thinking it was Kool Aid. And vomiting.

Then the time before that, Jimmy wasn't paying attention and ran into the back of Miss Granola's horse, who got spooked and bucked her off. Miss Granola not only fell down and broke her crown, but her left forearm and front tooth as well.

"Fine. I'll talk to Toby later when I get home," I say.

"Call him now. Tell him to swing by the store later today," Mr. Whitehead says, grinning as he gently places an iPhone on the counter. "Call him on your new phone."

I stare at the silver and white device.

He pushes it toward me and continues, "It's yours, Allison. About time you get with the program and get connected. This is for you."

I have an old laptop at home but never had an interest in owning a cell phone.

"Thanks, but no. This is expensive, Mr. Whitehead. You know I can't afford one and not even sure I want one."

"No, it's yours. Think of it as a company phone, an employee perk. My cell phone carrier gave me a free iPhone and extra line for the store. So here, you take it."

He picks it back up, pushes the side with his thumb and the bitten apple appears for a few seconds. Neon squares of colorful apps pop up and cover the screen.

I take it from his calloused hand, this sleek, sliver of the latest technology.

"Seriously? This is mine?"

"All yours, so call Toby. Tell him about the float," he says with a quick wink.

"I don't have his number."

"When are you gonna see him again? Tonight?"

"Hope so."

"Well, when you do see him, get his number, and tell him about the parade, please."

"Thanks, Mr. Whitehead. For the phone and all. I'll do what I can about the parade, too."

"You do that, Allison. We'd all appreciate it."

~~~

About seven p.m., after showing Bob and Grandma my phone, I take Maple out for a walk to see my favorite tree.

Outside of town, there is one, tremendous oak tree that lords over a corn field. The glorious branches spread almost as wide as the tree is tall.

When I was young, Grandma would tell me to go outside and play with the neighbor kids. Instead, I'd just run over to this tree, my tree, and lay under it for hours, staring up at the dark umbrella of leaves, so heavy with foliage not a shard of sunlight could shine through.

I sit under my tree as Maple runs off chasing a brazen prairie hen. She stops briefly to take a whiz, then gallops off again. The mosquitos are angry, out in full riot and the circus of locusts are louder.

Around here we say 'the corn is knee high by the fourth of July', but this one isn't. This field remains untilled and tangled over by creeping charlie, wild johnny jump-ups and dandelions. Farmer Henderson died two years ago, and his three sons are still fighting over the hundreds of acres worth millions.

I hear footsteps quickly crunching up the dirt road toward my tree. It's Toby. He's beaming, big, and breathing hard from running.

"I was hoping you'd be here," he says, dropping down in the weeds next to me.

"How'd you know where I was?"

"Stopped by and asked Bob."

Maple trots over and sits in front of us, panting hard. She then bolts off after a flock of arrogant Canadian geese that seemed pissed we are sitting nearby.

I hold out my new phone as if cradling a porcelain Christmas tree ornament.

"Hot damn, look at you, Ally. Congrats and welcome to the 21st century," he says, nudging me with his shoulder. "Call me now."

"I don't know your number."

"Okay, I'll call you then."

"I don't know my number."

He snatches my phone, swipes and taps the face. He hands it back to me and does the same with his own. The phone in my palm then vibrates like a nervous fish.

"Answer it," he instructs. "Swipe the bottom of the screen and answer it."

I do. It stops shimmying as I hold it up to my ear.

"Hello? Who is this?" I ask curiously, like I don't know who it is, even though he's sitting right next to me.

"Hello?" he answers, "Who's this?" playing along.

"It's me!"

"Hello, me!" he says, laughing. "Do you want to go out for pizza tomorrow? Just me and you?"

"Like a date?"

"Not like a date, but a date."

"Uh, sure. And before I forget, Mr. Whitehead and the entire Granola American Legion are planning to put you on their float for the Independence Day parade," I say.

"Nope."

"You were invited, or I should say, they elected you."

"No. I don't care much for parades and all that."

"Why?" I whisper into the phone.

"Because."

"Because why?"

"Because."

"The fireworks? Mr. Whitehead said some vets don't like fireworks much."

Toby lowers his voice, "Their not my favorite thing."

His knee knocks against mine, and I knock his back.

Staring straight ahead, both of us on our phones talking to each other, I ask, "What do you like, then?"

"You," he answers.

I knock his knee again, and he knocks his back harder.

The butterflies stir inside my stomach, lift higher and flutter up my throat. If I were to open my mouth, they would float out, and fill the sky.

"Ally?"

"Yes?"

"You're the sweetest girl I've ever met, and so pretty. You're so, oh, I don't know," he says, drifting off.

"Oh so what?" I ask, dying to know, then not wanting to know the answer.

I hang up. He lays his phone down also.

We get up and walk back to Granola holding hands before he says he's gotta get home, too.

Once I'm upstairs in bed, I text Steph my new number. Grandma's snoring in the next room and it's drubbing through the walls. Maple is next to me, chewing on the corner of my pillow.

My phone flitters to life a minute later. A series of rapid fire messages light up the screen, obviously from Steph:

Hay!

OMG

Call me!!!

I call her back, and she answers out of breath, "You finally got a frickin' phone? Congrats, girlfriend!"

"Thanks, I think I'll get the hang of it just fine."

"Oh, you won't believe this. I got fired tonight from Chik-n-Frys," she says.

"Why? Didn't you just start there a month ago?" I ask as Maple groans. I'm starting to wonder if having a cell phone is such a good idea, especially at eleven at night.

"This new dumb chick tells me to change out the french fries, then turns and rubs her fat butt on me. I told her to stop rubbing her nastiness on me, so she throws down the fry basket, hot oil goes flying, and she says, 'You wanna piece of this?' And I say, 'Why would I want a piece of lard?' and she says, 'You wanna fight? Let's go', so I say, 'Lesbo? You're a lesbo?' ready to take her on, then the manager steps in and tells me I am fired because Chik-n-Frys is LGBT sensitive."

"Dang, that's not good, Steph. Sorry about that," is all I can think to say.

"I know, right?"

I hear her son crying in the background. There's some banging, shushing, panting, a quick 'quiet hush stop it go to bed', then footsteps and a slamming door.

"Gotta go, Allison. So glad you finally got a phone. Talk to ya later," she adds, and then quickly hangs up.

I roll over and pull Maple's solid, warm body closer to me. Her marquis-shaped diamond eyes are snow-blue and shine full of soul. The millions of tiny muscles surrounding them flick, revealing unlimited emotions. Perfectly.

Her viciously cropped ears stick up like Batman's. The right one had an additional, awful cut. It has a poorly healed, wide, V-shaped slit on the edge.

There're gouge scars on both sides of her ample hips. Maybe when she was being used as a breeder girl, the males had too long of toe nails.

I can see how someone could look at this type of dog and feel intimidated. But it's not aggression. It's intensity.

She's full of extreme love and forgiveness. Now with eyes shut tight, her broad chest rhythmically lifts up and floats down as we both fall asleep.

CHAPTER SEVEN

A mosquito zings into the kitchen window screen. A moth ricochets off too. A fly buzzes by as the oven's timer dings.

I pull the Boner's frozen pizza from the oven. I figure since I'm going out for pizza with Toby tonight, might as well make Grandma and Bob one before leaving.

"Automation!" Bob yells from the living room.

Grandma walks down the steps, her eyes straining from the light, just up from her daily nap. She sinks into the couch next to Bob.

"Supper's ready," I say, placing the greasy, sliced pizza on the dining room table. Pulling off a tiny pepperoni, I toss it down for Maple. It lands on the top of her snout, then slides down to rest on her jowls. She slurps it in.

There's a knock on the door.

"Run! Hide your wallets! It's the evil Herbalife lady!" Grandma says, now fully alert.

Maple cowers down, not wanting to get involved with anything other than licking pepperoni off her mug.

"Mrs. Albertson stopped selling Herbalife last year. And she wasn't evil, just overly persistent," I answer, coaxing Grandma to take her seat at the dining room table.

"Ethylon, calm yourself and eat your supper," Bob says, turning down the volume.

I open the front door and Toby is on the porch, slapping off a mosquito.

Having never been on a date before, I tug on my nose, like I do sometimes when I'm nervous.

"Come on in," I say, stepping aside.

He's wearing a purple polo shirt and designer jeans.

"Butter my butt and dip me in gravy! Don't Toby look nice tonight," Grandma calls from the dining room.

"Why, thank you, ma'am," Toby answers, smiling.

"Bob, what about my needs? Why don't you ever take me out to Grimoire Reaper's Pizza?" Grandma asks.

"Because you never ask me to take you," Bob answers.

"Maybe I'd like to go out for pizza some time."

"You wanna go out tonight instead, sweetheart?"

"Hell no. I don't wanna go out because I hate people," she answers as she runs upstairs with her plate of pizza.

Bob grabs a slice of Boner's pizza, returns to the couch and turns the volume of *The Dating Game* back up.

~~~

"Let's go for another driving lesson before chow. How about you drive us over to the Price Wackers parking lot and we'll practice there," Toby says.

"Will you please at least back it out of the garage?" I ask, tossing him the keys.

"I already know how to do that. You're the one that needs to learn," he says, throwing the keys back to me.

We get in, Maple hops in back, and I chunk the gear knob into reverse. The old Buick floats out of the garage like a slow barge.

"Turn the wheel to the right once the back tires hit the street," he instructs.

I do.

"Not bad, Ally," he says. "So far so good."

We clunk forward as I grind the gear knob into 'D'.

"Now, slowly apply the brakes," he coaches.

I do, but not slowly. We both launch up, then collapse back into the vinyl upholstery.

"Ally, you're in control of this vehicle so you need to treat it with respect," he says, rubbing his neck.

Flustered, I answer, "It's not my fault if the car doesn't do what I want it to do."

"No, no. Don't think that way," he says. "This car will not magically do what you want. It only responds with what you do *to* it. If you operate it correctly, it will respond correctly. If you slam on the brakes, grind the gears and get mad, you'll go nowhere fast."

"Fine," I say under my breath, and calm down.

Off we go.

I'm the only car on the road as we head up to the main intersection that will lead us out of town toward Grimoire Reaper's Pizza.

We pass by Chik-n-Frys, Chub and the little roadside souvenir shack that sells over-priced weird stuff like gold painted cow patties, Kirby Puckett bobbleheads, and bags of Minnesota wild rice tied with green ribbons to travelers on their way north to the cabin or back from Duluth.

Driving as careful as I can, I blow through the last intersection's red light and end up in the middle of Price Wackers parking lot.

"Hooah," he says with one hand on the dashboard. "Mostly great job. Yeah. Let's move on to something else."

"Okay. Like what?"

"Let's practice using your blinkers and turning."

I flip up the blinker and it ticks like a bomb. I smack it down, diffusing it.

"Blinkers," I say.

"Roger that."

"Turning and blinking."

"Actually, it's blinking, then turning. Don't be one of those people that don't signal their turns," he adds.

In the parking lot of the bygone and boarded up Price Wackers, cracks bulge up like scabs, weeds scratching to get out, the faded lines have bled away. Crumbly cement parking blocks are itched raw by years of weather.

I keep driving around, back and forth, up and down, practicing turning on the blinkers left and right. Gradually running over less curbs, I get the hang of the blinkers.

"Okay, Ally. Now, you're going to learn how to park the car," he says.

I slam on the brakes.

He groans, rubbing the back of his head after it flies forward, whips back and forward again. His hand then moves to the rear of my seat.

"Can I ask you a question, Ally?"

"I guess so."

"What ever happened to your parents?"

"Who?" I reply, wanting to avoid the question.

"What happened to your parents?" he repeats.

"You know, things happen. A lot of things happen. The church ladies say everything happens for a reason."

"Tell me what happened to them," he says again.

"My dad died when I was about five," I answer. "It just happened. He was young, only thirty. They did an autopsy and said it was a brain aneurysm. My mom died, uh, in her sleep a little bit later. Why, where is your dad?"

"Sorry about that," he says quietly. "My dad was killed when I was a little baby. They say he loved Harleys and was riding home from work on a summer evening. He never made it home. The truck driver said he never saw him. My mom never remarried, never had more kids. That's all she wrote."

"Sorry about that, too," I say.

The old Buick rumbles. Without a word, I drive towards Grimoire Reaper's Pizza. The traffic light flips to red when we approach, so I slam on the brakes. Putting the car in park as the light turns green, I get out and walk around to Toby's side. He grins a little while shaking his head, slides over and takes the wheel.

Off we go again.

~~~

"Do you know how to pump gas, Ally?" he asks about five minutes later as we approach the interstate crossroads.

I tug on my nose and keep my eyes straight ahead until he stops looking at me. I don't answer.

He adds, "I take that as a no?"

Dear gawd, he's going to show me how to pump gas. I don't want to know how to pump that stuff. The car might explode, or it might get on me and I'll burst into flames.

"No, I don't. And I don't care to learn."

Toby pulls into the Git-n-Split station at the farthest pump from the green, checkered building.

A portly guy ambles out with a loaf of white bread in one hand and his keys jangling in the other. A woman in a navy blue skirt and a tight suit coat is walking in, her matching pumps clicking on the concrete. There's a Volvo SUV next to us, loaded with four kids in back and mom in the passenger seat, all busy tapping on their phones.

Maple hangs her head out of the window, eyeballing the whole place. Her nose quivers, not liking the smell of petroleum and strange interstate people.

"Come on, Ally. I'll show you how to do it," Toby says with a wink.

I open the door and dreadfully walk over to his side of the car as if I'm on death row. I don't want to do this. I don't want to put my hand on that slippery, dirty, rubber-coated pump handle, with the hot, silver spout and deal with gasoline.

"Grab the handle," he says, swiping his credit card at the pump.

The pump dings, readjusts, and announces, 'You may now begin fueling'.

"No," I say, more to the pump than Toby. "I do not want to begin fueling."

"Do it. Put your hand on the nozzle."

Okay. I do that much.

"Now, lift it off."

I don't.

"Lift it off, Ally. Just lift it up and out."

"No."

"Just do it. Pull it out," he says louder, like an order.

I do.

"Now, with your other hand, open the gas cap."

"No."

"Flip open that little door on the car, unscrew the cap and put the nozzle in the gas tank."

I glance up at him, not enjoying this at all.

"You're doing good, Ally. You got this. Now squeeze the lever."

"No."

"Yes."

Fine. I trust him. I squeeze.

The rush of fuel goes gushing into the car. I can feel it moving through the hose. I can smell it. And I'm in control. I exhale. I did it. And it wasn't so bad.

After I slam the nozzle back into the pump, I screw the gas cap back on and push the tiny door shut.

"Proud of you, Ally," he says, smiling.

I've never batted my eyes before, but think I just do. Then, like a needle scratching off a record album, even though I don't think they make record albums anymore, he adds, "Let's go inside and buy a bottle of motor oil. I'll show you which kind, and how to check the oil. It's too easy and something you need to know."

"As educational as that sounds, I don't want to handle any more flammable liquids today, Toby. I really don't," I answer, my school girl blush fading to pale.

"Naw, it'll be fine. I'll buy you a pop, my treat."

I reluctantly follow him into the store.

He leads me to the rear and starts discussing oil. What's best for summer, what's best for winter, and how I need to use the right 'weight' for the old Buick. I try to act as interested as I can as to not hurt his feelings, but wander over to pick out a glazed donut and Dr. Pepper.

Oh no. Dang it. Oh no no no.

At the register, the cashier is Devin Clancy, the creep rapist from church camp. I haven't seen him in years and thought he went off to college somewhere.

"Well, lookie who's here," Devin says. "Is this the equivocal and enigmatic Allison Couch?" he asks, grinning like the doll Chucky in the movie *Child's Play*.

I don't say anything. I only wish I still believed in Jesus so I could ask him to strike Devin with a lightning bolt right between his beady eyes.

"Do you even know what those words mean, little Miss Couch?" he adds, louder.

"I see you got a new pair of glasses," I answer.

"How's it going at Whitehead's?" he answers, leaning on the counter. "Still working as nothing but a clerk at a hardware store? What an exciting life you must lead…"

"Just as exciting as your gas station job, I imagine."

"I'm only home for summer break, helping my dad out. He owns this station, ya know. I'm finishing up my Master's degree at Tufts University. That's Ivy League out east. And you?"

I look down at the floor.

"Tufts ain't Ivy League," Toby drawls, stepping up to the counter.

"Like you would know?" Devin scoffs, eyeballing him with high and mighty contempt.

Toby turns to me, concerned and asks, "What the hell's wrong with this guy?"

Devin sneers and says, "I see you're into black dudes now, Allison. I should've known you like that dark meat."

In about zero seconds, Toby has one hand on Devin's throat, nearly pulling him over the counter.

Devin's hotshot smirk dissolves into his blotchy, red cheeks. He's wheezing, like an asthmatic cat barking up a clump of fur.

"You owe her an apology," Toby says, slow as sin, pulling Devin closer.

"Actually, I think he owes *you* an apology," I say.

Then, I realize Devin probably can't apologize to either of us because Toby is crushing his vocal chords.

"Asshole owes you both an apology!" a trucker yells, standing behind us in line.

Toby doesn't release.

The trucker steps forward and whacks his pack of Starbursts on Devin's head for good measure.

Devin's hands have gone limp and his tongue is lolling out of his mouth, covered in bubbly saliva. His deep shade of red has turned to dark purple, like a fat eggplant.

Toby's gonna kill him if I don't do something.

"Let's go. He's not worth all the paperwork Sheriff Goldberg would have to do if you kill him," I say, with my hand on his shoulder.

Toby seems to come out of a trance and releases his grip. Devin collapses on the counter, gasping back to life, wheezing for air.

I lay a ten down next to his sweaty face, grab our stuff and we walk out the door.

Toby throws me the car keys. I drive us west out of town, as the sun slowly sets. Both of us want to go as far as we can from what just happened. He stares out the window, squinting into the fading light.

I'm unsure what to think. I've never felt so valued in all my life. He makes me feel safe, comfortable, but worried for him at the same time. Maybe that's the feeling of falling in love, which is the scariest, most beautiful and dizzying thing in the world.

I turn on a long, grated dirt road with cornfields and cow pastures on either side. Every once in a while we pass an old farm house and broken up barn. A black Ford pickup truck approaches, and the old man gives us the country salute, which is two fingers up from the steering wheel, like a peace sign.

Twangy country music is blaring from KDOT. Maple has her big head out the back window, ears and cheeks flapping in the warm wind. The lush fields go on forever, luxuriously, like a hand-sewn quilt, fluffed out carefully and full. I could drive like this forever…

"Incoming!" Toby yells.

I swerve to the left, then back to the right as he yanks up the hand brake to stop us. Too late.

THUD

Maple is thrown nearly into the front seat.

"Fuck," he says.

Shocked, I look back and see a deer twisted in the shallow ditch off to the side of the road. It must've darted out of the cornfield and straight into the side of our car.

"Oh no," I whisper.

"Damnit," he says, getting out of the car. Maple jumps out and follows. We drift through a surreal cloud of disbelief, back about five yards.

I groan.

The deer is a doe, laying on her side. Blood is oozing from her velvet, twitching ears, slowly like lava. Her black eyes are wet marbles, spiritless, staring at something far off, or nowhere. Somehow, she's still trying to breathe. Her broken body rises up in agony, then deflates with each desperate whelp.

"What should we do?" I whisper.

A crow crackles, flits down near the deer, then flies off, alarmed. Toby doesn't answer. He's staring at the agonized animal like it's a thousand miles away.

I flip through the options.

"We should call 911. Or the forest department. Or road department. Or Sheriff Goldberg," I say.

The doe rattles in a spasm and pain.

"We could take her to the animal hospital," I add, not realizing how ridiculous that sounds.

Reluctantly, Toby pulls out a pistol from a holster somewhere under the back of his jeans. He aims it at her head, thumbing down the lever.

God's green earth inhales.

He fires.

She stops trying to die.

And dies.

I exhale.

"We couldn't leave her here to suffer, I guess," I say.

He doesn't answer.

A long time ago, a strawberry moon overhead in central Minnesota signaled to the Indians the perfect time to gather ripe fruit. But the rosy moon now shining tells us something else. Just go home. The day is done.

Maple jumps back in the car, spooked.

We turn around without words and drive back to Granola, not stopping for pizza. I'm mentally exhausted and want to go home and sleep for a long time. I think he is, and does, too.

So much for our pizza date.

CHAPTER EIGHT

Grabbing my red apron, I'm relieved to get back in my routine after such an intense night.

"Good morning, Mr. Whitehead. Are you going to show me how to make the keys today?"

The old man blows on his coffee in his yellow mug while shaking his head.

"No, not today, Allison. I have to fill a couple custom orders for those home building contractors. Did you have a chance to ask Toby about the parade?"

"Uh, I was going to ask him last night but then some other stuff came up instead. But I'll today, promise," I answer, writing my time on my card.

As soon as I flip over the OPEN sign and unlock the door, Jungle Jim comes barreling in.

"Is he or isn't he?" he asks.

"Who?"

"Toby. Who the hell else am I talking about?"

"I don't know who or what you're talking about most of the time, Jimmy. That's why I asked," I say.

"Is he going to be on our Independence Day float?"

I walk back to start the popcorn, answering, "I don't know. I didn't ask him. Didn't have a chance, but will."

"I told those old pukes at the American Legion that I wanna be on the float, too. Bob can be the foam hammer. Why can't I ride on the float with Toby?" he whines.

Mr. Whitehead comes out from the back, swinging his yellow mug of coffee around in the air.

"Because he's the Silver Star kid, not you. When you damn near get your butt blown off saving American lives, you can be on our Independence Day float. Until then, you are the foam hammer."

Jimmy plops his shoulders down in resignation and says, "Fine. But can you at least make the face hole bigger? So I can at least see out of that stinkin' thing and not bang my nuts into the fire hydrant like I did last year?"

Mr. Whitehead changes his tone and says, "Sure, Jimmy, will do. And ya' know, I really appreciate your help, bud," he says.

"Okay, I'll do it," he answers, and walks out the door.

~~~

July Fourth begins with 70 percent humidity by seven a.m.

"When does the parade start?" Grandma asks the next day as Maple and I return from our morning walk.

"Noon, Grandma. I'm leaving in a minute, and Bob is on his way over here now. He said last night that he already put the lawn chairs out on Main street. You'll have the best seats in the house. He also has a cooler of Grape Shasta and some venison jerky for you."

"I hate venison jerky," she says, sitting down at the dining room table.

"You love venison jerky, Grandma. You eat it all the time. You asked for it."

I push a cup of coffee towards her, hoping she will calm down and wake up. The doctor prescribes a lot of pills for her to sleep or she'd be up all night climbing the curtains with hairspray and a lighter. However, in the mornings she's like a bear coming out of hibernation, angry and confused.

After she takes a few sips and calms down, I pedal over to the Granola American Legion parking lot where the Independence Day parade is being staged.

~~~

Down Main street, the local German matrons are selling goulash, cabbage buns and bowls of chicken noodle soup with butterballs from a tented concession stand.

Old Mrs. Reifenberger scurries up to me wearing crisp, pull-on jeans and a navy blue blouse spangled with red stars. Gold plastic bangles jiggle around her gray wrists and white dot earrings dissolve into her gooey lobes.

"Where's your grandma, Allison dear? How is Ethylon doing these days? I haven't talked to her in months. I stopped by your house last week but she screamed at me to get off her lawn. She accused me of trying to steal her pink flamingos. I figured she was in one of her moods again," she says, tapping the side of her head.

"Yes, probably so, but she will be here later. I'll tell her to stop by your stand."

"You do that, Allison. You and Bob take care of her, dear. You're all she's got," she says, handing me a small box of hot apple and cream cheese strudel before I leave.

"Thanks, Mrs. Reifenberger, I sure will."

Along the street, families from the Cities, devotedly trying to create unplugged memories for their high tech and wired children, cluster on lawn chairs and blankets, drinking gas station coffee or sucking on sippy cups.

By mid-morning, the Scandinavian town ladies have taken over the inside of the American Legion.

They've brought in loads of Tator Tot hot dish, simmering crock pots of bacon scalloped potatoes, along with pans of creamed green beans covered with french fried onions. Deviled eggs, sprinkled with paprika, float around on silver trays like little boats in a harbor. Bags of ripple chips and Top the Tator dip cover the bar.

Minnesota went non-smoking a few years ago. NO SMOKING. No restaurants, no bars, no parks, nowhere.

But the law doesn't seem to apply inside the Granola American Legion. No one gives a rat's patootie. They smoke pipes, cigarettes and cigars anyway. I guess if these gentlemen fought off Nazis, Commies and Islamic terrorists, smoking is the least of their health concerns.

Morton is whizzing around in his electric wheelchair. He loves to reminisce about 'those damn kraut boys' seventy some years ago. One of his favorite stories is of coming upon one of 'those damn kraut boys' who was severely wounded.

He doesn't talk about the heroism or glory or gore of WWII, but only this one German soldier. Morton said he initially wanted to 'finish him off', but couldn't get over the look in the enemy soldier's eyes. The German desperately mumbled something to Morton, but he couldn't understand what. Then, the 'damn kraut boy turned his head and died'.

Morton is still wondering what the young German soldier said to him, seven decades later.

Sheldon flits around the tables, his eyebrows fluttery and white like snowy butterflies. In Korea, he told everyone in his infantry battalion that he was a catholic priest. He held mass in the field and gave last rites unfortunately to many who died in combat.

Except, he isn't catholic, much less a priest. He's jewish, and was in Talmud Torah school to be ordained as a rabbi when he got drafted. But he knew he had to fill a need at that time, so he said he 'improvised', like 'all good soldiers do'.

He said 'sometimes, something is better than nothing,' as it gave great comfort to those who needed it at the time.

When he returned home to Granola after the war, he married his sweetheart, Golda, and went to school to become a veterinarian.

He says only animals have souls because humans sure the hell don't. He also gave up religion. Sheldon is now the only Atheist in town that lights menorah candles.

The American Legion post commander is Tommy, who was a Navy Seal in the Gulf War. And he actually was, not like every other homeless guy holding up a sign claiming to be. But he never talks about it.

He married Hannah, who was a finance clerk in the Marines. She's the only female veteran in Granola and now the American Legion treasurer.

Their two daughters joined the Navy and are stationed out in California.

Their son went to cosmetology school. He now works as a hair stylist for an Aveda salon in Minneapolis. That's why Tommy and Hannah always have the trendiest, best smelling hair in town.

Tommy's standing in the background, wearing silver, mirrored sunglasses, arms folded across his barrel chest and watching everything like a bald eagle. He sees me and calls, "Allison! Where's our Toby at?"

"Not sure, Tommy. He might be coming, but probably doesn't want to ride on the float," I answer, shrugging my shoulders.

"What kind of answer is that, Allison? Might? Not *might*. Probably? Not *probably*. We need that man on our float. He deserves to ride on our float. And I'm gonna go find him now," he says, storming out the door.

Mr. Clancy slithers over to me.

Oh no. He's going to say something about the Toby and Devin episode at the gas station.

"Good morning, Allison," he says, sounding how stale soda crackers taste, mealy.

"Morning, Mr. Clancy," I say just as Morton whirls up in his wheel chair.

"Gawd damn it, Clancy. Get that TRUMP button off your shirt," Morton yells. "I didn't fight the Nazis just to have pinheads like you go elect one for president."

Clancy looks down at the crippled old man, sickly amused. "Now, now, Morton. It's a free country, isn't it?"

"And we need to keep it that way," he answers, and runs the wheel of his heavy electric chair up and on Mr. Clancy's foot.

"Get off! Get your chair off my toe!" Clancy screams, cringing in pain.

"Not until you get that button off your shirt!"

"Freedom of speech," Clancy hisses.

Morton narrows his eyes, shakes his head, and moves his wheelchair forward a few inches so it's off Clancy's toe. Then, he moves it forward again so it runs up and on his other toe. He waits a few seconds, then pushes forward and buzzes away.

Clancy takes a deep breath and starts to tweak up and down on his feet, apparently trying to get some feeling back into them.

"Now then, Allison," he says. "When did you get that pit bull of yours?"

"I don't have a pit bull," I answer.

Mr. Clancy folds his fat, freckled arms across his big belly and leans back.

"You have a pit bull. And a large one at that," he says.

"No, I don't."

Everyone in Granola knew about Maple, but no one did anything. When Toby and I liberated her and I started taking her around, people fell in love with her.

Except Mr. Clancy.

I heard at the last city council meeting, Mr. Clancy introduced a bill to start a bully breed ban in town, meaning any bulldog, boxer, bull mastiff, bull terrier, mix or cross, would be sent over to St. Cloud to be euthanized at the humane society. Thankfully, the mayor has a boxer named Rocky, so he put a stop to that nonsense.

"I see you walk that big-headed beast all the time. It's always barking upstairs when I come over. Other people see you too, with that dog every day," he says.

"No. I don't have a dog. I have no idea what you're talking about, Mr. Clancy," I answer, glaring at him. "Besides, why are you coming over to our house anyway?"

"It's my job. I'm the county building inspector."

"I know that. But our house don't need inspecting. Neither does Whitehead's Hardware. And especially not the dog we don't have."

"You're getting as crazy as that loony bird grandma of yours," he says, tapping his link sausage finger to the side of his sweaty temple. "Is it any wonder your mother jumped off the deep end."

I clench my mouth and don't answer.

"There's another issue we need to discuss, and it isn't pleasant. You need to tell that grandmother of yours to stop pooping on my lawn," he says.

"Excuse me? Did you just say what I think you said?"

"You heard me. I don't have proof. But I don't need it. I just know it's her," he answers, cringing, buckling up on his sore toes.

"How do you know it's Grandma's, much less people poop?" I ask.

He steps back and says, "If anyone knows poop, it's me, Allison. I know everything that goes on in this town."

"So, you're also a poop inspector?"

"No! I am not!" he says, frowning at me. "But it's something your grandma would do!"

The silence between us is acrid, thick, suffocating. I need some fresh air after this awful conversation.

Turning around without saying another word, I hurry outside to look for Mr. Whitehead.

Elaborate floats, classic old cars, marching bands and shamrock green John Deere Tractors pack the parking lot behind the American Legion.

Sheldon and Mr. Whitehead are busy laying out the foam hammer suit on the side lawn. They're too old to lean all the way over, so they're kicking it around and pushing it with their feet. The costume smells of funk; rolled up too tight and stored too long in a hot shed out behind Mr. Whitehead's house.

"Where's Toby?" Sheldon asks me.

"Sorry, Sheldon, but I'm not sure where he is."

Toby texted me late last night that he'll stop by, but doesn't want to be on the float. Hopefully, he changed his mind.

The float is on a flatbed, with red, white and blue streamers looped around the sides. There is a beautiful banner that reads:

Staff Sergeant Tobias Davenport, US Army
Operation Enduring Freedom, Silver Star Recipient

The Granola Boy Scout troop built the float, handmade with much care and even more pride. The boys constructed a tank turret out of cardboard, painted it camouflage and carefully secured it on top.

One scout, Charlie Sherpa, made a bench for his woodworking merit badge, especially for Toby to sit on.

All the scouts carved their initials on the legs and want Toby to take the bench home after the parade is over.

The flatbed is hooked up to Tommy's Ram 2500 pickup truck. Tommy doesn't brag about being a Navy Seal, but sure does about his truck with dual rear tires.

Every chance he gets, he mentions he has a 'dually', and is thrilled to show it off in the parade. No one is quite sure why he needs such a monstrous, powerful truck. He only drives it back and forth to the American Legion, or over to the St. Cloud VA, or down to Minneapolis for his monthly haircut at the Aveda salon.

"Call him, Allison. Call him now and get him here," Mr. Whitehead says.

The boy scouts are looking at me, eager and hopeful.

I try a few times, but no answer. I'm disappointed but not surprised.

CHAPTER NINE

Jimmy shuffles up, a cigarette balanced on his thin lips, holding a purple tomato the size of a baseball.

"Chutzpah! Jungle Jim! I told you to stay out of my vegetable garden. I saw you in there the other day swiping a green bell. Now you schlep off with one of my prized, heirloom tomatoes?" Sheldon asks, shaking his cane and rushing toward Jimmy.

Jimmy takes a bite out of the tomato as if it's a juicy apple, then looks at me.

"Allison? Did I ever tell you that tomatoes are fruit? Sheldon wisecracker here thinks tomatoes are vegetables," he says, taking another bite.

Sheldon turns as bright as the tomato in Jimmy's hand.

"What are you going to do next, Jimmy? Slurp on my salt lick out back along with the deer?" he asks.

Jimmy puts the half eaten tomato down next to his crotch and says, "How about you slurp on my salt lick right here, old man?"

Sheldon stumbles forward keeping his balance with his cane. He then flicks it up and smacks Jimmy on the side of his head, which sends him flying to the ground.

Cowering, Jimmy covers his face with his hands, and hollers, "Incoming!"

"Stay out of my garden!" Sheldon says.

"I wasn't in your garden!"

"Schmuck!" he answers, smashing his cane down on Jimmy's back.

Jimmy rolls over into the fetal position and cries, "Uncle! I say uncle! Sorry!"

"May you lose all your teeth except one, and that one should ache, you putz!"

"I said I was sorry!"

"Good. Now, if you want a tomato, come over end of August. I can't give them away fast enough. Come on over any time before that if you want. I'll make you a tomato, green pepper and cheddar sandwich. But stop sneaking around my garden. You think you're back in 'Nam crawling through the jungle or what?"

Morton whizzes over in his chair and adds, quite loudly, "He wasn't in 'Nam. They sent him to Thailand to run a USO brothel and eat stir-fried pineapple."

"You ever tried to break up a fight between a pissed off ladyboy and a drunk Marine? I saved the lives of more than a few good men," Jimmy says, his eyes wide, rubbing the side of his head.

"All of you need to calm down," Mr. Whitehead says, rushing into the middle of everything, trying to restore some order.

I feel a warm hand on my shoulder.

He's here.

It's Toby.

"Sorry I'm late. Mrs. Swenson, Mrs. Anderson, and Mrs. Peterson wanted me to try some of their bars," he says, wiping crumbs from his mouth.

"Date, lemon or seven layer?" I ask, relieved.

"All of them. And besides that, Tommy put me in a head lock and promised to kick my ass to Sunday if I didn't do this," he answers, grinning.

"Yeah, Tommy gets excited sometimes," I say.

Toby is wearing blue jeans, red and white striped retro Nikes, and a Vikings jersey. The shirt looks new, just unfolded with the creases still showing.

"Toby," Mr. Whitehead sighs. "Thank God you're here. You see this float? This is our float. Your float."

"Yes, sir, and its' a beauty. The scouts did an amazing job. I sure appreciate it. It'd be an honor to represent you gentlemen in this parade," he answers.

Everyone in the parking lot exhales. The grey, silver and balding heads bob up and down in relief.

"Well, you best get up on it because we're lining up now. We got a couple Eagle Scouts that are going to sit on the back and throw out the candy," Mr. Whitehead says, pointing to the awestruck boys.

The scouts stand up, straighten their uniforms and give the three-finger scout salute. Toby snaps to the position of attention and returns the salute.

Turning to Jimmy, he slaps him on the back and says, "Come on, buddy. Ride with me."

Jimmy's mouth drops open. He swallows hard.

"Who? Me? You talking to me?"

"Yes, you. Let's you and me do this," he answers, hopping up on the float.

"Hell ya!" Jimmy says, giving a little fist pump. He jumps on and takes a seat next to Toby on the bench.

I've never seen Jungle Jim smile so big before. He's happier than a pig-tailed girl with a chocolate sprinkled, double dipped, ice cream cone.

"But who's going to be the foam hammer?" Mr. Whitehead asks to no one in particular.

Just then, Bob comes waltzing up with a corndog in one hand and a half eaten bratwurst in the other.

"Hey, Bob," Mr. Whitehead says slyly. "Come here a minute. You gotta do me a big favor..."

~~~

The parade lines up, and the Harley guys from the Minnesota Patriot Guard rumble through first on their big bikes, breaking off every twenty feet to line the parade route with American flags.

The American Legion honor guard leads the way. All four gentlemen are wearing starched black pants and crisp, white shirts, traditional envelope flight hats loaded with gold embroidery, patches and other hoo haw.

One of them is Jump Master Mike.

Jump Master Mike was a career 82nd Airborne paratrooper, but that ended in Panama when he jumped out of a plane and crushed his spine landing. He needs a walker now, but that don't matter. He stands as straight as his broken body can stretch and has his rifle strapped to his sunken chest.

The second in line are the 4H farm kids with their project animals. Two beautiful black heifers, three annoyed llamas, and several goats. They're on leashes, led by the fresh faced and freckled teen-aged girls. The animals have brilliant, blue ribbons, won at the Minnesota State Fair last year attached to their harnesses. One llama is trying to eat his ribbon, so the girl removes it and stuffs it in her pocket.

However, as soon as the parade starts, everyone realizes it was a bad idea to put the animals second in line.

Obviously agitated, the livestock start blowing out chunks of diarrhea which pretty much covers the roadway for the remaining floats.

Third in the parade is a '69 Chevy convertible with a Git-n-Split gas station banner, driven by Devin Clancy.

Mr. Clancy, wearing a goofy cowboy hat, is sitting on the trunk with his feet in the back seat, swinging his arms high like amber waves of grain. He's throwing out handfuls of candy corn that he must've bought half-price after Halloween last year. Most of the kids scoop up what they can and throw it back at him.

Next in line is Pete Peterson, Mrs. Peterson's son, of Peterson Insurance. He's driving his beige Ford Escort with two poster boards masking taped to the sides, displaying his phone number.

His cute little girls are in the back seat throwing full size Milky Ways and Hershey bars with his business card taped to them, out at the people lining the street. Pete always gets a ton of new business after each parade.

And here comes Whitehead's Hardware giant foam hammer. The kids rush toward Bob, kicking and hugging him at the same time.

Bob slowly topples over, and the kids jump on him, laughing and screaming. Sheriff Goldberg, who is standing nearby, runs over to help him back up as the kids scatter.

Miss Granola, Miss Grimoire County and the Granola High School prom queen are next on three, American quarter horses. Both the graceful horses and young ladies are equally poised and beautiful.

Next, a couple of gigantic John Deere tractors from the farm implement store outside of town, roll through.

Then comes the Granola High School Marching Band and one of the best in the Upper Midwest. The students are loud and proud, and in perfect precision. Covered in pimples, yes, but the type of teenagers that don't slam the door in their mother's faces, or steal their dad's booze, or get hickeys, or think everything is 'boring' or 'stupid'.

They're marching to a tight drum cadence.

Suddenly, the big cymbals crash and they begin playing *The Army Goes Rolling Along*.

The crowds along the streets jump to their feet.

The American Legion float is next with Toby and Jimmy. The boy scouts dangle their feet over the back, jumping off and on to pass out Kit Kat bars.

Tommy drove over to Costlo in St. Cloud last week and spent over three hundred dollars on Kit Kats. He said, 'Hell, I'd give my life to this great country, so what's a couple hundred bucks in Kit Kats, damn it.'

All the adults place their hands over their hearts or salute, cheering as the float passes by. Toby waves back, but Jimmy gets carried away in the patriotic moment. He stands up and throws his arms to the sky. But he's not wearing a belt, and his shorts drop to his ankles.

Jimmy's a little too patriotic.

He's commando.

A bunch of little girls run up towards the float, pointing and yell, "Ewe! Yuckie! What's wrong with his Mister Winkie? Gross!"

"Pull your freakin' pants up, Jimmy!" Toby says, trying not to laugh. The Scouts on the back look over their shoulders, sniggering, "Dude, dude, seriously, dude?"

Jimmy tries to pull up his pants, but loses his balance and falls on his back. Toby stands up, leans over, and unscrews the whole screwed up mess Jimmy is in.

Half a block later, Jimmy is back on the bench next to Toby, like it didn't even happen.

The parade lasts about an hour, and when the finale, the Oscar Mayer Weiner truck drives by, it's over.

Back in the American Legion parking lot, Mr. Whitehead is holding a flimsy shopping bag of colorful paint samples, grumbling that he forgot to give them to Bob to hand out to the parade-goers.

"That's for the best," I say. "The kids would've licked them, so you saved yourself a couple of lawsuits, for sure."

He thinks for a moment and nods his head.

Grandma appears from behind the building with Maple bounding by her side.

"Allison," she calls.

Maple runs up to me, head butting my leg, and tries to be a good girl by sitting but is too excited to sit, so squats down to pee instead.

"What the hell was Jungle Jim doing up on that float? He looked like a retarded caterpillar, wiggling around, trying to get his pants back on," Grandma says.

I shake my head.

"At least Toby looked nice. And Bob did a good job being the foam hammer," she adds.

"Let's go inside and have some lunch," Mr. Whitehead says. "The ladies made quite a spread for us and Hilda, the waitress, brought her homemade double dill pickles."

He puts his arm lightly around Grandma and we all go in and wait for Toby, Jimmy and Bob to return.

CHAPTER TEN

The American Legion is vibrating with excitement. Either that, or beer-buzzed gentlemen too old to be getting drunk. They're all laughing about the Jimmy fiasco, which has already become a funny story in the past.

Maple finds the nearest air conditioning vent. She lays directly on it to take a nap.

Morton and his wife, Vera, are settled at a table like two doddering love birds. I don't see his wife often as she has some 'old person' ailment. I forget which one but she hardly leaves the house, except on special occasions.

Morton drops his gnarled, sun-spotted hand down on Vera's. His own arthritic thumb somehow manages to curl under her palm to hold it.

Johnny Cash comes on the muzak.

"Allison? Did you know my sweet Vera here is the first gal I ever kissed?" he asks.

"I better be the *only* gal you ever kissed," she says to him while winking at me.

"It was over at the Granola Drive-In. Do you remember the first time we kissed?" he snickers.

"Dear, of course I do. We were in row E, watching Bogart in *The Treasure of the Sierra Madre*," Vera smiles, looking down at her lap.

"I think it was row N, for *NO!*" Morton says, laughing.

"It was row E, honey. Because you tried absolutely *everything*," she giggles.

Morton shakes his head.

"We should have kissed in row F. You know, *forever*," he whispers to her.

His small, shriveled shoulders inflate back to the solid melons they once were. Vera sits up and her wizened breasts ripen. But only for a moment.

She leans over and puts her old gray head on his and closes her eyes softly.

"You're still so full of beans," she says.

They fall in love all over again, sixty-five years later.

"Well, if you ever need anything from the hardware store, you just give us a call, Vera. I can drop anything off at anytime, okay?" I say.

"Allison, do they sell penile implants?" he asks.

"Morty!" Vera says, blushing.

Finally, Toby, Bob and Jimmy swoop into the American Legion through the side door.

"Wow, that was a doozie out there today," Jimmy says, taking a seat at our round table. "Glad it's over with."

Toby wipes his brow and says, "You and me both."

"How hard is it to keep your pants on, Jimmy?" Grandma asks. "No one on earth wants to see your little worm. You're lucky a hawk didn't swoop down and pluck it off thinking it was bait."

"It wasn't my fault," Jimmy says.

"Then who's fault was it?"

"You know what, Ethylon? It could've been worse. It could always be worse, so let's forget about it," Bob says, trying to keep the peace.

We all fall quiet. No one wants to talk about Jimmy's junk. Ever. Never in our entire lives. Ever again.

Hilda the waitress brings over cans of pop, paper plates and sets of plastic-ware wrapped in napkins like little mummies.

A few minutes later, Steph bursts through the door like a sizzling firecracker. She's wearing a red and white striped halter vest and cut off, jean shorts. Star spangled from head to toe, even her acrylic, blue nails sparkle.

"She looks like a Yankee Doodle DO ME," Grandma says under her breath, but I tell her to keep quiet.

Steph sits down with us. Grandma adds, "You certainly look 'dandy' today, Steph."

"Hi, Miss Ethylon. It's nice to see you, too," Steph says, fanning herself with her paper plate.

Grandma just hmphs.

Many vets come over and slap Toby on the back, saying 'how damn proud' they are of him, and thank him for his service. Toby stands up each and every time, replying, "Thank you also…You who served before me had it so much worse….Thank you also…"

This goes on for a good ten minutes before we're able to eat our Sloppy Joes, coleslaw, mustard-potato salad and ripple potato chips.

"Needs more salt," Grandma says, and grabs the shaker from Bob. She then winks and adds, "You sure got a nice foam hammer there, Bob."

"You know I will always foam for you, Ethylon," he answers, then plucks a red carnation from the centerpiece and elegantly hands it to her.

"Give me a break, you two. I'm about to lose my lunch," Jimmy says, grabbing his plate to go load up on more food.

Steph chuckles and kicks me under the table. I kick her back. Mr. Whitehead is oblivious and Toby just takes another bite of his Sloppy Joe.

Hilda the waitress waddles over to the table and plunks down a Mason jar brimming with double dill pickles. Her ruddy, round cheeks pop with rosacea.

The dill seed stalks are sticking up from the jar. She pulls them out and shoves them into the centerpiece vase to stand alongside the red, white and blue flowers. Then, she licks her fingers.

"Eat up, Allison," she says, throwing two bumpy dill pickles on my plate.

"Thanks, Hilda. They look great," I answer.

"Pass them pickles to me, please," Mr. Whitehead says, holding out his hand without looking up.

Hilda smacks a fat pickle right in the middle of his palm. He takes a big chaw from it, then another.

"Hey, Toby. My new boyfriend Chad wants to join the Army too, just like you," Steph says between bites. "He talks about it all the time."

Her bleached teeth are flecked with tiny pieces of sauced hamburger and red lipstick.

"That's cool. I hope he does," he answers.

"He wants to be an Airborne Ranger," she says. "And then join the Navy Seals and Delta Force. And after that join the CIA."

"Really?" Grandma asks. "Chad Knutson that works at Taco Gong?"

"Yep, that's him, Miss Ethylon."

"That's a bunch of baloney. I know that boy. I know his mother. She used to go around to the tables after the bar closed and swill down everyone's left over booze."

"Grandma, please, let's not bring all kinds of stuff up now," I say. "Let's just eat this delicious lunch, okay?"

"Everyone knows about Chad except you, Steph," Grandma says.

"And what about Chad?" Steph asks, tensing up.

"He's a pot head," Grandma states.

"He is not," Steph says, squeezing her Sloppy Joe.

"Even Jimmy and I never smoked that much ganja…"

Steph throws down her napkin and says, "I'll have you know Chad is on expert level in *Call of Duty*. Plus, they said they would promote him to assistant manager if he shows up on time for a full week."

"All that kid does is smoke wacky weed behind the dumpster at Taco Gong when he's probably saying he'll take the garbage out," Grandma says.

"That's not true, Miss Ethylon."

"How many whiz bangin' times does the garbage at Taco Gong need to be taken out, Steph? Oh, he'll take the garbage out, all right."

"What are you talking about, Miss Ethylon?"

"Your new boyfriend, Chad. He takes the garbage out every hour because he's smoking and joking with his best friend Bob Marley out by the dumpster," Grandma says.

"How do you know what he does behind the dumpster, Grandma?" I ask.

"You think I don't know? That dumpster is downhill from my bedroom window. What the hell else do you think I do all day beside stare out my bedroom window?"

"Grandma, I thought you came here to the American Legion to play Bingo everyday, not sit and stare out of your window."

"I don't play bingo with anything except my butt."

"Why have you never told me this before?" I ask. "You know you can't sit in your room all day. You told me that you play bingo."

"I don't like bingo. But Chad likes bongo."

Silence.

"Pass me the pepper, please," Bob mutters.

Without looking up, Mr. Whitehead hands him the grinder.

Steph is about to cry, so Toby takes a deep breath and says, "Well, Steph, people change. Usually for the better. Tell Chad if he wants to talk to me anytime about the Army, give him my number. I go for a run every morning, and he can come with me if he wants to prepare."

Steph sniffles and nods her head.

"Who the heck names their kid 'Chad' in the first place?" Jimmy asks. "No wonder he's a pot head."

"It's short for Chadwick," Steph mutters.

"You mean short for Chad wet-my-pants," Jimmy says.

"Shut up, Jimmy," Mr. Whitehead says.

"Chad sounds like something you find in a fat guy's dirty underwear," Grandma adds.

"Both of you, please, just leave that boy alone. It's not his fault his mother named him when she was drunk," Mr. Whitehead says.

"Now I'm curious. I can't wait to meet this guy," Toby says, grinning.

"Well, this conversation certainly took a turn for the worse in a record fifteen seconds," Bob says, looking at his wrist watch.

"Will you please pass me the pickles, Allison?" Steph says, looking to the side, obviously wanting to end this conversation as well.

"Sure," I say, handing her the jar, vinegar spilling over the top.

Grandma, me and Steph all lean back in our chairs.

Steph just found out her new boyfriend is another pothead. I just found out Grandma does nothing but stare out her window when I'm gone. And Grandma, well, she hasn't heard anything she doesn't already know.

CHAPTER ELEVEN

The next morning, despite the cotton candy residue still hanging in the hot, humid air, the town is spotless.

The trendy parents and young children have long driven back, licked up in traffic heading toward the Twin Cities. They left Granola neat as a pin, following the recycling bin rules to a tee.

I heard there were complaints that the Granola matrons did not offer vegan choices, or gluten free options along with their home-cooked dishes. And peanuts and dairy were floating amok causing havoc with allergies. Other than that, I'm sure they will all be back next year.

Maple and I walk to the field, and I throw her ball as far as I can. She takes off, kicking up clouds of dust under her big paws before bringing it back like Dale Jr. cruising a victory lap. Dropping the drool covered ball at my feet, I throw it again, and off she goes towards the horizon.

I wish I could feel the absolute joy of a dog running in soft dirt, chasing a ball. Bringing it back, and going out again to get it, not mad that the same ball is thrown over and over and brought back over and over.

I open up the store at nine, but Mr. Whitehead calls and says he'll be in later. Most everyone in Granola, including him, is probably home nursing a hangover.

"Good morning, Allison," he says, shuffling in the front door about noon.

He doesn't even bother going to his office.

He adds, "Say, I'm going to close up a bit early today. Need to get over to the American Legion for a meeting. Gotta wrap some things up after the parade. Why don't you take the afternoon off, too."

"Sounds good, Mr. Whitehead," I say, taking off my red apron. "We didn't have one customer all morning, not even Jungle Jim."

"Alrighty. I'll see you bright and shiny tomorrow."

"Bright and shiny for sure."

After I send a text to Toby, I stop by Chub to get lunch for Grandma and a book of postage stamps for our bills.

A frumpy woman with thin, feathered hair hangs over the customer service counter. The store manager bustles over. The lady, manager and cashier get into a very nice Minnesota argument. The woman is now banned from returning food without a receipt, because she's been doing it everyday. It's unspoken, but she's been getting food from the food shelf and returning it here for the cash.

After the cashier politely takes the return for the last time, the lady leaves with her dignity.

At the deli counter, Maggie Root is busy slicing the salami. I've known her since high school, and she always gives me the scoop on what salad is the most freshly made.

"Hey, Allison," she says, shutting off the machine and peering over the glass case.

"Hey, Maggie. What's good today?"

"Anything but the crab salad. That nasty crap is gonna get up and crawl back to the ocean any minute now. But I just made the bow tie, tuna & pea salad. It has a little kick to it, too. Pinch of chili powder. But don't tell anyone. I'm suppose to follow the recipe. Corporate rules, ya know."

"Mums the word. And I'll take two quarts. Thanks."

Lots of kids in school called her carrot-head. Not for having red hair, but because one day she proclaimed herself a vegetarian. So, Devin and his friends started chasing her around the cafeteria with hotdogs, or whatever else kind of meat we were served at lunch.

Finally, fed up with the torment, she ended up eating her lunch in the girls bathroom for the rest of the year.

Maggie married her high school sweetheart, John Root.

John went to vocational school when he graduated and is now the busiest and best plumber in Grimoire county.

When John was about twelve years old, he threw a M80 cherry bomb down a open manhole in front of his house. It ignited the methane gas down there and blew up everyone's toilet for a whole town block.

His parents had to take out a second mortgage on their house to pay for all the repairs and new toilets. Mr. Clancy wanted to send him away to a juvenile detention center, but Sheriff Goldberg didn't press charges.

Instead, he put John to work around town. For an entire year, he had to mow the affected neighbor's yards in the summer, rake in the fall, and shovel their sidewalks in winter to make amends. The neighbor's quickly forgave him, and still laugh about it.

John said the whole experience is what sparked his interest in plumbing. He makes good money too, and has long paid back his parents.

Neither Maggie nor John are much to look at, but nature sure blessed their two boys. A model scout saw the kids at The Tasty Spork a few years ago. He offered them both a modeling contract on the spot.

Once a month, Maggie drives them down to the Twin Cities for 'gigs' and photo shoots. The boys are always in the Target store flyers on Sundays, or in advertising for the Mall of America.

~~~

I pedal home with the salad. Grandma is out by the side of the garage, watering her morning glory garden.

A few years ago, Bob tacked chicken wire all the way up the side of the garage. One single morning glory plant took off, and now the entire side is a thick carpet of heart shaped leaves, twirly vines and the deep purple trumpets.

"Toby was here but I told him to get lost," Grandma says, shutting the water hose off.

"Grandma, really?" I ask, holding up the Chub bag so Maple won't snap at the food.

"Just kidding. He treats you good, Allison. Handsome too. You sure he ain't related to Denzel Washington?"

"He already told you he's not."

"He brought over some fancy cinnamon-caramel ice cream. He said it's GEE LAW TOE. I told him to go buy me a case of Coors Light for dessert instead."

"Grandma. Just stop."

"Fine. He's actually inside watching a game show with Bob," she answers, as Maple follows us into the house.

Once we all start eating, Grandma looks at Toby and asks, "You gonna help Allison get her license or what? It'd be nice if she got it before I kick the bucket."

"That's what we're working on, ma'am," Toby says. "We'll go out today for another practice run."

"I'll take the test as soon as I am ready, okay?" I answer, mad with myself for not getting it long ago.

"About time you get your license," Bob chimes in.

"I know that." I sputter, stabbing a mayonnaise soaked noodle as hard as I can.

"I wouldn't pressure her," Toby says.

"That's right. We all know Allison don't like pressure," Grandma says.

I throw my fork down and glare at her. "What's that suppose to mean?"

"It means you don't like pressure, Allison. That's all I said and all I meant."

Bob takes a big gulp of milk and says, "Who likes pressure? I sure don't."

I sit back and fold my arms across my chest.

"Ally, are you ready for another lesson?" Toby asks, trying to keep the peace.

"That would leave me with the dishes," Grandma says.

"How hard for you to throw these dishes in the dishwasher so she can go get a driving lesson, Ethylon? How hard is that?" Bob asks, turning towards her.

"How hard are you?" Grandma answers with a wink.

"I'll wash your dish anytime," he says, grinning back.

I can't handle this mental picture so run out the door with Maple on my heels. I jump into the Buick. A few minutes later, Toby appears, pulls up the garage door and sits in the passenger side. Maple leans over the back seat and starts to lick his fingers, then slops on his neck.

"Let's practice driving on the interstate," he says.

"No way," I answer, now in a bad mood. The car rumbles in neutral after I back out of the garage.

"Come on now, you can do it, Ally," he says, pointing through the window. "Turn right at the interchange, and then merge onto the interstate."

"People drive too fast on the interstate."

"It's easy once you do it, so let's give it a try. Don't make this a bigger deal than it is."

"Fine," I snip. "I'll get on the interstate if that makes you happy."

Toby grins and says softly, "Ally, I'm already happy enough being with you. All I'm saying is we need to do some highway driving practice."

I look over at him, so patient and calm, and my icky mood melts. It's impossible to be pissy with him.

Driving up the road, I turn right, down the entrance ramp onto I-94.

"You *do* know the difference between yield and merge, correct?" he asks.

I slow the car down to about twenty miles per hour.

He continues, "You merge onto the interstate. Yield means prepare to stop, but merge means pick up the speed. You need to get up to the same speed of all the other cars so they don't, uh, run into you."

He stares into his side view mirror and continues, "Like I said, pick up speed. Give it some gas so you, we, don't get plowed over by a semi, like that one barreling up our ass right about now."

The driver of the eighteen-wheeler lays on his horn, hits his brakes, yanks up the reserve brakes and swerves to the left lane as I enter into the right lane.

The noise of the giant truck trying not to kill us is deafening. An SUV honks, and swerves over too.

"Well, that was a little rough. But you'll get the hang of it," he says, and I wonder how a black guy can turn as white as a ghost.

I eventually do get the hang of it, cruising down the interstate, making sure to keep exactly at 60 mph, not one notch over, not one less.

About ten miles from Granola, he points towards the approaching exit ramp and says, "Why don't you get off at this next exit. Be sure to signal."

"That leads out to the old Granola Drive-In. The owners burned it down to collect insurance money about five years ago. I'm not sure what's out there now."

"Well, let's go see then."

I take the unappreciated gravel road, leading out east, passing a neatly ordered apple orchard. The farm house next to it has a confederate flag being used for a living room curtain and four cars on blocks in the front yard.

The sun starts dimming as thin fingers of grainy clouds reach across the sky. I keep driving, doing good because it's more or less a straight shot to nowhere.

Suddenly, the car heaves.

Bang, okay okay okay, bang, okay okay okay, bang, okay okay okay, bang.

"Pull over, Ally," Toby says, wrinkling his brow. "We have a flat tire."

We stop. Maple jumps out and dashes off into a cow pasture after a quarrel of sparrows.

We both squat down next to the rear left tire.

"That looks flat," I say.

Toby pulls his lips back, slowly answering, "Yes, it is."

"Flat as a pancake," I add.

"Yes, flat as a pancake."

"I think it's actually *flatter* than a pancake."

"Probably so."

"I think it's the flattest tire I have ever seen."

"You got a spare?" he asks, but I can tell he's getting annoyed with me.

"Spare what?"

"Spare tire," he says, getting more annoyed.

"Uh," I answer.

"Open the trunk," he says, now officially annoyed.

"How?"

Toby plucks the keys from the ignition and opens the trunk. He lifts out a bag of Goodwill clothes that never got dropped off, a Bigfoot snow shovel, a box of silver metal ice cube trays, a laundry basket of Encyclopedia Brittanica books, then pulls up the bottom of the floor.

He yanks loose a spare tire and a wrench, along with a ratchety sort of tire jack, covered with cobwebs.

"Finally," he says, throwing the tools to the ground.

I kick the wrench and ask, "Now what?"

Kneeling down, he carefully pushes rocks away from around the flat tire.

"Do you know how to change a flat, Ally?" he asks sharply, pulling the spare towards him.

"Nope."

"You're gonna learn how right now, so pay attention," he says, pointing to where he wants me to stand.

"Yes, sir."

"When changing a tire, it's of paramount importance that you loosen the lug nuts first. If you undo them while the car is on the jack, you run the risk of knocking the car off it," he says as he starts to loosen the nuts.

"Don't take them all the way off," he adds. "Just crack the nuts open."

"Like a little squirrel," I say.

"If you say so, Ally. Now look. See this tire jack? You open it like this, and set it up under here like this, then you start pumping."

I stoop beside him and watch as he yanks the jack up and down as hard as he can. Slowly, the car's rear lifts up.

"Next, you undo the nuts the rest of the way with your fingers." Then he adds, "Like a little squirrel."

"That's what I was thinking," I answer.

"Good. Now watch me."

He puts the lug nuts in a neat pile, pulls off the flat tire then pushes it under the rear door.

"See what I just did? If you want to keep your legs, you use the flat tire as a back up cushion if the main jack fails. You see how I'm doing this?"

"I see," I answer, getting bored with this all.

He puts the spare tire on and says, "No, you don't see. You need to be prepared and know how to do this. You don't ever want to be stuck in the middle of nowhere by yourself with a broke car. So get your cute butt down here and do it for yourself."

I spend a few minutes putting the lug nuts back on, then he shows me how to jack the car down, and further tighten them up.

"I think I got it," I say, out of breath.

Toby smiles, does that wink-blink thing with his eyes, and says, "I knew you could do it. Good job, Ally. Do you want to practice it one more time?"

"I'm sure I got it. Thanks for showing me how, Toby."

He throws the old tire in the trunk along with everything else. Maple, him and I pile in the Buick and head back to Granola.

The sun is having a hard time calling it a day, lingering on the edge of the world, not wanting to take her business anywhere else but Minnesota. I roll down my window and take a deep breath. I wish I believed in Jesus again so I could thank him for putting Toby in my life.

CHAPTER TWELVE

"Good morning, " I say, grabbing my red apron.

"Yes, it is, Allison," Mr. Whitehead answers, sitting back. He takes a sip from his yellow mug.

"Are you going to show me how to make the keys?"

"Not today. I gotta run to Grimoire and pick up some special order items from Farm Depot. Mrs. Albertson needs some triangle door hinges. This other lady, a young mother, needs a rubber bumper for her baby stroller."

"Like you always say, Mr. Whitehead, we deliver."

"Yep, we sure do. I'll be back by five. Will you call the customers and tell them the delivery will be here after that? Just don't tell them I went to Farm Depot. We don't want anyone to know about my secret source."

"Nope. You're secret's safe with me," I answer.

"All right, see you in a bit," he says, clicking off from his computer. He hoists himself up and plods out the door.

As soon as I flip the OPEN sign over, in rushes a young woman with a baby stroller. She's sporting a neon pink top, capri leggings and her glossy brown hair is pulled back in a cute pony. Mascara clumps in tiny chunks at the ends of her long lashes. Her running shoes look bouncy. She's bouncy. I wish I had her sparkling teeth.

But she's grimacing. Her forehead is tightly bunched in a worried knot.

"Where's my rubber baby buggy bumper?" she demands, eyes narrowed at me.

"We got that under control, ma'am. It should be here by five, because we're all about customer service at Whitehead's Hardware," I answer, taking a step back, not wanting any of her anxiety flaking off on me.

Her eyes widen. She repeats, "Five?"

"Yes ma'am. Your buggy bumper will be here by five."

Throwing her hands up in the air, she begins babbling; "I can't get here at five. I can't. I have a baby and my husband will be home about that time. Then, we have a family style meal and a pleasant evening enjoying each other. You know, precious moments like that. Gawd, I still don't know what to make for dinner. I love kale but my husband hates kale. He says it tastes like poverty, calls it 'crap salad'. He says only Bernie voters eat crap like kale. He only wants iceberg. Can you believe it? Iceberg lettuce? There's no nutritional value in iceberg!"

She then covers her face with her manicured fingers, squeezing her forehead.

Woah.

This woman is way too upset about kale, and baby buggy bumpers, than any normal person should be.

As reassuring as I can sound, I say, "No problem, ma'am. The bumper probably isn't that big, so if you live in town, I can drop it off on my way home today. You just tell me where you live. I'd be happy to do that for you."

"Really?" she exhales.

"Really."

"Promise?" she asks, straightening up, calming down and takes a deep, slow breath.

"Promise," I nod reassuringly. "If you stop by Chub today, it's five-bucks-a-cluck. Rotisserie chicken. You get a whole one. Grab a package of mashed potatoes, you know, the pre-made stuff, and a jar of gravy. Then, you don't have to worry about what to make for supper."

She doesn't say anything so I add, "Chub brand corn cans are about .89 cents, too."

"Thanks," she says, calming down. "That actually sounds good. Sure. It will be 'comfort food' night. And my name is Kristin McCarthy, by the way."

She scribbles down her address.

"Alrighty then. I'll see you a little after five," I say.

Kristin nods, then turns, her pony tail trying to keep up, as if hanging on for dear life. She runs out the door with her stroller toward Chub.

~~~

After work, I pedal over to Kristin's house. She lives in the pristine, new development on the southern edge of town, Castle Court Estates.

Twenty giant houses have been built so far with more planned. The homes are as big as small apartment buildings, gabled and garish. It's amazing how one family could take up so much space.

But the driveways are puzzling. The three stall garages open to the side, so you have to drive up and make a hard turn to get into them. I guess that's the trend now.

A glass and curled wood table is arranged between two rattan peacock chairs on her porch. An elaborate cast iron pig, potted with azaleas and marigolds, smiles back at me.

I press the doorbell. It chimes the beginning of Beethoven's Moonlight Sonata. After a minute, she throws open the thick, oak door.

"Just in time before my husband gets home. Thank you so very much," Kristin gushes.

I hand her the rubber baby bumper I somehow balanced on my bike to get here. Her house whiffs of Chub rotisserie chicken and something pungent and sour.

"Oh, and I got the chicken you suggested, but I don't do corn. Too starchy. Got the fresh asparagus instead," she says, standing in the doorway, still in her in running attire from this morning. She couldn't be much older than me, probably the same age, mid-twenties.

She continues, "I'd love to give you a tip, but recently, my husband doesn't give me cash. He wants to see everything I buy charged on a credit card."

I pull out my phone to check the time to make sure I'm not back in the 1950s. Nope. I'm good. So, I say, "I don't need a tip, Kristin."

"What's your name, by the way?" she asks.

"Allison. Allison Couch."

"Like the thing you sit on in the living room?"

"Yes. Exactly like the thing you sit on in the living room," I answer.

"Thank you, Allison," she says, grabbing the stroller parked on the side of her glorious entryway. She starts jiggling it back and forth like a dry martini. Or kale protein shake, in her case.

"What's your baby's name?" I ask, trying to sneak a peak but don't see the baby under all the blankets.

"Daniel. But I like to call him Little Danny Bo Bumpkins Doo Doo man."

"Can I see him?" I ask.

A glint of horror flashes over her face, then she pulls her lips back into a forced smile.

She doesn't answer that question, instead says, a little too proudly, "He's a beautiful, healthy, baby boy. We decided to go gender color neutral. No blue or pink. Only greens and earth tones. Muted, but no pastels."

She pauses, then adds, "Secondary colors are in. Citrus, kumquat, and a little plum for contrast."

"Uh, I bet he's cute," I answer, gritting my teeth at the bundle of blankets and plush purple caterpillar on top.

"Yes indeed he is. Adorable. We're actually trying to get pregnant again," she says, patting her stomach.

"Who's we?"

She hesitates, then answers, "My husband and I are, of course. We're trying to get pregnant."

"Men can't get pregnant."

"I know that, Allison. What I mean is, marriage is a team effort. So is having a child together."

"Sure," I say, backing away. She's starting to creep me out, so I turn and walk back to my bike to get home.

"Allison?" she calls to me as I swing a leg over.

"Yes?"

"Thanks again for dropping this off. I appreciate it. Maybe I'll come down to the store tomorrow. You can help me pick out some new baby safe outlet covers. The ones my designer chose are cheap plastic and I worry so much about little Danny and electricity. You know... turn your back for one minute and ZAP!"

Oh my.

I swallow hard and say, "We got a nice brand, Baby Bee Safe, like the bee, you know, the little logo is a bee. I bet you would like those."

"I heard about them, saw them online just a few days ago. You carry Baby Bee Safe?"

"We sure do, and we can special order anything else you need for little Daniel."

Her shoulders suddenly drop and she slams the door.

Something isn't right with Kristin and Little Danny Bo Bumpkins Doo Doo man. I'm missing something. Not sure what, but something just ain't right with her.

~~~

I pedal as hard as I can to Chub to buy some five-bucks-a-cluck chicken also, then get on home with the bags swinging off my handle bars.

I pass by Sheldon's house. He's out in the yard watering his prized collection of fuchsia pink, bright yellow and blood red teacup roses.

"Good evening, Sheldon," I call.

He waves the hose up in an arc, then whips it down again, creating a rainbow over him.

"Great day in Minnesota," he calls back.

When I get home, Maple barks from the inside before I even reach the porch. Bob's screaming at the TV.

"Hi ya, Bob," I say, shutting the door as Maple rushes towards me. She's always deliriously bonkers when I come home, acting like I'd never return, relieved when I finally do. Or maybe she just smells the chicken.

"Chick chick chicken," Grandma yells from the kitchen. "Just don't throw the bones away again. We need to boil them and make stock afterwards," she adds, grabbing the bags of food.

"You don't make no stock," Bob says. "All you do is keep the carcass on the counter for a week before it turns moldy and I have to pitch it out in the swamp behind the house for the 'coons. You don't want Maple grabbing it and choking to death. You can't feed dogs chicken bones."

Grandma storms over to the couch, grabs the remote, and smacks Bob on the head.

"I ain't never fed no dog no chicken bones. I only want to make stock but you throw the bones away before I get a chance."

"You get all the chances in the world to make your dang stock. But every week you don't."

"You're missing my point, Bob, you Repubturd!"

"What do chicken bones have to do with my politics? Anybody was better than your gal Hillary. Tell her to send me an email. Oh wait, she deleted them all."

"You leave my gal Hillz out of this!" she says.

"You started it."

"Did not!"

"Did too!"

Stepping between them, I quickly grab the remote from Grandma before she whacks Bob again.

"Both of you, please. Let's have supper and worry about politics and chicken bones later," I say.

Bob simmers down. Grandma does also so we finally pull the chairs to the table and eat.

~~~

Afterwards, by the time I get to the field with Maple, Toby is already sitting under the tree. His legs are sticking out in front of him, feet flopped to either side.

Maple runs up and head butts him before zinging off to chase a wild turkey, ducking into the fringe of trees on the far side of the field.

I sit down next to him. He has a small bottle of Jim Beam between his thighs. The sweet stink of alcohol fills my nose. He tucks the whiskey around to his side, not trying to hide it much, while staring straight ahead.

His profile is outlined by the setting sun, smooth and graceful, but angry. It's the side of him I saw at the gas station with Devin Clancy.

"Hey," I say.

"Hey," he answers.

Maple is barking in the distance. A wood thrush lands nearby, takes off, circles around and comes back. A chickadee chirrups, as if saying, 'Don't come 'round here, Don't come 'round here.'

"Fuck everything," he says.

I don't know what to say, so don't say anything.

"Sorry, Ally. I start thinking sometimes..."

"About what?" I ask.

"I don't know."

"I don't know either."

"Yeah," he says.

"What the heck are we talking about, Toby?"

He holds his breath, then exhales, answering, "I went to the VA today for my appointment. Every time I go there, they ask the same stupid question, 'Do you have thoughts of harming yourself or others?'"

"What's wrong with that?"

He shakes his head and mutters, "No shit I do. How about I tell those fools, 'Why, yes, sir. I do. Every other God damned day since I got back.'"

"Just tell them that, then," I say, hiding my shock. Toby seems like the most balanced person in Granola. But then again, he could of easily killed Devin with one hand.

"Yeah, right. I'll just say, 'Oh, yes doctor. My biggest accomplishment since I've been back is not harming myself or others every other day.'"

He takes a long drink and adds, "Here's what they need to ask, 'How can we *help* you deal with your thoughts of harming yourself or others?'"

"Maybe you should suggest that to them."

Toby turns and glares at me, his black eyes frenzied with electricity.

"Seriously, Ally? You think I should just put that in their little suggestion box?"

"Do they have one?"

"No, they don't have one," he guffaws.

Then, as if asking if I ever tried sushi, he asks, "Have you ever wanted to kill yourself?"

I feel like he slapped me into his hidden world. I'm terrified and honored. Not knowing what else to do, I tell him the truth.

"Yes. I have. I think most people have thought about it. Everybody hurts, sometimes. Grandma once told me 'you haven't lived if you've never wanted to die.'"

Toby finishes off his booze.

I continue, "But I don't think it's about wanting to kill yourself. No one wants to do that. I think it's about wanting to end the feelings that are making you *want* to kill yourself. If that makes sense."

"Yep. It does," he says, throwing the empty bottle as far as he can. It thuds in the dirt and bounces into the weeds.

A crow dives down, lands, cackling at the sky.

"How would you do it?" he asks.

I shrug and answer, "I'd probably just take a bunch of pills and go to sleep. Definitely not a gun or knife. No blood. Nothing messy that someone has to clean up. Clorox bleach wipes are too expensive unless you got some good coupons."

He nods, squints, and almost laughs. "If you say so, Ally. Nothing messy unless you leave behind coupons for bleach wipes…"

"But it wouldn't end anything," I say. "If you kill yourself, it doesn't end a thing."

"Yes, it would."

"No, it wouldn't. All the demons would just latch on to someone else, whoever's left behind."

"They could go back to Hell."

"The Devil don't want them back. They would latch onto other people instead. My mother killed herself. That didn't end anything. It just transferred all the pain to Grandma and me. It's like an inheritance we have to drag around and can't buy anything with."

The wind is tender, picking up hints of rich dirt and dusty ragweed. Gypsy moths glide by, hover around us. Toby nods his head quietly.

But what I really want to do is shake him, scream into his ear, his head, as loud as I can, *Because when the sun rises the next morning after a bad night, and you climb out of your black hole, your temporary insanity, understanding all those thoughts were a vicious lie, whispered by a demon that hates you, and you see the shore, no longer immobile, and can swim, grateful, and look up at the sky, and appreciate the brilliant blueness and thank it for being there instead of cursing it's arrogant glory.*

Maybe he heard me.

His dark cloud dissipates, and he emerges from his horrible mood. He nods his head a little. I glance at him, then up toward the sky…and all it's glory.

He puts his hand on mine. I turn mine up toward his and clasp, intertwining our fingers. The songbirds become louder. Maple lays down in front of us, and for the next hour, we just hold hands before walking home.

On my front porch, we hug for too short of time.

"Thanks for listening," he says quietly.

"You need to go home and get some sleep. Promise?"

"Alright," he says, and gives me a quick, light kiss.

Watching him slowly disappear down the sidewalk, he dissolves into the fuzzy shadows of the night.

~~~

Back in my room, I fall on my bed next to Maple.

I wonder what it would be like to really kiss Toby. Maybe I should have invited him in but I can't imagine how wonderful it would be to have sex with him. I never had much practice.

Steph tried to teach me a long time ago. She made me practice French kissing on her mirror, and even told me the sounds I was suppose to make.

The only time I had sex was back in high school at our graduation party. It was a six kegger down at Big Loon Lake. This cute guy, Billy Tollefson, asked me if I wanted to play 'bop the bishop'.

We ended up in the back seat of his Cadillac Cimarron, even though neither one of us knew what we were doing. I guess that's how it goes with first times. He got mad at me because I wouldn't move. So, I started to wiggle around, but he said, "No, not side to side. You're suppose to move up and down." I said, "Since when are you Dr. Feelgood the sex expert?"

He told me I was suppose to moan and make some noise. So I did. He got mad again and told me I sounded like a yipping chihuahua.

"Stop yipping!" he said.

I told him he sounded like he was dry heaving up a dead squirrel. Afterwards, we both got out of the car and went our separate ways.

A few summers ago, I wanted to have sex with this smarmy guy named Vinnie Cardello. I thought that would be the coolest last name ever to have. Marry him, get rid of Couch and change it to Cardello.

Vinnie was from St. Cloud, working nearby on probation, doing his 'sentence to service' time. He never told me what he got in trouble with the law for, just said he was 'as framed as Michelangelo.'

After the project was over, he never came by the store again even though he said he would. I'm glad I didn't have sex with him after all.

I text Toby to make sure he's home and safe. He texts back with a simple, 'yes,' and a 'good night'.

My thoughts finally slow down and I fall asleep.

CHAPTER THIRTEEN

At work the next morning, Lexi Hooper marches in. She's holding the hand of a dainty little girl. In the other, she's toting a car carrier seat with a sleeping baby that looks like a miniature Winston Churchill.

Her over-sized sweatshirt is smeared with not only her breakfast, but her baby's and toddler's as well. Black coffee, peanut butter and something orange.

Lexi's a few years older than me. She got a college scholarship in gymnastics when she graduated from high school. However, she had to come home after the first year. She had begun puking too much to keep her weight down and had to be hospitalized.

"Hey, Allison," she says.

"Hey, Lexi."

She drags the girl and lugs the carrier up and down the main aisle. The toddler begins to whine. The baby punches its rebellious fists in the air harder than punks in the front row of a Metallica concert. Lexi heaves in desperation, peering down the aisles.

"Something I can help you find?" I ask.

"Nails. I need some nails," she answers as the child screws up her face, holding her breath.

"Do you want common brights, cement coated sinkers, galvanized casing, finishing, underlayment, cut clasp, ring shank drywall, round heads, oval heads, box heads, split proof wood siding, hardened pole barn, dry spirals, duplex bright or galvanized roofing nails?"

"Mommy!" the child erupts.

"Just give me about a dozen nails. For pictures. I want to hang pictures," she answers curtly.

"How heavy are the frames? Are you sure you don't want the picture hanging nail kit?"

She scowls at me, wanting to rip my eyes out for wasting sweet, valuable time with all these questions. But Mr. Whitehead always told me to up-sell to the customer. Why sell her twelve nails at four cents apiece when I can sell her a few picture hanging kits at $5.99 apiece?

"Gawd, Allison. All I want are some fucking nails to hang some pictures," she hisses through clinched teeth.

"Mommy said the F word! Mommy said the F word!" her child hoots.

"Alrighty then," I say, grabbing three packs of picture hanging nail kits for her.

At the counter, Lexi whacks down a credit card. The child kicks her shin, trying to pull away, but Lexi keeps her locked close with a vise-like grip around her wrist.

Ruffling up, the baby is ready to crow bloody murder any second now. Then does, at full squawk. Lexi skims a scribble across the receipt as a signature, throws her Visa in her Vera Bradley bag, and charges out the door.

Mr. Whitehead emerges from his office holding his clipboard and saunters over to the green Grillgreats we have displayed near the front. He fondles the handle on one of the grills. After running his fingertips over the gleaming dome of one, he wipes off the smears with his shirt. People around here love looking at them Grillgreats, but no one has ever bought one.

He glances at his watch and says, "Well, you better go get some lunch. I'll watch the front for a bit."

"Steph told me she got fired from Chik-n-Frys, but just got a new job at Sub Station. She said if we come in today, she won't ring us up for everything. Give us a deal."

"Bring me back a meatball foot long, please," he says, tossing a twenty dollar bill on the counter. "Get yourself one too, but pay for them, for gawd's sakes. We don't need to get Steph fired on the first day of her new job."

Jimmy bumbles through the front door, holding a smoldering cigarette stub.

"You want a sub sandwich today, Jimmy? I'm buying," Mr. Whitehead asks.

Jimmy sticks the cigarette butt into his pocket. "Hell no. I don't want no Sub Station sandwich. Have you seen the owner, Gerald? He looks like a shifty-eyed big mouth trout. A perv. I know all about pervs and he's one."

Mr. Whitehead and I cringe as he continues, "That dude looks like he would sniff ladies's bicycle seats."

"That's enough, Jimmy. All I did was offer to buy you lunch but you're making me lose my appetite," Mr. Whitehead says. "You need to stop talking like that."

"Sorry. I'll take a hot tuna melt, with pepper jack cheese, and pickles and that's it," he answers. "And throw on some bacon and jalapeños. Extra mayo. And lettuce and onions. Do they have cucumbers? Some cucumbers. Olives too, both black and green if they got 'em."

I pull off my red apron, grab the twenty dollar bill and ask Jimmy, "Is that it then?"

"That's it, I'm not fussy. But if they have some ranch dressing, tell them to give it a squirt. And tomatoes."

"Anything else?"

"Nope, that's all. Unless they have guacamole, I'll take that. And mustard. The yellow kind, not that brown stuff that has little beads in it."

"You want the kitchen sink on it too, Jimmy?" Mr. Whitehead asks.

"No, just some pepperoni."

Lunchtime is busy at the strip mall near the interstate. Family vacationers, sick and tired of each other, fresh off the road, refuel on gas and eat fast food. Lots of road construction men, sitting around smoking Marlboro Reds and drinking anything with caffeine.

But the truckers use the Come-n-Pump gas station on the other side of the interchange. Mr. Engeson, the owner, has the long parking lots for the semi trucks to pull in.

He also built a huge, special bathroom addition to the store, but only for the truck drivers. It's equipped with lockers, free use of towels and shower stalls. He got his buddy who owns a construction business to install high end granite tiles and counter tops.

Dorothy, his wife, owns Granola Floral, so she's always over there planting flowers around the store in huge terra cotta pots next to the pumps.

But what Mr. Engeson is most proud of, however, is the dispenser soap. He says the soap is specially scented with mint and chamomile. That's suppose to wake the truck drivers up but calm them down at the same time.

Mr. Engeson calls the soap, 'Trucker's Delight.' He pays a lot of money for it, so only truckers that fill up their tanks can use the shower and special soap for free.

The guys come from miles out of their way, on their routes to somewhere like Chicago or Idaho to refuel and shower with the special soap.

When a female truck driver stops in, Mr. Engeson kicks all the men out just so the lady can have her peace for as long as she wants.

Grandma says Mr. Engeson also has 'floozy hookers' over there that give special body massages too, but I don't want to know about that.

When I get to Sub Station at the strip mall, the line is about six deep. Steph is standing behind the counter in the middle. Not the bread-slicer and cheese and meat put-er on-er, but the veggie-laying condiment-squeezer, who then passes it to the end cashier. I can tell she's mad because she wants to be the cashier, the one in charge.

"Hey, Steph."

"Hey, Allison," she says, smiling when she sees me. "Sorry you gotta pay for these sandwiches this time. But the assholes won't let me cashier on the first day. They don't trust me yet. Can you believe that?"

"No problem. How are you liking your new job?"

Steph makes a face as her piece of Bubblicious falls out of her mouth and lands on Jimmy's sandwich.

She picks it off, pulls the lettuce from it, and sticks it back in her mouth.

"Not bad. We get free pop when it's not busy." She then adds softly, "Girlfriend, will you stop back later? Please? I gotta tell you something in person, not over the phone. This is serious."

"Sure, will do, Steph. Hang in there," I answer.

After moving through the line, I then ride my bike back to Mr. Whitehead's with the heavy bag of sandwiches.

CHAPTER FOURTEEN

I hear Mr. Whitehead slam down his phone. He walks out of his office, his big belly covered by a meatball stained napkin. He wads it up and tosses into the trash.

"Morton hasn't been able to move the past few days. Hasn't been at the American Legion at all. I stopped by his house last night and he's just been sitting in his Lazy-Boy, can't even manage to get in his wheelchair," he says.

"Oh no. I'm so sorry to hear that. Morton is as good as they come," I answer.

"Damn shame to see him so helpless. He was a tanker in Patton's army. One of the last still alive."

"He's a good man," I agree.

"I'm going to buzz over to his house to make sure everything is okay. I might have to drive the old fart to St. Cloud, put him in the Veteran's nursing home there, if they got room. His wife, Vera, isn't in much better shape."

"You do what you need to do, Mr. Whitehead. I'll hold down the fort here for as long as you need."

"Lock up if I'm not back by five," he calls over his shoulder as he goes out the back.

About an hour later, Kristin bangs the front door open with her new rubber bumper on her baby buggy.

"Hi ya, Allison," she says.

She has on a tight blue tee shirt with a white camisole underneath, expertly draped over her tiny tummy that she seems hellbent on getting rid of.

"Hi, Kristin. How're you doing today?" I ask.

"Beautiful afternoon in God's Minnesota, isn't it? I want those outlet covers you were talking about. Say, do you also have baby gates? The real wooden ones, not the cheap metal. I prefer mahogany. Where are they?" she asks, peering over the store like a beacon in a lighthouse.

Her neck turns sinewy, veins pressing out from her skin. For a split second, she appears grotesque.

"Sure," I say. "We can special order them. Here's the catalogue you can look through," I answer, pulling it out from under the counter.

Kristin begins thumbing through the magazine, gushing 'awe' and 'oh'. She then shakes her head softly, closing her eyes. Freezing in place, she doesn't move. For what seems like an eternity, she remains frozen in time before thawing into human animation again.

"Yes, I'd like these right here. These in dark mahogany," she says, tapping on a photo. "I need twelve of them. No rush, but when can you get them?"

"Sure. Might take a few days, though."

"My son is still so young, but they grow up fast, don't they? In a blink of an eye, they're gone. Just like that, they're gone. Poof."

She raises her hand, clamps her fingertips together, then releases them. Poof.

"Yes, just like that, I guess," I say softly. "Poof."

"You wanna pay now or when they come?

"Bill me," she answers over her shoulder and rushes to the door with her stroller.

Mr. Clancy holds it open for her, leering. As soon as she leaves, he turns towards me and scowls.

He looks angrier than usual.

"Allison. Can I have a word with you?"

I hide my hands in the pockets of my red apron, and don't say anything. I wish Toby was here. I wish Mr. Whitehead was in the back room. I'd give anything for Jungle Jim to stumble through the door so I wouldn't have to be alone in the store with this awful man.

He clears his phlegmy throat and says, "I'll take that as a yes, so I'm about to give you a little advice."

"I don't want no advice," I answer.

"Listen to me," he spits, and he puts his hands on the counter. Gross. Once he lifts his palms, there will be puddles of sweat that I'll have to clean off.

He leans over as far as he can, his face a few feet from mine. There are two hairs sticking out of his left ear like antennas, and three out of his right nostril.

He thinks I'm intimidated by him, but it's only disgust.

I can tell he is going to get all lawyerly on me. With both of my hands still in my apron pockets, I lay them quietly on the counter.

"We all know it would be easy for me to get your grandma taken away to Rolling Acres," he says, moving his face closer.

I look down at the counter.

"Let's make a little deal. Mr. Whitehead will only sell this eye-sore building to you. So, you need to make that happen. And then you will sell it to me. Simple."

I shake my head and mutter "no." Clancy has always been persistent about Mr. Whitehead selling the store, but today he is off the chart hostile.

"If you don't make this happen, I will cause a boat load of bad problems for you, Allison. I will flush your boring little life down the toilet. I have too much money invested in that strip mall for this dump to stand in the way."

"That sounds like you are threatening me."

"No, Allison. No threat at all. I'm only making you a deal. And here's a few more," he says. "Your vicious pit bull will suddenly bite me, oh! ouch! when I happen to walk by your house. Then, by law it will be euthanized."

"Is that so," I say.

"You do know what the word, 'euthanized', means, don't you sweetheart?"

"Yes, I do."

"And tell that colored boyfriend of yours if he ever comes near my son again, he'll be sitting in prison where he belongs. In a cage with all the rest of them. He's lucky the security camera wasn't working the other day at my gas station. I heard all about what happened."

I look down at my red apron pockets.

"Bottom line, honey, I need this property. And unfortunately you're the only person that can get it for me. So get it."

"Are you done spitting on me yet?"

Apparently he's not.

"Nuts don't fall too far from the family tree, do they Allison? You're just like your mother," he sneers before finally leaving.

I pull my phone out of my red apron and switch off the record button. I export the entire conversation to an audio file and email it to Sheriff Goldberg.

Sure enough, about half hour later, Sheriff Goldberg's squad car pulls up to the store.

"Good afternoon, Allison," he says as he walks through the door.

"Good afternoon, sir," I answer sheepishly.

"Where's Mr. Whitehead?" he asks, looking around.

"Went to St. Cloud. He had to take Morton to the hospital there," I answer.

"Is there anyone else in the store?"

"No, sir."

I'm getting nervous. Maybe I shouldn't have tape recorded Clancy. And I'm not quite sure why I did. Maybe that was illegal or something.

"Good. Now, listen to me, dear," he says, dropping the formalities.

"Yes, sir."

"Are you listening?"

If I had only one person to get advice from for the rest of my life, it would be Sheriff Goldberg.

"Yes, I'm listening," I answer again.

"I got your email. Do not send it to anyone else. Do not let any one else listen to it. Do you understand?"

"Yes sir."

He rubs his eyes and says, "You obviously think Mr. Clancy is doing more than being a bully. And you're right.

I forwarded your email on to the federal agents. They have an open investigation on Clancy."

"For what?" I ask, not too surprised.

"Some questionable issues regarding his investments. All allegedly at this point. But it could turn out serious."

"Good."

"The feds probably won't need to talk to you, but if they do, I'll let you know."

"Okay."

"Do not, and I repeat, do not, tell a soul about this audio. Do not take matters into your own hands. Do not record him again because he might catch you and, well, we don't want that. Just let Lady Justice and Madam Karma do their jobs."

I exhale.

"Promise me," he adds.

"I promise."

He's right. If I told Toby what Clancy said, he'd choke him too the next time he saw him. If I told Steph, she'd slit Devin's car tires. If I told Mr. Whitehead, he'd probably whack Mr. Clancy over the head with one of our Bigfoot snow shovels. Jimmy would probably urinate on his porch and Grandma, well, I don't want to think about what she'd do. Bob would just agree with the sheriff and tell me to keep my mouth shut.

"Okay. Thank you, Sheriff."

"How's that dog of yours doing?"

"Great, fits right in with the family. How's your wife getting along?"

"She's doing well but had to retire a little early. Getting some arthritis is all."

"Grandma drinks warm water with blackstrap molasses when her flairs up. Maybe she could try that."

"I'll let her know."

"Hope she gets better."

"Me too. Have a nice day, Allison."

"Yes, sir. You too."

~~~

The Price is Right is blaring when I get home. Grandma is clanging pots and pans in the kitchen, not cooking but swearing up a storm. Bob waves up the remote, his forehead glistening in the yellow glow of the TV.

"How can I make supper with all this fruit?" Grandma asks as I walk into the kitchen. "All we got around here is fruit. I don't like fruit. In fact, I hate it. I told you that."

"Grandma," I say, pulling a bunch of bananas from her hand that she has already squished. The yellow paste is oozing out of their sorry ends. A bruised orange rolls under the cabinet.

I continue, "Grandma, the doctor said you need more fruit, that's all. That's why I bought all this for you. If you don't like bananas, I got some strawberries over there..." and point to the counter.

Except the plastic pint of strawberries are smashed, juice dripping off the countertop, down the drawers and pooling on the floor.

Maple runs over to lick up the bloodied berries.

"How about you go relax and I'll make us some scrambled eggs and sausages for supper instead," I answer, hiding the box of blueberries behind the toaster. I know they'd be her next victim.

"Nothing like breakfast for supper. Thanks, Allison," Bob says as Grandma simmers down, taking a seat on the couch next to him.

I appreciate Bob, as I never met Grandma's husband, my Grandpa. He died in a freak farm accident but Grandma doesn't ever want to talk about it.

I never met my dad's side of the family either, as they're all wealthy professionals from New Hampshire. They never bothered with me. Never made any attempt to contact me or anyone after my dad, their son, died.

They were angry at my dad, who was raised Catholic. He married my mom, a protestant. That was a big no-no not so long ago. They were also disappointed that their son never did more with his life than move to a hayseed town like Granola.

My parents met at a Blue Grass festival in Wisconsin. They were young when they married, and had me about six months later. The fact he did the right thing and married the woman whom he got pregnant didn't seem to count for much in their eyes.

When my dad died, they insisted on flying his body back East to bury it out there. No wonder my mom was depressed. They still don't want anything to do with me.

"By the way, Grandma," I call from the kitchen a few minutes later. "I talked to Mr. Clancy at the parade a few days ago. He told me he thinks you poop on his lawn."

"Excuse me? What did you say?" she answers, but it sounds like a mouse squeak.

Bob grabs a pillow, hits himself in the face with it a few times, sighs, then focuses back on the TV. Neither one of us is putting it past her.

"All I'm saying is, be careful what you do around Clancy because he watches us very closely," I answer, thinking about what he said today.

"They should make a special planet for crybabies. Then, Mr. Clancy can get his buffalo butt in a rocket ship and go live on Planet Crybaby where horrible men like him belong," she huffs.

"I'm not blaming you for anything, Grandma. I'm just repeating what I heard."

"Holy hell. Do you think I'd do that?"

I don't answer, so she continues, "Do you really think I would run over there and squat on his lawn? I'm not stupid enough to do that, at least not in broad daylight."

"Calm down, Ethylon. Just calm down, sweetheart," Bob says, hitting himself with the pillow again.

"Don't tell me to calm down," she says. "Do you want to know the truth about Clancy? I'll tell you all you need to know about him. He's a sick and twisted bastard. As bad as they come. You wanna know what him and Gerald, the owner of Sub Station used to do when they were younger?

They'd go cow-popping. Do you know what cow-popping is, Allison? It's when you sneak into a field of cows and pull their tails so hard up over their backs that their tails break out of their sockets. **POP!** "

"He's going to hell on a full ride scholarship," Bob says, throwing the pillow at the TV.

I rub my eyes and fall silent.

Clancy really is worse than I thought.

CHAPTER FIFTEEN

July in Minnesota is sticky, thick and hot. Sometimes we're hit hard with a hail storm but usually beat with heat and humidity. The only place to be is inside under air conditioning or in one of our 10,000 lakes.

The next morning, Grandma's up at seven a.m. banging on my door, informing me that we're going to take her to Big Loon Lake.

Although it's Friday, the hardware store is closed. Mr. Whitehead said to take the day off. He wants to bring Morton's wife, Vera, to visit him at the Veteran's nursing home in St. Cloud.

"Who's driving?" I ask from under my pillow.

Maple whines.

"Bob is. And Jungle Jim is sitting outside on our porch wearing a Speedo looking like an emaciated crack whore. So get up, Allison. It will be fun."

I roll over, and only want to hug Maple for a few more hours. I'm exhausted, not so much physically, but feel like my brain is running on fumes.

"Sure, I'll be down," I mumble as I throw on my swim suit and clothes.

I send Toby a text to see if he wants to join us. I wish it was only us two going but Grandma doesn't get out much. If she wants to go somewhere, I try to make it happen.

"Did you get some breakfast, Grandma?" I ask, walking down the stairs.

"Bob has danish rolls for us to eat on the way. A big box of them from Newton's Bakery. The raspberry and lemon kind, so let's go," she answers.

We cruise over to Toby's house and pull up in the driveway. He's pushing the mower around the yard. The scent of fresh cut grass wafts through our open windows.

"Come on," Bob yells from the car as Jimmy pipes in, "Let's party hardy, dude!"

Toby pulls his phone out of his pocket, taps on it, obviously just reading my message. He smiles up at us.

"Sure, I'll be right there," he calls before running into his house. A few minutes later, he runs out again and hops in the back seat next to me and Grandma.

His leg touches my knee, so I move mine over so it doesn't. Then, I move it back so it does. One thigh is muscular, smooth with little curly-cues of black hair all over it, disappearing into his swim trunks. The other leg is riddled with scars, some deep, some triangular. Pink gouges on his dark skin. From Afghanistan, no doubt.

We stop at Chub. Bob and Toby go in for picnic supplies. It's an unspoken agreement that I wait in the car with Jimmy and Grandma to keep the peace. Bringing them both into the store together would be too risky. No telling what kind of trouble those two would make.

Half an hour later, Bob and Toby lumber out, arms full of bags of food and ice for the cooler. Finally, we get on the road toward Big Loon Lake.

"I can't believe you're wearing that swim suit, Jimmy," Grandma says. "That's so tight I can see your religion."

Jimmy quickly turns toward Grandma and bellows, "You want me to take it off, Ethylon? Is that what you want? You want me to take it off right now?"

"Hell ya, baby!" Grandma answers, egging him on.

Toby stares intently at the road ahead, pursing his lips, trying not to laugh.

And sure enough, Jimmy pulls off his swim suit and throws it on Grandma's lap.

"Get it off! Get this cootie-crawly thing off me now! I'm going to get herpes!" she screams.

I grab the Speedo and throw it on Bob.

Bob grabs it and throws it on Toby.

Toby throws the Speedo at Jimmy, who quickly puts it back on. A few minutes later, he then opens the box of danish rolls.

"Did you do what I think you did, Jimmy?" Toby asks.

"What he didn't do is wash his hands," I say.

Jimmy wipes his mouth and asks, "Who, me? I didn't do nothin'. Why? What do you think I did?"

"Did you suck the lemon filling out of that danish and put it back in the box?" Toby asks.

"I don't know what you're talking about," he answers, yellow jelly glistening off his mustache.

"Like hell you don't know. You just put your lips all over the pastry," Grandma says. "We're all gonna get gonorrhea now."

"I only did it to one," he says, as if that makes it okay.

"That's uncouth, Jimmy," Bob says, shaking his head.

"What does that fancy word even mean, Bob?" Grandma asks. "Who you trying to impress?"

"It means 'rude, gross and tacky.' I saw it on a game show yesterday."

"Jimmy, will you eat the one you sucked on, and leave the rest alone so we can all have one," I ask. "None of us has had breakfast yet."

He picks out the deflated, somewhat soggy danish and hands me the box.

Bob turns on the radio, flips the station and Adele's beautiful voice fills the car.

"Why does she always sing about calling up some boy she broke up with ten years ago and then gets mad when he isn't happy to hear from her?" Grandma asks. She then turns to the radio and yells, "He's moved on, Adele! And so should you! Get over him!"

Bob says, "Well, I think a lot of people have regrets over relationships that happened years ago, and don't realize it until much later in life."

"That's all fine and dandy, but Adele is a stalker. She said she called the guy a thousand times who doesn't want to talk to her. That's called being a stalker."

"Grandma. I'm sure Adele isn't a stalker. Just listen to her amazing voice. Forget about the lyrics," I say.

"Well, Ethylon, if you ever broke up with me, I wouldn't stalk you. I would just die of a broken heart," Bob says. "You're the apple to my pie."

"And you're the ham to my cheese, sweetie," Grandma says, sitting up to kiss him on the back of his head.

About an hour later, we arrive at the sandy beach of Big Loon Lake. A family of red-marked loons glide past as the sun slides above the horizon. Thick blade grass, garlic mustard weed, and foxtail surround the water's edge. A black hawk circles overhead as Maple leaps into the lake after a skipping sunfish.

Bob drags out a small grill from Grandma's trunk. Toby carries over the bag of charcoal and they quickly light it up. Jimmy pulls over the cooler and I bring the Chub bags of brats, buns, chips and dip.

"Let me have the tongs," Jimmy says to Toby, trying to grab them. "If anyone knows the art of barbecue, it's me."

"Sure, you can be the meat master extraordinaire, Jimmy," he answers, handing them over with a flourish.

"He ain't got no meat in that Speedo of his, that's for sure," Grandma says.

"I might not have the wiener but still have the beans, Ethylon," Jimmy answers, beaming.

Toby wrinkles his forehead, mutters "WTF?" under his breath, as he empties the charcoal briquettes into the grill.

By eleven a.m., the grill is smoldering. Bob drops down a big sack of corn ears in front of Jungle Jim and tells him to 'get to huskin'.

"Why me? I don't even like corn," he answers.

Grandma takes the bag and puts it on the side of her lawn chair. Grabbing an ear, she pulls down the silk-lined leaves and throws them at Jimmy.

"Let's go for a swim," Toby says, grabbing my hand and I follow him into the clear water.

The lake bottom is sludgy, slippery slime. The water is cool below and bath tub warm on the smooth surface.

Elegant dragon flies flit near by, one flutters past, as if to check us out. Overhead, a white grid pattern covers the pastel blue sky, jets somewhere too high or too far away to make a noise, only leaving their puffy trails.

Toby and I throw a tennis ball back and forth, playing 'monkey in the middle' with Maple. She always gets it from me, so I'm suppose to be in the middle, but Maple refuses to give up the ball.

Water drips from Toby's chin. His eyes are black oil, reflecting the morning light. I want to run my fingers over the hard curves of his shoulders, and explore his beautiful landscape. He pulls me around to a small cove in the lake, hidden by pussy willows and cattails.

"I've been wanting to kiss you all morning," he says, and we immediately lock lips. His solid body envelopes me. I have never felt so dang horny since, well, never. He obviously is too.

"Allison! Toby!" we hear Bob call from the beach.

"We better go before they start to wonder what we're doing," I whisper up into his ear.

"Right," he says after one more kiss, and we paddle back around toward the barbecue.

He grins and says, "I can't quite get out of the water yet, Ally. Just give me a minute."

"Why?"

He throws his eyes down, then up at me quickly.

"What?" I ask.

"I'm kinda pitching a tent right now."

"What does that mean?"

"My private is standing at attention."

"What? Oh...you mean...*that*."

"Full salute," he says, laughing.

"Oh my gawd, Toby, just hush now. You're almost as bad as Grandma."

On the beach, the grill is glowing orange, but for whatever reason, Jimmy grabs the lighter fluid can and spurts the contents out on the embers. It erupts into a scorching yellow and blue fist of fire.

"Holy macaroni!" Bob yells, stumbling backwards as Grandma jumps out of her chair. Toby runs up to help and I stay in the safety of the lake water. Maple splashes in next to me, whimpering. She's obviously wondering why humans do these sort of things.

Devoured with licking flames, the grill is engulfed. The cheap metal melts and caves in. Bob and Toby throw sand on the rage, trying to keep it contained.

Finally, the burning heap collapses into a smoldering pile of regret.

"I swear Jimmy, when God was passing out brains you must have been hiding behind a damn tree," Grandma says over the pillar of stench and smoke.

"I just thought it needed a bit more juice," he answers, wiping his eyebrows but most of them, now singed, flake off on his fingers.

"You're like King Midas. Except everything you touch turns to shit," Grandma adds, watching the grill smolder.

Toby puts his hands on his hips, looking over the entire sorry situation.

"Let's build a regular camp fire. We can still roast our brats and wrap everything in foil to cook. I think we can still make this work," he says.

"Like we have a choice..." Grandma grumbles.

"Bob and I will grab all those big rocks down there and we'll put them in a circle. Ally, will you please bring me the rest of the coal briquettes? Grandma, will you please wrap all that corn in foil. And Jimmy, will you please not do anything? That would be great."

We get busy, building an old-time campfire and we're back in business.

"Here," Jimmy says to all of us with his head bowed and shoulders slumped. He holds out five long sticks that he has debarked and whittled down to pointy ends.

Bob grabs one, skewers a brat on his, and holds it over the fire pit. We all do the same. The corn is delicious, the brats are perfect, and we eat and relax in the glorious sun for the rest of the afternoon.

CHAPTER SIXTEEN

The next morning, Grandma barrels down the steps as soon as she hears the doorbell.

"It's the Beelzebub Messengers again!" she says, her skinny face haloed by frazzled hair. "Shut the curtains, lock the doors. We're not home. They preach about Ukuleles chapter two and want to save me from myself."

"If it were the Jehovah Witnesses, I'm sure they would have heard you by now," Bob mutters from the couch.

"No, Grandma, it's only Toby at the door. Yesterday he said he would come over this morning," I say, trying to calm her down.

I lead her to the dining room table and pour her a mug of coffee, with almost half being milk, so it's cool enough to drink immediately. I shove her pills into her hand and she gobbles them up.

When I open the door, Maple barrels over to Toby, trying to lick him to death. He takes a knee to play *Who's a good girl?* with her for a few minutes.

After taking off his high tops, he stands back up and sneaks a kiss on my cheek. Maple grabs one of the shoes and runs upstairs.

Toby sits down across from Grandma at the dining room table and hands her a bag of warm bagels.

"They're potato bagels, Miss Ethylon. Just picked them up from Newton's Bakery," he says, with a half smile. "Got some whipped honey walnut cream cheese for them, too."

She's calm now, slurping her coffee, and sweetly says, "Allison, get our guest some coffee, will you please?"

Slowly, he dunks his bagel into his cup, smirking. I think he's up to something.

"Today, Allison is getting her license," he announces, which is news to me. "We're going to drive over to the DMV. You know, the Department of Motor Vehicles and she's going to take the test and get it."

"Like heck we are," I answer.

"Like heck we ain't," he says.

"It's Saturday. They're closed."

"Usually, but they are open one Saturday a month. And this Saturday is the day. But only till noon."

"I don't think I'm ready, Toby," I say.

"Are you saying I'm not a good teacher?" he smiles.

"You're the best teacher there is, son," Bob says. "Or at least the bravest, getting in a car with Allison behind the wheel and all."

"What's that suppose to mean, Bob?" I ask.

"Relax, I'm just teasing you a little," he answers.

"Good luck, Allison. But I hope that crazy witch Helen isn't working today," Grandma says, pointing her bagel at me. "She's the one that gave me my driving test the last time I was there. She's the one that failed me. I think that old hag must be possessed or something. You should have seen her. Old Helen's head spun around 360 degrees like that evil girl in the Exorcist. Just because I ran into that thing that was in my way."

I take a deep breath and place my hand on hers.

"No, Grandma. You actually spun Bob's car around 360 degrees. The thing that you ran into was the side of the DMV building. They revoked your license because they figured it would be safer for you and the community if you let someone else drive you around instead."

"All the more reason why you need to get your license, Ally," Toby says calmly.

Grandma slams down her coffee cup, jumps up and puts her hands on her scrawny hips. "You tell Helen-from-hell at the DMV to get a license for that broom she rides. Then she can fly over here and revoke my expired ass."

She grabs the bag of bagels and cream cheese, and plunks down on the couch next to Bob. He puts his arm around her and changes the channel.

"You ready?" Toby asks.

"As ready as I'll ever be. Let's go."

I look back at Bob and Grandma.

Bob waves the remote in the air as a good-bye. "You'll do just fine, Allison," he calls from the couch.

"Good luck and knock 'em dead!" I hear Grandma yell as I shut the door.

"But that's just a figure of speech, Allison," Bob adds. "Don't really knock anyone dead!"

~~~

Sobbing. Bawling. Blubbering.

I don't know why I'm taking it so hard. Toby was very supportive and encouraging on the way to Grimoire.

But I flunked the driving test. Badly.

Grandma was right. Helen took way to much pleasure in the fact that I failed.

"Now we know what to expect and what we need to work on," Toby says. He's back in the driver's seat, holding my hand as we drive home to Granola. "At least you tried, and that's a big step right there. Next time will be a piece of cake, I can guarantee you that."

"I honestly don't think I was that bad except for the fake rubber kid they threw in the road," I whine.

Wiping my eyes with the back of my hand, I add, "Why the heck would they throw a fake rubber kid out in front of me? Seriously? Why would they do that? That wasn't fair. That wasn't fair at all."

"I guess they threw the dummy out in the road to see if you would safely avoid it. Or run over it, back up over it, then run over it again. Kind of like what you did. But I wouldn't bug up about it. Just make sure you don't do that to real kids, okay?"

"Might as well of been a real kid with the way old Miss Helen freaked out. She got on my very last nerve, Toby. She gave me a massive headache before we even started," I sniffle. "Grandma was right about her."

We drive a few miles before he answers, "Naw, you need more practice, that's all. We'll get you up to speed."

Then he adds, "I don't mean up to speed, speed wise. I mean that rhetorically. You know, how when someone says 'up to speed' but they don't mean flooring the gas pedal and running shit over."

"I don't want to talk about it anymore," I say, and end the conversation by sticking my head out the window like Maple, all the way back to Granola.

Right outside of town about ten minutes later, Toby pulls over onto the shoulder near a fresh vegetable stand.

It's not really a stand, just Chuck Hernandez sitting on a flimsy lawn chair by his Toyota pickup, surrounded by a wooden boxes brimming with potatoes, tomatoes and jalapeño peppers.

Chuck is a skinny man with a thick top of curly grey hair and black eyebrows. He's the only Hispanic guy around for miles and miles. Now a backyard farmer, he was once the mail man in town for more than forty years before he retired.

His real name is some lovely lilting Spanish name that everyone in Granola butchers beyond recognition. So, a long time ago he told everyone to just call him Chuck. Like the ground beef.

His wife died ten years ago. His grown children and their families are constantly trying to get him to move to Florida or New York, but he refuses and stays in Granola.

His son, Rio, is the one in New York City, and works in public relations for the Yankees baseball team.

Cielo, his other son, moved down to Florida, got a doctorate in amphibians, then became a hippy professor. He figured out how to breed the endangered Button-nosed Thai gecko in captivity. Apparently that's a good thing, as Cielo made the international news because there're only about four Button-nosed Thai geckos running around loose in the world.

"Hola, Farmer Chuck," Toby says, getting out of the car.

"Hola war hero especial!" Chuck answers, excitedly pushing himself up from the flimsy chair.

"I ain't nothing special, sir," he grins.

"Get yourself some vegeetabullz and peenyoz, son."

Then he looks at me and calls, "Bonita! When is your granny going to kick gringo Bob to the curb and go out with me instead?"

"I doubt those two will ever break up, Mr. Hernandez," I yell from the car. "But you'll be the first to know if they do, I promise."

"Tell your granny to call me day time and night time! Ettie-lon is picante just the way I like 'em! I love Ettie-lon so much much much!"

"Sure will, Mr. Hernandez, sure will," I answer.

Chuck loads Toby up with two plastic Jollymart bags, bursting with bright tomatoes, suede-tan potatoes and glossy jalapeños.

"You make patatas bravas tonight, you two love birds. And tell my hot hot hot Ettie-lon I will die for her," he says and theatrically puts his hand on his heart, swooning.

Toby pays Farmer Chuck and thanks him. Then he hands me the keys, apparently tired of me pouting, and tells me to drive home.

"You need the practice," he says, sliding into the passenger seat as I move over.

"Obviously," I grump.

The sun is drifting down, disappearing behind the abundant fields, yet there're still sharp rays poking through the rows. We pass by red barns and white silos, ruffled grouse and ring necked pheasants. Although I've lived here all my life, some days Minnesota's beauty still takes my breath away.

Now, Toby's the one sticking his head out the window as we wind our way to Granola.

"You wanna come in for supper? I'll fry up Farmer Chuck's potatoes and tomatoes. Or better yet, I'll make you a grilled peanut butter and mayonnaise sandwich," I ask, pulling into Grandma's garage.

"A *what* sandwich?"

"You'd like it. It's my special comfort food. I always eat one when I feel like a loser."

"You're not a loser," he says, grabbing me for a long kiss. "I'm proud of you," he adds. "But I need to get going. I promised my mom I'd hang her new TV on the wall. I'm sure she's waiting."

"Moms first. Okay, and thanks for putting up with me and making me at least try. I appreciate it."

"You bet, Ally," he says quietly. "And don't worry about the test. You'll get it next time."

CHAPTER SEVENTEEN

"Good morning, Mr. Whitehead. Are you going to show me how to make the keys today?" I ask, tying my red apron, back at work on Monday.

He's paging through a nuts and bolts catalogue with one hand and jotting down notes with the other.

"Good morning to you too, Allison, but not today. I have to do some paperwork back here and then go to Farm Depot again to get those special orders."

"Sure," I answer, and walk up front to flip over the OPEN sign and start the popcorn.

Jimmy walks in, out, then in again a minute later holding the door open for Kristin and her baby stroller.

"Hey Allison. Did my baby outlet covers arrive yet?" Kristin asks in a huff, looking around the store.

"You can never be too careful with small children," Jimmy says, bounding up to her. "When I was a kid, I ate an entire loaf of bread dough that my mom left on the kitchen counter to rise. It started rising in my stomach, and up my throat. I couldn't breathe. Bread dough was coming out of my nose. My mom rushed in and grabbed me by the hair and made me drink Draino so I'd throw it up."

Kristin yanks the buggy back, looking at me horrified.

"Thank God for moms," Jimmy adds.

I clear my throat, smile sweetly at Kristin and say, "No. Your baby orders haven't arrived yet, being the weekend and all, but will today."

I then glare at Jimmy, wishing he would back off.

But he doesn't.

"One time my brother tied a garbage bag around my neck and made me jump off the roof. Parachute, like an airborne ranger. Got a bad concussion. Blood was squirting out my ears like a water fountain."

"Jimmy, please," I say.

Mr. Whitehead comes marching out of the back room, his yellow coffee cup swinging in one hand and a clipboard in the other.

"Why the heck are you talking to my customers like that, Jungle Jim? Unless you want to buy something, or get some popcorn, get out of here," he says.

Jimmy grins, shakes his head and walks out the door, mumbling something about Richard Nixon.

"Sorry about that, ma'am," Mr Whitehead says. "Good morning to you and that cute little baby somewhere under the blankets there. If you need any assistance, Allison will help you. And if she can't, I will. You let us know. Quality products and excellent customer service are our goal here at Whitehead's Hardware."

Kristin jiggles her baby stroller. After an awkward silence, Mr. Whitehead trudges back to his office and shuts the door.

"So, anyway," she says, gently patting down the baby blankets in her stroller while staring at me.

"So anyway," I mimic, then add, "Yes. Your order will be in later today, about five p.m. If you want, I can swing by your house on my way home and drop them off. Or call you, or whatever you want."

Her grip on the buggy gets tighter. She starts pushing it back and forth so quickly it's almost vibrating. But under the fluffy chenille blanket covering every inch of her baby, he doesn't cry. He must be fast asleep.

"That would be great. By the way, do you have any home security cameras? In a blink of an eye Daniel will be walking, so want to get some now. You know, be prepared for kidnappers and whatnot."

"No, I think you have to get a company to come out and install those. But I'll bring your electrical covers over tonight, promise."

She smiles painfully, then bustles out the door into the bright morning.

I'm missing something about Kristin but don't know what. I can't put my finger on it. There's something she's not telling me but I don't know her well enough to ask.

"Thanks, come again," is all I manage to say.

A few hefty road construction guys come in soon afterwards. I overhear them swearing about one of their co-workers, whose job was to operate the truck that paints the lines on the road. He got drunk at lunch yesterday and now the lines are screwed up for a few miles. Now they have to fix that mess. They end up charging nearly $900 on their company card, so I'm sure Mr. Whitehead is going to be happy about that mistake.

The next customer waltzes in. He is thirty-ish, impeccably dressed, wearing a grey suit with a polished, grey tie. He places both hands on the counter, leans over, and says in silky words, "I need some cable ties."

"Cable ties," I answer, biting my lip.

"Cable ties," he says again.

"You must, like, be into cable," I say, sounding stupid.

"Yes. I suppose you could say that."

I hesitate. Keeping my hands under my red apron, but over my crotch for some reason, I lead him to aisle four.

He chooses the economy pack of 120.

I twirl around, and bite my lip again.

"Golly. You need anything else?"

"Rope."

"Rope?" I ask, biting the other side of my lip.

"Rope."

"You must, like, be into rope," I say, and lead him to another aisle, and warily hand him a bundle.

"Anything else?" I ask, biting my lip again.

"Duck tape."

"Sir, it's *duct* tape. With a 't.'"

The gentleman's eyes practically goggle out of his head. He obviously doesn't like to be corrected.

"Okay, then I'll have some *duct* tape with a 't'," he says smooth as a fistful of worms.

I grab a roll and toss it to him.

"Here's two inch wide grey," I say, then rush to the register to ring him up and get the sleazy creep out of here.

~~~

Before noon, I pedal over to Sub Station to grab lunch.

Steph told me they have a new Sriracha Chicken salad,

laughed and said, 'It's made with cock sauce!' Then she reminded me I had promised to stop by to talk to her in person, anyway.

I reach the shop as it opens at eleven.

The front is empty except for Steph. She is hanging her head over the little sink on the back wall behind the counter, splashing her face with water.

"Hey, Steph. How's it going," I ask as the glass door slowly eases shut behind me.

She keeps splashing her face, holding her fingers under the water, then pressing them on her eyes.

"What's wrong?" I add.

She stops for a second, head still over the thin faucet.

"Hey, Allison. Nothing. I got jalapeños in my eye, that's all."

"How did you get jalapeños in your eye?"

"I was slicing them. And wouldn't you know I rubbed my eyes and now their burning."

She splashes more water, her back slightly shaking. I see her mouth, grimacing.

"Your cheap jalapeños come in a big jar already sliced, Steph. What's really going on, huh?"

She listlessly shuts off the tap, tugs a wad of coarse brown paper towel from the roll above and dabs her face. With the messy handful still on her eyes, she keeps her head down and whispers, "I think I'm pregnant again."

I go through the swinging kitchen door so I can get behind the counter and give her a big hug. Poor Steph.

With two kids already, from two different guys, working at fast food for minimum wage, she don't need nor can afford another little person to take care of. If she was, it would throw a huge wrench in her plans for LPN school, among everything else she juggles.

She stops crying and says, "I think it's Chad's, the cute guy at Taco Gong. He's great in bed, but he's too broke all the time to even buy minutes on his cell phone. I already have two kids by losers, I don't need another one."

"Did you pee on a stick yet to find out? You can get the test strips at Bull's Eye Drug in Grimoire. They even come in economy value-packs."

"No. I tried those before and they don't work. I made an appointment at the county clinic tomorrow at eleven. Can you come with me?"

"Absolutely, Steph. No problem. Why don't you come by the store about ten or so. I'm sure Mr. Whitehead won't mind if I take an early lunch. This is more important than work," I answer.

She straightens up and stops sniffling. A dad in cargo shorts and two young daughters in soccer cleats come through the door. I leave, but it's hard when she's still upset and possibly pregnant again.

Peddling back to Whitehead's, I think about my best friend, Steph. In high school, when we were younger and dumber, with braces and permed hair, we were sitting in her bedroom, filled with Coty's Vanilla Fields perfume.

It was the night of the Junior-Senior dance. She was trying on a white, low cut shirt. I said it didn't make her look fat and slutty at all. She took it off, threw it me and tried on something that made her look sluttier. But I didn't tell her, didn't want to hurt her feelings.

'The purple velvet one makes you look mysterious' I remember telling her instead.

She told me to put on the black one and cackled, 'Girlfriend, you are going to burn down the house in that hot outfit.' I got so embarrassed, I was going to take it off but she made me wear it.

Laughing, she then asked, 'Did I tell you I broke up with Tyler? A few days ago he said he wanted us to watch a pornographic video. Then, he wanted me to get on my knees and give him a blow job like in the porno. So, like, I started. When I looked up, he was still watching the video and eating a bag of sour cream and onion flavored potato chips at the same time. I thought that was so rude. I grabbed the bag of chips and threw them at the TV.'

I agreed that it was so very rude.

'I know, right?' she said, then lit a Virginia Slim. I took a puff, and had to lay down for a few minutes because of the head rush. She thought that was so funny and called me a 'light weight'.

She put a Prince CD in the player and said she wanted to go down to First Avenue in Minneapolis and meet Prince when we turn twenty-one. We started caking on our make up and singing with him at the top of our lungs.

Then she asked, 'Why don't you ever kiss Charles? He likes you. If it wasn't for his acne, crooked teeth, greasy hair and dirty clothes, he'd be cute. He's a fixer-upper, but what's his dad in prison for again?'

'Making meth in his tool shed,' I answered.

'That sucks,' she said.

I had wanted to kiss Charles back then, but that never happened. We liked each other, but neither knew how to make the first move. We just talked a lot during study hall.

One time after winter break, when I asked him how his Christmas was, he told me his mother got drunk again and rammed the entire tree, ornaments and all, through the living room window.

She snapped the head off Baby Jesus from the nativity set and chucked it through the broken window too. Then all the presents. Sheriff Goldberg came over and hauled her off to detox because she puked all over the floor.

Charles and his two older sisters spent the rest of Christmas Day cleaning up vomit and taping garbage bags on the window to keep the snow from coming in.

A week after we graduated from high school, Charles left for the Marines without telling anyone. He left town quietly and no one has heard from him since. Not even his own family. I bet he's doing just fine.

~~~

Later in the afternoon, a neatly dressed, young but weary looking man walks into the store.

He's starting to bald, but the short blonde hair he still has is expertly greased up and over. I wonder if he has his eyebrows waxed, because they are perfect. In one hand is a cell phone and a set of car keys in the other.

"Good afternoon," he says, without looking at me.

"Good afternoon," I answer. "How can I help you?"

He scans the place like a desperate periscope, his thin neck reaching up and methodically peering, here to there to back again.

Walking over to the counter, he clicks down his cell phone and keys, finally locking eyes on me.

"I think my wife has been in here," he says, almost apologetic.

"I don't know," I answer, sensing something is going to come crashing down.

He licks his dry, pasty lips and says, "My wife, Kristin McCarthy. Her. Has she been in here?"

"Kristin and baby Daniel?"

He winds up tighter than a guitar string and answers in a staccato voice, "Yes. Kristin, my wife. The woman with the baby carriage. Her."

"Yes. She has."

"Yes she has what?"

"Been here. Shopping."

He relaxes a bit.

"Shopping for what?"

I don't know what to say except the truth. So I answer, "Stuff."

"What kind of stuff?"

"Hardware stuff."

"What kind of hardware stuff?"

"For Daniel. You know, buggy bumpers, baby outlet covers, safety things for when he gets older."

His eyes click shut like snapping fingers. Squeezing his mouth, his lips bleed pale. His healthy tan fades to chalk.

After a few seconds, he mutters, "Really…"

"Yes. She's obviously a loving mom. I can tell that for sure. And worried. About everything. All the time…"

He shoves his phone and keys in his pockets, slams down his business card, straightens his tie, all the while keeping his eyes closed. He slowly turns towards the door as if stuck in sludge.

"Please," he whispers over his shoulder. "Our baby died shortly after he was born. He was our Danny boy for only three hours. That was six months ago. We moved out here to get away from everything. So…"

He pauses, grows weaker, he continues, "Understand that please and give me a call…when she comes in again. Call me right away."

He then walks out the door.

"Oh no," I whisper to myself.

I wish I still believed in Jesus so I could ask him to send some comfort to Kristin and her husband.

Mr. Whitehead walks out from aisle one, head down and gently places his coffee mug on the counter.

"I overheard that," he says.

"Oh dear. I can't imagine the grief. No wonder Kristin is, was, I knew something was wrong with her."

"People grieve in different ways," he says. "I'm sure you still grieve for your parents."

Gritting my teeth, I say, "I'm not really thinking of me right now, Mr. Whitehead."

"I don't know Kristin. But I know you. And you don't like to talk about things."

I don't say anything.

"Like I said, you don't like to talk about things," he adds. "But if you ever do, I'm all ears."

"It's been more than twenty years, so not much left to talk about," I answer.

"All I know is that you were your mother and father's shared joy. They fought a lot but it was still clear they loved each other very much. When your dad died, your mother couldn't handle it. Kind of like Kristin, I suppose. Pain and love mixed together plays horrible tricks."

I look at Mr. Whitehead. At how intently kind he's gazing at me. His old face soft, weathered, and concerned.

"Okay," is all I say.

"Okay, then," he answers and walks slowly out the front door to get some fresh air. I know he's wishing that he still smoked because I'm sure he'd light one up.

One of my few memories of my dad was how his breath always smelled like spearmint gum. But he would never give me a whole piece. He'd pull a piece out and I'd leer at the shiny, silver sliver of foil sliding from the slim pack. When it was half way, he'd snap it off and give me just half. Only half.

I remember bawling, having tantrums because all I got was half, not a whole. He would laugh, and tell me I don't have a big enough mouth yet. And as if to prove him wrong, I'd scream louder for the whole piece.

One time, he told me I was spoiled and popped the other half piece in his mouth, along with two additional pieces, and laughed at me for crying.

'Give her a damn piece of gum, Steve,' my mom said. 'Stop spoiling her,' he answered. 'I'm not,' she said. 'Yes you are, like you spoil everything….' he said.

Steve was my father, and Caroline, my mother.

My dad had a penchant for all things motorized, so he got a job as a mechanic at the Amoco station when he moved here to marry my mom.

Mom sold Avon, worked part time at Grandma's beauty shop, and every Saturday drove to St. Cloud to clean the Super Seven motel to make extra money. The owner let her stay in a room, if one was available, so she could work on Sunday also before coming home.

My dad didn't like the fact my mom left for the weekends and stayed over in the 'big city.' I think he worried about her meeting other men.

They fought a lot about that. 'Maybe if you didn't spend so much money we'd have enough. Maybe you just like getting out of Granola to meet other men.'

Mom was a Northern beauty. Solid, with long, thick legs. Blonde hair and dark, blue eyes. Her face was bright, imperfect, wide. Her two front teeth overlapped slightly.

Sometimes one of those teeth had a smudge of pink from her lipstick. I was always fascinated how her mouth would instantly turn from a worried frown up to a smile whenever she looked at me. Going from nothing to brilliant in a short second.

I know I made her happy. But I didn't make her happy enough to stay.

Grandma often stormed into our house, and shoo me to my room while all three of them screamed at each other.

Once in awhile, Sheriff Goldberg would come over, and I'd be whisked out of my room by Grandma and spend the night with her at her house.

In my room now, I have three photos of my mom and dad and me, but none of us all together. There's one of my mom next to a Christmas tree holding up an electric hand mixer. I guess my dad had given her that as a present.

The second photo is of me and my dad. I'm sitting on his lap in a lawn chair, and I'm holding a Barbie doll. I had cut all of Barbie's hair off, so it was short, just like mine.

The third is of me and my mother, a close up of my face when I must have been three or four, missing a front tooth. My mother is hanging her head over my shoulder looking in my ear for some reason.

Grandma has boxes of photos downstairs. I've never had the guts to go look at them all. I want to keep those memories in boxes, downstairs and put away. I simply couldn't handle it. Grandma goes down there and looks at the photos, but she ended up crazy as hell.

After my mother killed herself, Sheriff Goldberg called my school to make sure I would 'get help.'

That year I had to talk to the school psychologist every week. He made a special trip to Granola Elementary from Grimoire just for me, Charles and a few other struggling kids. We had to sit in a little room off of the nurses office, which was plastered with bright posters about 'feelings'.

One had a red, fuzzy monster. He was Mr. Anger. Another, a blue rain drop was Miss Sad. There was a happy, smiling face. He was Sir Laugh-a-lot.

I was only six, but Dr. Schmidt wanted me to keep a notebook and draw if I ever got angry or sad. I was suppose to draw, since I wasn't too good with my writing or letters at that time.

Weekly, I had to show him the notebook. He'd look at the drawings and want to discuss them with me. He finally got sick and tired of me scribbling black crayon all over the pages and me refusing to talk about anything, he gave up.

At the end of the school year, he wrote a report that stated I was making significant progress and he didn't need to see me anymore.

I retreated into myself even further. At school I was known as the weird 'orphan' kid, even though I was living with Grandma. As the years went by, most kids forgot what happened to my dad and mom. I was then weird for no reason. Everyone thought so, even the teachers.

Grandma once told me if I ever feel like I'm going through hell, don't stop, keep on going.

So I did.

By eight grade, I had English class with Steph. We were assigned to be partners during first quarter poetry and creative writing. When we had to write haikus, she'd write the dirtiest ones ever. I'd tell her, 'No! You can't hand that one in!' giggling until we got in trouble.

English class with Steph was the first time I laughed in a long time. She gave me a tampon when I didn't have one. She called it 'a plug', and that made me laugh too.

At lunch, she wanted me to sit by her and her friends, and would tease me about liking Charles. Although we never talked about my mom, because I didn't want to, she understood that.

We talked about boys, bands, acne, clothes and school instead. Normal stuff that teenaged friends talk about. And I started to feel normal, for once in my life. Thanks to her.

More than twenty years have passed since my mom killed herself, and not much longer since my dad died. What I miss the most are the memories I was suppose to have with them. I miss the things that never happened. I miss the future, not the past.

My mom will always be one of those Russian nesting dolls that you twist open to find another, and yet another, only to discover the last solid one inside is missing.

I bet Kristin is missing the future also. So she keeps lifting up layers of chenille crib blankets looking for her beloved Daniel. But he's never there.

~~~

At the end of the day, I sign out and go home.

Grandma is sitting calmly at the dining room table, knitting. Knitting a scarf into infinity. It's about twenty feet long, and she won't stop.

"Say, Grandma. Why don't you hook off on that scarf and start another? I think it's long enough."

She keeps clicking the needles, only faster.

"She's knitting a scarf for Godzilla," Bob calls from the couch, not moving his eyes away from *The Price is Right*.

"No one is getting this scarf. I'm saving it for my first grand baby," Grandma answers, her blue-veined fingers spinning the purple yarn. "You should marry Toby and have babies. Then we'd have a bunch of little Denzel Washingtons running around the house."

"Grandma. Please stop talking like that."

"I see how you google-eye him. And how he plays tiddlywinks with you."

"That's not true. I don't google-eye him."

"Yes, you do. And he's always looking at that cute fanny of yours."

"Both you and Toby act like we don't know what's going on," Bob says, staring at the TV while smiling.

"Cute asses are hereditary in our family, don't ya know. I used to have a cute ass like yours when I was your age. You get yours from me. And you get your pretty hair from me too, so thank me very much."

"Stop talking about this, okay?"

"Nothing wrong with getting married and having children, Allison," Bob says.

Bob was married back in the early '70s, to whom he refers to as, 'Satan's retarded daughter'. She left him after a year and took all the money, the cat, his collection of vintage fishing bobbers and the bundt cake pan.

He'd said he wanted kids, lots of them. Instead, his wife moved to the Twin Cities and started hanging out in 'patchouli stinkin' coffee shops'. The last he ever heard from her was when she called for bail after being arrested for throwing a brick through an Army recruiter's office in the Uptown area of Minneapolis.

"I'll get married and all when I'm good and ready. I'll get there when I get there," I say, and then call for Maple.

We both run to the field as fast as we can. As I plop down under the tree, a text from Toby dings in.

'Be there in a few,' it reads.

After I throw the tennis ball for Maple, Toby appears. He lands beside me like Superman to save the day.

"Hey," he says, sitting down next to me.

"Hi," I answer, trying to yank the ball out of Maple's mouth. "How's it going?"

"Could be better," he answers, looking up and away at a formation of geese commuting overhead.

"What's wrong?"

He shrugs, keeps looking up and says, "Have a hard time sleeping. I get in these damn moods sometimes."

"You want to know what helps me when I start getting depressed and angry? I imagine people walking around with thought clouds above their head," I say.

"What the heck are you talking about now, Ally?"

"You know in cartoons? When people are thinking, they have three bubbles above their heads with a cloud. I imagine people with thought clouds above their heads."

"Yeah? Then what?"

"Like at Chub, when someone is taking up the aisle or standing around in your way, staring at the yogurt case or Hamburger Helper," I say. He nods, so I continue, "Imagine they have a thought cloud above their head, and it reads, 'If I don't make something good for supper to impress my husband, he'll leave me because I think he's having an affair,' or 'I somehow survived stomach cancer, but now can't eat solid food for the rest of my life. So, what should I eat?' or 'I only have forty dollars to make supper for my three kids for a week, what should I buy?' Then, I end up feeling lucky when I think like that."

"I suppose," he says, nudging my shoulder with his.

I know he's been in combat, got shot at, and killed people. I've only seen it in the movies. He's been around the world and back. I've hardly left Granola. He's black and I'm about as white as they make 'em.

But I remember the color wheel that Mr. Cunningham taught us about in tenth grade art class. And how a color goes best with the two colors on either side. But it coordinates just as brightly with the color directly opposite. Maybe that's what it's all about.

Toby twists the mangled ball from Maple and wails it across the field.

"You wanna come over for supper?" I ask.

"Thanks, but my mom and I are driving down to the Cities pretty soon, to visit some of our cousins down there. How about tomorrow? We still never had our pizza date."

"That's a deal."

He gently puts his arm around me and walks Maple and I home.

CHAPTER EIGHTEEN

"Good morning, Mr. Whitehead," I say, tying on my red apron. "Do you think I can take an early lunch today? I'd like to go with Steph to her doctor's appointment. Um, it's kind of a female thing."

Nodding his head without looking up, he says, "Steph? Damn it. Is she pregnant again?"

Sucking in my lips, I hold my breath, not wanting to answer the question.

He glances up and says, "She's a nice girl. I thought she was going to school now."

"She is, but just not yet. She needs to figure out a couple things first. Ya know, feminine matters."

"Sure, Allison. You go do your feminine matters, then. I might just close down for a few hours anyway. I've got a meeting over at the American Legion. Some things are more important than work."

"Thanks for understanding, Mr. Whitehead," I say, signing my timecard and go start the popcorn.

At about ten-thirty, Steph pulls up to the store in her red Chevy Gran Prix. It has a little spoiler on the back trunk, which doesn't make sense because the car starts to shimmy and rattle if she gets it over 50 mph.

One door is beige, because it had to be replaced after she slid into a light pole. She put in an insurance claim, then kept the money and had one of her boyfriends find a door from the scrap yard and do the work for her.

Last winter, Mrs. Halverson was driving her Lincoln, skidded on some ice going to Chub and hit Steph in the rear. Steph put in another insurance claim and got almost 1500 dollars. But she didn't get the repair either. So, it's still smashed up in back.

"Hey, girlfriend," she says, walking through the door.

She's wearing a tight, pink shirt with a low neckline. Her poor thighs swoosh together, sounding like sand paper scraping with every step. I wonder how she does it, walk in those jeans. The seams on both sides are barely holding her in. Maybe that's the actual sound I'm hearing, the threads of the inseams wincing in pain, trying to keep it all in, when she just wants to burst out.

Plunking her fake Louis Vuitton purse on the counter, she scrunches up her face. "You can take off now, right? My appointment in Grimoire is in about thirty minutes."

"Go ahead and go, Allison. And good luck, Steph," Mr. Whitehead calls from his office.

Outside, I yank open the beige car door, and throw a ton of candy wrappers, happy meal boxes and sippy cups out of my way. Brushing off Cheerios and half eaten Starbursts stuck to the seat, I eventually have a space to sit.

When we pass the Git-n-Split, she abruptly turns in.

"No! Not here!" I scream.

She slams on the brakes and stares at me.

"What the heck, Allison? All I want is a diet Dew."

"Devin Clancy works here," I answer.

"You mean that jock rapist from high school?"

"Yep. Toby got into a fight with him a few days ago. It wasn't good, Steph."

"I hope Toby punched him in his smug face."

"Well, let's just say Toby left him speechless."

"I thought I saw dickhead Devin driving around the other day. But didn't he go off to college somewhere?"

"Yes, blah blah, home for summer break."

"In high school, he got voted *Most Likely to Succeed*, and him and his football friends said I was voted most likely to get an STD. Remember that crap he said, Allison?"

"Remember on the bus, he called me a dumb 'c' word, so you grabbed his Sony Walkman and threw it out the window," I answer, snickering.

"Oh yeah, and he started crying like a little girl."

"Didn't you get suspended for a week?"

"Three days, but it was worth it though, I'll tell you that much. He thinks he's hot shit on a silver platter but he ain't nothing but a cold turd on a paper plate," she says.

This is why I love Steph so much. We both hate the same people.

She now glances around the parking lot, then points like a laser toward a black BMW.

"Is that his car?" she asks.

"Yep."

Slowly, she pulls up as close as possible to his. There's a *Tufts University* sticker centered on the back window.

"What the hell are Tufts?" she sneers.

"More like Turds University."

She opens her door as hard as she can into his car. She shuts her door, then bashes it open again. And again. And again, leaving four, deep gouges in his side door.

His car alarm goes off.

"Steph, we've got to get out of here!" I yell.

She throws the car in reverse. We zoom out of the parking lot just as Devin comes zipping out the door.

Turning up the radio, we sing along with Prince until we get on the county road towards Grimoire.

"Did you or didn't you?" she asks, suddenly turning down the music.

"Did I or didn't I do what?"

"Did you or didn't you have sex with Toby yet," she asks, purposely swerving back and forth on the highway singing *Little Red Corvette*.

"Steph, just stop it. And no, we haven't."

She regains control of the car and asks, "Seriously, why not? You're crazy not too. Or is he the one crazy? Does he have that PTSD like all those Iraq army guys do?"

"He wasn't in Iraq. He was a few countries over in Afghanistan," I answer.

"Be sure to wear a condom so you don't catch PTSD."

"Pretty sure you don't get it that way."

"Is he crazy like he has it?"

"I wouldn't say crazy, but he sure thinks about Afghanistan a lot."

"Back to the first question. Why haven't you done it?"

"We just haven't got around to it, I guess."

"You're the one that's crazy, then. How do you *not* get around to it with a gorgeous man like that? I'd do him in a heartbeat if he wasn't so into you."

"We've kissed, made out a little, but just haven't yet, that's all. Not that I don't want to."

"Then you need to stop being shy and jump on top of him. Guys love it when you jump on them."

"I'm not going to jump on him."

"Here's what needs to happen. Give Grandma an extra dose of pills and kick Bob out of the house some night. Invite Toby over and answer the door wearing nothing but some lacy panties and a smile. Do you have some sexy lingerie? You wanna go to Jollymart afterwards and I'll help you pick some out?"

"No, I'm just going to let it happen. You know, I just like being with him."

"O M G. I get it now. I think you are in L O V E."

"Shut up, I don't want to talk about it anymore."

"Allison and Toby sitting in a tree…K I S S I N G," she chants as she turns the music back up, grinning ear to ear.

Finally, we get to Grimoire.

After pulling into the parking lot of the medical clinic, Steph turns off the car. Her *Hello Kitty* keychain slowly swings. She slowly melts into the reality of why we're here. Her face turns red. I can tell tears are ready to flow.

"Gawd, I don't want to be pregnant. I can't do it. Not again. But I couldn't get rid of a baby either," she sniffles.

"One step at a time, Steph. Let's go and see what they say. You probably aren't, so don't worry. Most of the stuff people worry about ain't never gonna happen, anyway. But if you are, we can deal with it. Okay?" I say, gently squeezing her hand.

Taking a deep breath, she yanks *Hello Kitty* out of the ignition, rubbing it like a good luck charm, but doesn't say anything. We get out of the car and go inside.

Shortly after checking in, the receptionist calls for 'Stephanie Gunderson.' Steph gives me a weak smile, then follows the receptionist back through a swinging door.

I thumb through a *Newsweek* and a *People* magazine, both dated a year ago. I read a pamphlet on how to quit smoking, flip through a Spanish language brochure about immunizations, then stare off into space until she's done.

An hour later, she springs out higher than Tigger in The Hundred Acre Woods. She obviously isn't pregnant.

"Hell yes! I mean, hell no!" she shouts, fist pumping in sweet victory.

"Congrats!" I squeal.

"Quiet!" the receptionist shushes.

"See ya! Wouldn't want to be ya!" Steph yells, and we run back to the car.

"And you know the best part?" she asks, pulling out of the parking lot.

"You're going to be more careful next time?" I ask.

"Yeah, that too. But the doc gave me this shot, and the birth control lasts three months. I used to be on the pill, but I'd get high and forget to take them. One time the dog ate the entire monthly pack and I never got around to getting more. So, this is a lot better option for me."

"Sounds like a good plan," I nod, turning on the radio.

About five miles from Granola, I squint my eyes toward the side of the road and say, "You gotta be kidding me. I think that's Jungle Jim."

He's standing on the shoulder, hitchhiking.

"Seriously, how does that doofus even manage to tie his shoes in the morning?" she asks.

"He only wears slip-on shoes."

"Is he homeless? He does live somewhere around Granola, doesn't he?"

"He lives in Mrs. Halverson's basement."

"How the heck does he pay her any money for rent?"

"Mr. Whitehead said the VA gives him a benefit check every month so he can live on his own. They want to keep him away from the St. Cloud Veterans Home because he's too annoying."

Jimmy last held down employment about fifteen years ago. Bob got him a job working for the Minnesota roads department. He couldn't be trusted with a snowplow like Bob, so they wanted him to be the dump truck counter over the winter season.

At the gravel pit outside of Granola, the snow plows and other big trucks from the county drive in to fill up on the sand and salt mix to spread over the roads after they've been plowed. Jimmy was suppose to sit in a little hut and count the trucks going out, to keep track of how many loads were used. His supervisor gave him a note pad and a pen along with a thermos of coffee.

He had one job. He was to make a tally mark for each truck leaving. But Jimmy drank too much peppermint schnapps that night. He passed out within the hour and his note pad fell on the space heater. His supervisor barely got him out of there alive before the entire shack burned to the ground. And that happened on the first and only night.

Steph pulls over to the side of the road. Jimmy runs up to my window and leans in, along with a burst of cigarette smoke and a belch of beer.

"Hot diggity! Isn't this my lucky day! Being picked up by the two, best looking ladies in Granola!"

"Get in, Jimmy. I gotta get back to work," I say.

He reaches for the back door, but Steph pulls ahead and stops. He walks to the car again, but she takes off, then stops again. With his hand almost on the door handle, she gives it some gas and starts moving, picking up speed.

About ten yards down the road, Jimmy catches up. He takes a flying leap through the back door window. She slams on the brakes. Then, steps on the gas and off we go towards Granola, with Jimmy's legs sticking out of the window and his head somehow lodged under my car seat.

"I think he passed out," I say, looking at his contorted, cockeyed body.

"I'm not passed out. I'm mucked," he mutters from under my seat.

"He's fucked all right," Steph says.

"I think he means stuck," I answer.

"Pull over," he pleads.

"Sure, Jimmy. Hey Allison. Can I at least buy you lunch before you go back to work? We can drive-thru Taco Gong. My treat," she says.

I grin and say, "Sure."

After a few minutes, we're back in Granola and at the Taco Gong menu board. Steph is yelling into the speaker.

"We'll have four nacho cheese Loco Tacos and two large diet Dews." She then looks over her shoulder and asks, "Hey Jimmy, you hungry?"

"Yes," he mumbles from under the seat.

"Make that six nacho cheese Loco Tacos and three large diet Dews, please."

At the pickup window, the little doors fly open and her boyfriend Chad sticks his head out.

"Hi Steph! I thought that was your sexy voice," he says, smiling at her.

"Hey, Chad. You gotta come over tonight. We got some reason to celebrate and stuff."

"You know it, hot mama," he says, handing her a greasy bag of tacos and three gigantic cups of pop, refusing her money.

He then looks in the back seat, rubs his eyes and asks, "Whoa. Who's that?"

"Jungle Jim."

"Hey, Jimmy," Chad says.

"Hey, Chad," Jimmy answers from under the seat.

"See ya tonight," Steph says, blowing Chad a kiss before we leave.

Thankfully, we're only a block away from Whitehead's Hardware. But not close enough.

When I look back to check on Jimmy, I notice Sheriff Goldberg's squad following quietly but closely behind. Steph notices too, but keeps driving until we get to the hardware store. She casually pulls in.

I sit quietly and whisper, "Maybe he's going to arrest us for vandalizing Devin's car."

She takes a sip of pop, shrugs and says, "Doubt it. He probably just wants to know why there is half a person hanging out the back window."

Sheriff Goldberg walks directly over to Jimmy's door and pulls it open. He yanks him by the seat of his pants not just out, but up in the air, out and down.

"I think I have a caucasian on my head!" Jimmy cries.

"A what on your head?" Sheriff Goldberg asks.

"I knocked it real hard," he answers, rubbing his head.

"You mean a concussion?"

"Yes!"

"No, you don't, Jimmy," he answers, then stands in front of my window. "Steph? Allison? Should I even ask? Do I even dare ask what's going on?"

"Oh, hi Sheriff. We were coming back from Grimoire and picked Jimmy up hitch hiking. But he had a problem getting the back door open, so, you know, and then he just got in anyway," I say. Because it's more or less the truth.

Steph likes to push the truth a little and adds, "Yeah, that's right, Sheriff. We tried so hard to get him unstuck but it was impossible. Thank goodness you were strong enough to do it," she smiles, innocently.

Goldberg turns to Jimmy and enunciates quite clearly, "Jungle Jim. For one day. For just one. God. damned. day. Will you *please* stop acting like yourself?"

His radio squawks from the squad. He shakes his head, rushes back to his car, and leaves. I give Jimmy his tacos, and he saunters away down the sidewalk.

"Thanks for being there for me, Allison," Steph calls as she pulls away.

"Stay out of trouble tonight. Don't celebrate too much," I yell and go back to work.

~~~

Mr. Whitehead storms out of his office. He's mad as a sack of wet roosters.

"That damn Mr. Clancy. He just called me. He says the building isn't up to code because we don't have an automatic door for handicapped customers. Now I have to apply to get a variance or install one, so I'll be busy wasting my time with all that rigmarole."

"When Morton comes by, he just bangs into the door with his wheelchair and curses until I opened it for him. Why do we need automatic doors when I'm right here?"

"Apparently, it's a big deal," he answers. "Not up to code. I guess Mr. Clancy thinks there's a procession of crippled folks out there in wheelchairs trying to get into the store to buy hammers but can't because we don't have an automatic door. Sumbitch Clancy."

Mr. Whitehead is far too good-hearted and way too old to have to put up with all this. I wish I could tell him about what's really going on with Mr. Clancy; the audio file, the investigation, what Sheriff Goldberg told me.

"I wouldn't worry too much about Mr. Clancy anymore. A mean man like him can only last for so long before something backfires," I say, trying to be reassuring.

"I hope so."

"If he comes in today, I'll tell him you aren't here."

"You do that, Allison. Butter him up like a cob of corn and get him off my back for another day, will ya?"

"Sure."

"Then tell him to stick that corn cob where the sun don't shine, sumbitch," he says, shuffling back to his office.

Sitting on the counter, eating my Loco Tacos I glance out the window. Oh no. Kristin. Here she comes.

I loose my appetite. I don't want to deal with this. I don't know what to do. She's pushing her baby stroller toward the store, packed with nothing but fluffy, chenille blankets and delusional grief.

Her husband's card is still in my red apron pocket. I pull it out, then shove it back in.

"Hey, Allison," she says, breezing through the door towards me. "So glad you're here now. I came by earlier but you were closed. None the less, I need to order some motion-sensor night lights. And some child proof locks for the lower cabinets in the kitchen, so Daniel can't open them and drink poison when he's a curious toddler."

"Good afternoon, Kristin," I say softly.

"I also want to put some wallpaper borders up in the nursery, to cheer it up a bit. Bring it to life more, give it some energy. Do you have the peel and stick kind?"

I shake my head and say, "No. We special order them."

"Do you have a catalogue? Let's see the catalogue."

"Uh, sure, it's in back. Hold on, Kristin. Let me go get it," I stammer and quickly walk to Mr. Whitehead's office, shutting the door behind me.

"Oh gosh, Mr. Whitehead. I need to make a call about Kristin. She's out there now."

He bobs his head quietly but doesn't look up from his screen. He squeezes the computer mouse so hard I think he'll break it's back.

I pull out the business card and dial the number. Mr. Whitehead releases the poor mouse, sits back in his chair and rubs his eyes.

"Zach McCarthy," the voice answers.

"Uh, hi. This is Allison Couch from Whitehead's Hardware. You said to call you."

I don't know what else to say.

There is a brief silence, then, "Is she there?"

"Yes."

"What's she doing?"

"She wants to order new wallpaper borders. And child proof locks. And night lights for Daniel's nursery."

"Okay. Thanks. I'll be there in a few."

The phone goes dead.

I grab the wallpaper catalogue and return to the front, spreading it out on the counter.

With one hand, Kristin thumbs through the book, cooing and smiling, earmarking pages, and with the other hand, gently pushing the stroller back and forth. She looks so very calm, peaceful, lost in her own little world of what should have been.

About ten minutes later, her husband walks through the door,. He's holding back from puking a bucket.

"Kristin," he says, stopping in the middle of the floor, drowning in absolute misery.

Looking up, emotionally bleached and barren, she slowly shuts the catalogue.

Without a word, he holds the door open and she follows, pushing the stroller out. I see him folding up the stroller and place it sideways in the back of their Audi SUV. He gently guides Kristin into the front seat.

They leave, with her head buried deep in her hands.

~~~

Toby texts and says he's got homework and things to do around the house, so won't be by tonight. That's just fine with me, as I don't feel much like talking to anyone. Not even him.

Grandma, Bob and Maple are lounging on the couch when I get home. I walk past them without mumbling a word.

"Are you okay?" Bob asks.

"I don't want to talk about it."

Grandma grabs the remote, turns down the TV and says, "Allison. Life is funny sometimes. Sometimes it's a prime rib all-you-can-eat buffet, other times it's a cold shit sandwich with monkey-piss tea."

"Yep," I answer, and go upstairs. Maple follows me to my bedroom, and doesn't ask questions either. She lays down next to me, as close as she can. Wrapping one arm around her, I wrap my other around my own head.

I know how Kristin feels, to be gypped out of someone you love too early. But I will never understand why God would even send them down in the first place, only to snatch them back so quickly. Six years was not long enough to be with my parents. Three hours was not long enough to be with her child.

Don't make sense. I wish I still believed in Him so I could ask, but I don't feel like talking to Him either.

I fall like a brick to sleep before I break into pieces.

CHAPTER NINETEEN

Early in the morning, Maple and I head to the field as the sun stretches across the glowing horizon.

Toby's already sitting under the tree. Maple runs over to him, covering him with long licks, lifting one paw up, then the other, so fast she almost loses her balance.

But Toby's not looking too good. He obviously had a worse night than I had. With maroon moons under his half shut eyes, he's holding a Come-n-Pump cup of coffee.

It reeks of booze.

Whiskey? Who puts whiskey in their coffee at seven in the morning? Grandma would if I let her. Maple sniffs it, then runs off to the field, wanting nothing to do with the odd smell.

I give him a dirty look, but don't say anything.

"Can't sleep, been up all night again," he says quietly, without looking at me.

"Can't the VA give you something for that? You should ask them. You need some sleep, Toby."

He rubs his forehead and doesn't answer. He sets the styrofoam cup to the side, laying his hands on his wrinkled jeans. He's usually such a spiffy dresser, but he's wearing the same clothes from the last time I saw him.

Finally, he says, "The VA thinks pills are the answer to everything. They prescribed all kinds of medications, but I'm not taking 'em."

I'm not in the mood to be Minnesota nice, so say, "What's bad for your health is drinking all night. You think the VA doctor gives you a prescription because he wants to make you feel worse? What kind of logic is that? Seriously? This is the second or so time that I know about, with you up drinking all night and into the morning."

He sucks in his lips and keeps staring straight ahead.

"If you don't want medication, do they have a support group or AA over there?" I ask.

"I'm not going to some gay group run by a kumbaya intern that has no clue and don't know shit. I had to do that at Walter Reed hospital and it was a joke."

I thought about this long enough, for the past twenty years, regarding my mother. What if she'd gotten help. What if she'd went to a counselor. Something. Anything.

Not being old enough to understand or say anything to her then, I can to Toby now. There's no way I'm going to let him slip through my fingers, also.

I hate that he wants to be somewhere else, drunk, and soar, with eagles, and crawl, with the snakes.

"Well, you got to do something about this problem."

"Are you saying I have a problem?"

"Yes, I am. And you don't seem like the type of guy that doesn't do something about a problem."

He squints his eyes at the sunrise.

"If someone hands you a life jacket when you're drowning, don't you want to put it on?" I continue. "At least try whatever they have to offer."

"I get your point. I get it."

"Good. I know you probably lost friends over there. But you can't drink them back. I'm sure it just makes it worse. You don't want that. Either do I and neither do them. They wouldn't want this for you."

"You sound like my girlfriend," he mutters.

I might be naive, but I ain't a bag of rocks. I'm so mad at him right now I could spit. "*Like* your girlfriend?"

"Yes."

"I sound *like* your girlfriend. That's great. That's just whoop-dee-do great."

"What's that suppose to mean?"

"So. You have a girlfriend."

"What the hell are you talking about now?"

"You said I sound like your girlfriend."

"Ally. Listen to me. I don't have a girlfriend. Except you. I mean, if you want to be."

"Oh. I didn't mean to snap at you," I say.

"I didn't mean to snap at you either."

"Okay then," I whisper, relieved that we just had our first boyfriend-girlfriend argument.

"Can we be done fighting now?" he asks.

"Sure."

He puts his hand on my thigh. I cover it with my own. I want to say so much more and I think he does too, but we don't. Instead, we watch the opening day unfolding above us. Enough said.

Maple slops down next us, panting, keeping a protective eye on us and the trees. Toby squishes his cup, then lays his head on my shoulder.

When the sun finally breaks over the horizon in full force, we get up and walk home.

I stop on the sidewalk and ask, "You wanna come in for breakfast? I'll make you some butterscotch chip oatmeal. That's another one of my special comfort foods. I make it when I'm depressed. It's hard to be depressed when there's butterscotch involved. I bet you'd love it."

He squeezes his eyes with his long, elegant fingers. Then, flashes them open. The whites are yellow, spider-laced with pink, reflecting the light.

"I'm sure I would, but, no. Thanks anyway. I'm finally getting tired. But thanks again for everything."

"Promise me you will go home and get some rest?"

"Sure, I promise. And I'll be okay," he says.

"Why don't you come over tonight for supper? After you get some sleep."

Kisses work so perfectly when words just don't, so we do. He then disappears down the block.

CHAPTER TWENTY

After work, I'm in the kitchen with Grandma trying to wrangle the Hamburger Helper box from her hands.

I forgot how much she hates the 'goofy-ass' glove logo on the box. She hates him even more than the 'smug prick' Quaker Oats guy, or the 'creepy perv' Orville Redenbacher.

She punches the box and it explodes, spilling dried noodles all over. Maple wanders into the kitchen and starts eating the uncooked noodles scattered across the floor.

"Will you please leave the Hamburger Helper guy alone? Look, I brought home all the ingredients you need to make chicken fried steak. The club crackers. The onion powder, the oil, eggs, everything you need."

I pull open the refrigerator door and take out the steak that Bob won at the American Legion meat raffle yesterday. "Here, Grandma. Here's the steak," I add.

She hmphs.

Grandma sometimes walks to Chub to get groceries, but her cooking, besides her famous Chicken Fried Steak, is, well, a little different.

For example, she boils hamburgers.

I reminded Grandma before that hamburger should be fried in a skillet, grilled, baked in a meatloaf or cooked in Hamburger Helper.

Instead, she likes to boil up a pan of hot water, drop the patties in, scoop them out and put them on buns. Then, the buns turn soggy and disintegrate. We end up eating the hamburgers with a spoon.

Bob doesn't care. He puts the soggy bun, boiled hamburger, a squirt of mustard along with a slice of processed American cheese in a big bowl. He calls it Ethylon's Cheeseburger soup.

"I used to be a good cook but they hid all my pots and pans," she says.

"Grandma. I didn't hide the pots and pans. They're exactly where they've always been for years."

"I miss your chicken fried steak, Ethylon," Bob says, walking into the kitchen. His feet crunch over the spilled, dried noodles.

"Oh yeah, baby," Grandma answers. "It won a blue ribbon at the county fair in '81. It won another blue ribbon at the state fair down in St. Paul. But they wanted my recipe so I told them to kiss my chicken fried rump. I ain't sharing my secret recipe."

She starts tenderizing the steak by smacking it against the counter just as there's a knock on the front door.

Toby is standing on the porch, looking much better than this morning. He obviously got some rest today.

"Hi," he says, sheepishly.

"Hi," I answer. "Grandma's making supper tonight, so come on in."

"You're in for a treat, Toby," Grandma says, running into the living room, flailing a piece of raw steak in the air. Maple lunges, grabs it, then bolts to the basement.

"Beat the meat in the kitchen, Ethylon!" Bob yells.

"Beat your own damn meat, Bob!" she screams back.

"Toby, why don't you take Allison for a quick driving lesson first?" Bob calls over his shoulder as he steers Grandma back to the kitchen. "It's gonna be awhile 'till supper's ready. But it'll be worth it."

Toby smiles and does one of his wink-blinks as I slip on my flip flops.

"Just go," Bob adds. "The best supper will be waiting for you two when you return, I guarantee it."

~~~

After backing out of the driveway, Maple barges out of the house, licking her big snout. Toby opens his door and she lunges in, taking her place in the back seat.

"So, what are we going to work on today?" I ask, rolling down my window.

"Parallel park. That's part of the test that you failed, but that's my fault because I didn't teach you. Let's go to Price Wackers and we can practice there," he answers.

"I don't think I need to do that. No one parallel parks in Granola. People here just drive to where they're going and park as close as they can, where they can. You know, every which way to avoid having to parallel park. Sheriff Goldberg gave up a long time ago with giving out parking tickets because it took too much of his time."

"It's part of the test. And the entire point of driving is to go other places besides Granola. Places where you'll have to parallel park."

"Yeah. I know…but."

"No buts," he says. "I'll show you how, Ally."

Fine. I drive over to the deserted Price Wackers lot. Toby and Maple get out and he sets up two empty pop cans, a little more than a car length apart, then gets back in.

I keep staring straight ahead and say, "There's no other car to parallel park with."

"I know that. That's why I set up the cans. Pretend they're the bumpers to other cars."

"You didn't tell me that."

"I just did."

"Whatever."

"Now Ally, all you have to do is pull up, put the Regal in reverse, angle about forty-five degrees and back in. When you're even with the rear bumper of the other car, straighten your car out," he says. Then adds nonchalantly, "Pull up, then back in. Just like that."

"Just like that? Really?" I say, gripping the wheel.

"Just like that."

"I don't think I can," I answer.

He throws his head down, eyebrows up.

"Yes, just like that. Yes, you can. And yes, you will."

I keep looking straight ahead.

I don't move, so he continues, "Try it once. Do it once so we can at least see where you are with this."

I throw the car in reverse, knocking over both cans. Toby gets out, sets up the cans again, then calls for Maple to hop back in the car.

"She'd probably be safer in here until you get the hang of it," he says under his breath.

"I'm glad you finally got some rest," I say, trying to change the subject so we run out of time and I don't have to practice my parking skills. "What did you have for lunch?" I add.

"Ramen noodles and sour cream. My mom went out of town, so it's just me," he answers, grinning.

"Where did your mom go?"

"Visit her sister. She didn't want to go, is always worried about me, but I told her to go, she needs a vacation. I put her through a lot the past few years."

"Where's her sister live?"

"Just over in Wisconsin."

"I've only been to Wisconsin once. For church camp. I hated every single minute of it."

He hesitates, then puts his arm on the back of the seat.

"Ya know what, Ally?"

"No, what?" I whisper, thinking it's going to be some romantic moment. I'm hoping he lays a big kiss on me, and we do it in the back seat.

"You need to stop asking me questions and learn how to parallel park the damn car, okay?"

"You're the one answering so many questions."

He shakes his head, and points to the steering wheel.

We spend the next twenty minutes parallel parking.

As the sun is about to disappear, I finally do two perfect parking jobs in a row.

Then, Toby takes a bottle of Crown Royal out from nowhere, it seems, and downs a quarter of it. I hopscotch over being confused and go straight to anger. Wasn't he just drinking this morning? Didn't we already go through this?

He's not even hiding it from me. It's as if he wants me to confront him, wants me to care. Maybe I don't have the right to nag him. But then again, he did say I was his girlfriend. Maybe I shouldn't say anything. After all, he's a war hero with all this stuff to deal with. But he was drunk just this morning before I went to work. I don't know what to say except, "You need to stop drinking."

"I know."

"Does your mother know?"

"She's beginning to notice."

"You were drunk this morning. And when you sobered up at the end of the day, you start drinking again. Toby, that's not right. I thought we already talked about this."

"People drink."

"Yeah, but when they are celebrating a birthday or out with friends at a disco."

He smiles and says, "Really, Ally? A disco?"

"What I'm trying to say is you're drinking for the wrong reasons."

"I know."

His shoulders soften, so I add, "I think it's normal to be different after a war. You'd be crazy if it didn't affect you, but you gotta manage it a little bit better. And you can't do that alone, or by not letting people help you."

He's quietly staring straight ahead.

I add, "Everyone says you were in the hospital for a long time, because of what happened. I saw the scars on your leg, too. What exactly happened to you over there?"

"Nothing that didn't happen to a lot of people over there," he answers.

"Like what, exactly?"

I doubt he'll tell me. But he does. For a second, I appreciate the bottle of truth serum in his lap.

In a detached and deadpan monotone, he says, "Our team was on patrol looking for a suspected weapons stash. Our route was through a canyon with vertical walls to get there. Basically, an open tunnel.

We had to dismount and walk because the terrain became too dangerous to drive. It was barely morning, so we couldn't see too much anyway.

As we pushed in, we noticed signs of recent enemy activity. Something was really wrong. It became obvious something was really seriously wrong when I saw spent shell casings on the ground by this boulder.

I'm like, shit. We need to turn around. We need to get out of here. Just in the half second I'm processing this all, the Islamic fuckers opened up from the cliffs above with machine guns and sniper fire.

We couldn't tell where the bullets were coming from, though. We knew it was coming from above, but we were in a canyon, a bowl, so it could have been coming from anywhere. And it was. From everywhere.

Each shot echoed ten times more and louder. Four of our guys were hit plus our Afghani interpreter got hit in both legs. LT Nelson was hit in the side of his face. The others, they, I didn't...

We tried to find covered positions to engage, but the fighters on the cliffs above were hammering us. I took cover behind my Humvee and started treating Nelson but he was gone.

When Corporal Rodriquez managed to make it over to me, I asked him where Bright, our medic, was. He yelled back that Bright got hit, too, but he couldn't get to him.

As soon as Rodriquez said that, he was hit in the ass and it tore through his front, out his pelvis. His God damned penis blew off. I tried to treat him, the best I could. I even grabbed his dick that was splattered on a rock and shoved it back in his pocket.

The fight wore on and our guys were hurtin' bad. The gunship we called in for cover couldn't get to their targets because of the terrain. The medevac helicopter couldn't reach us either because of the incoming fire.

I got mad and managed to climb up the cliff to a point where I could see and shoot some of the hajis. I got into a knife fight with a few. Damnit. I don't know. It was ugly. I didn't take them all out, but enough to provide cover so we could get our guys out of the kill zone.

I took a lot of shrapnel in my leg. I was hit twice in my armor and once through my sleeve.

I remember everything. Everyday. We got out with four dead. That's about it. We got out."

"I'm so sorry," I say, because what else is there to say.

"People think I'm some kind of hero. But I don't feel like one. There's a clown jury, a box of bozos in my head that keeps telling me I'm guilty because I'm alive. And the jury don't stop replaying the evidence."

He rubs his eyes and adds, "They play it, on surround sound, then rewind and play it again. Play, rewind, play."

"It sounds like you did what you could in an impossible situation, Toby."

"I wish I could have saved them all, or none of them. Or kill all the Taliban, or none of them. I don't like the feeling of playing God, like it was up to me who I should save, or kill, or not."

His hands aren't shaking, but his soul seems to be.

"I didn't deserve that Silver Star."

"But you saved all those lives."

"We didn't gain one square inch of that unholy land. Instead, we lost four men with one sent home with his dick in his pocket. They're the heroes, not me."

"I'm so sorry Toby. I really don't know what to say. I am just. so. sorry."

"And then there's Jimmy. When we were on the float, he told me that he wished he was a hero like me. But no one should want that. It's not like that at all."

"Maybe you should just stop thinking about it."

Toby turns to me, incredulous.

"That's the problem. I can't stop thinking about it. All I want is one decent night's sleep," he says.

I wish I still believed in Jesus so I could suggest praying. Instead, I say, "Have you ever seen the YouTube video, 'Kid fails at obstacle course'?"

He rubs his face and asks, "What the hell are you talking about now, Ally?"

"You should watch it."

"Seriously? Why?"

"I don't know. But I like how the kid gets up and keeps living. It's not always easy to keep living."

He sighs quietly and mutters, "Okay, Ally. If you say so. I'll look it up on YouTube."

"Thanks for telling me what happened. Are you ready to go back to Grandma's and eat?"

"Yes. I'd like that."

I put the Regal in drive and we head home.

~~~

Who Wants to be a Millionaire is on when we return. Bob is swishing the remote like a symphony conductor.

"I could be a millionaire. It's *Gilligan's Island*. Who doesn't know that answer? It's *Gilligan's Island*," Bob yells.

A rich, meaty scent billows throughout the house.

"Supper's ready! Sit down, you two lonely doves. And you too, Bob. Let's eat," Grandma calls from the kitchen.

She carries out a heavy dish layered with flaky, juicy rounds of steak, a bowl of buttery mashed potatoes and a steaming cup of chunky brown gravy flecked with black pepper. She also plunks down a side dish of Hamburger Helper, a bag of potato chips and a tub of Top the Tator dip. There's not a vegetable in sight, and no one cares.

"This steak is amazing. I've never tasted anything so good, ma'am," Toby says with his mouth full.

"You want to know my secret ingredient?" Grandma asks Toby.

"I don't know if we want to know your secret ingredient," Bob says.

"Sure, Miss Ethylon. What's the secret? And I promise, I won't tell a soul," Toby says.

She leans forward and whispers, "Cocoa powder."

"Excuse me?"

"The unsweetened kind. A dash of cocoa powder in anything savory makes it royal, brings out the flavor."

Toby nods his head, taking another bite.

"Put some in your spaghetti sauce, or gravy, or beef stew, and thank me later," she adds.

Maple grunts loudly, staring at us, obviously wanting someone to drop a piece of steak under the table. Grandma doesn't wait that long, and tosses her an entire piece of meat. She gobbles it down in about ten seconds.

"She's gonna get the runs, Ethylon," Bob scolds.

"She ain't going to get the runs," Grandma answers.

"She will so. You can't feed the dog table scraps."

"Shut your trap, Bob. When I grew up, there was no such thing as twenty dollar bags of foo foo dog food. Our dogs ate table scraps and they all lived to sixteen years old," she answers. "Except Lucille Ball. She got run over by the neighbor's tractor. And Buster Keaton, the big german shepherd. He turned feral and ran off to live with a pack of wolves. But we think he was part wolf anyway. And then there was General Eisenhower, the chihuahua. We don't know what happened to him. He just took off one summer day into the far alfalfa field and never came back."

"Grandma, let's not talk about this anymore," I say, going toward the kitchen to start the dishes.

Toby grabs a wet towel to wipe the dining room table clean, then brings the rest of the plates to the sink.

I want to hug him. So I do.

Turning my head to the left side, he turns his head to the right. His breath that now smells comforting, so much better than the sharp bite of booze.

I inhale deeply, sigh, then breathe him in again.

He burrows his head further into me as I lay my head up on his shoulder. I wish we could hug this way forever. Absolutely forever. But I can tell Grandma and Bob are watching us.

"Why don't you go and get some sleep, Toby. I'll finish cleaning up, but do, please, text me later."

"Of course I will," he whispers in my ear.

Toby calls 'thanks again' on his way to the door and I follow him to the porch. I watch him walk away, wishing he would turn and look back.

Look back.

Just look back.

He does. I quietly wave, and watch him dissolve into the night as it begins to rain.

~~~

About eleven p.m., my phone vibrates.

"Hello?"

"Hello?"

"Hello?"

"You up?"

"Toby?"

"Hey."

"Hi."

I glance over at Maple who's crashed on most of my bed, snoring. Her front legs are stretched out and rear legs flared, her tail arched over her back.

"Did you get my text?"

"Nope. I can check if you give me a minute," I answer, trying to perk up.

"I can't sleep. Can I come over and sleep with you?"

"If you want," I whisper. "The back door is unlocked, just come in quietly. Grandma is snoring and Bob is gone."

"Okay."

"Okay."

I touch to disconnect.

Laying in the bed in the dark, rain tapping on the roof, I'm nervous, anxious, motionless. I can't wait for him to get here but at the same time, hope he doesn't show up.

About fifteen minutes later, Maple startles, barks, but I quiet her down. My bedroom door clicks open, then gently closes.

In the soft glow of my night light, I see him take off his socks, but nothing else.

"Hi," I say quietly.

"Hey," he answers, and lays down next to me, on top of the sheets, fully clothed.

I fold my hands on my stomach.

"Can I say something?" I ask.

He leans over me. I smell his freshly brushed teeth in the dark. Into my ear, he breathes, "Of course. What?"

"If you want to have sex, I wouldn't mind. That is, if you don't mind."

"Seriously, Ally? Are you for real?" he answers, and covers me, and pulls off my jammies, and I rip off his shirt, and we try to be as quiet as we can, but wheeling around on my bed with him is the best feeling that I never could've imagined.

There is nowhere else to be.

Because we're Hollywood movie stars, and Astronauts, and Billionaires, and Olympians, and Kings and Queens, and I bet we could discover the cure for cancer, save the whales, make the perfect omelette together and finally clean out the junk drawer.

And the rain beats down.

There is nothing more I think is worth doing other than being with him.

I want him to be the forever

I want to cry

Laugh

So relieved

Moving in slow motion

Speeding up to kiss

Tighten my thighs around him

Ankles locked high above

Warm, green sheets

Handfuls of everything

Around and around

Until the whole universe explodes

Into shattering rainbows

After the storm

He comes soon after

Toby rolls over on his back next to me, catching his breath, then moves down to lay his head on my chest. Clinging to me, he doesn't want to let go.

"When I'm not looking at you my hands are curled into fists and get cold," he whispers. "I love you, Ally."

I know he does.

"I love you too."

Because I do. I found someone that makes me feel beautiful. His eyes are endless miles, not the easiest to walk through but I want to try.

Life is funny sometimes. Toby, a perfect stranger a few weeks ago, is now the best part of my little life, making it bigger and better.

I nudge him off because I have to go pee.

When I return, he's fast asleep on his back, holding Maple in one arm. I fall into his other. Wide open and waiting for me.

I've never slept with a man before, as in sleep in a bed. I've slept with Grandma when I was younger, and her bed smelled of sweet, Avon perfume. I slept dozens of times with Steph when I used to go over there in high school for slumber parties. But as soon as she would fall asleep, she'd push me out somehow, and I'd end up on the floor, her pink shag carpet for a mattress, a wad of dirty jeans for a pillow and her thick bathrobe as a blanket.

But never a man. It's a present I always wanted but never thought I'd get. He snores like Maple, but doesn't drool like her.

The pattering rain suddenly dumps into a midnight downpour. I sleep deep, safe and content, grateful he is next to me.

When the early summer rays peek through my curtains the next morning, Toby is already gone.

CHAPTER TWENTY-ONE

I breeze through the back door of Whitehead's Hardware and dreamily grab my red apron. The delight of last night is humming over me still.

Mr. Whitehead creaks his chair around, blinks hard at me, leans back and says, "Good morning, Allison."

"Yes indeed it is. It's beautiful out. I love Minnesota in the summer, especially after a good, hard rain."

Taking a sip of coffee, eyebrows up, he asks, "Are you okay, dear?"

"I'm just peachy."

"What's gotten into you?"

"Nothing. Toby and I just had a nice date last night, that's all. The best date ever, actually."

He spits his coffee back in his mug and says, "Is that so. I'm glad you finally did, I mean, had, I mean, are having, a good morning."

"Yep."

"He's sure a lucky man. I always said if you just keep on being you, someone would eventually catch on."

~~~

About noon, I run, forgetting my bike, over to Sub Station to say 'hi' to Steph. I gotta tell her about last night, even though I know she'll throw a conniption fit of happiness about me and Toby finally having sex.

The line is three deep, but Steph sees me over the crowd.

"Hey, Allison," she calls, waving her plastic-gloved hand and blowing a bubble.

"Hey, Steph," I answer.

She wipes her nose, scratches her hair, then goes back to making a customer's meatball sandwich. One of the meatballs rolls off the counter and lands on her shoe. She kicks it off, Italian sauce goes flying, and it rolls all the way across the floor.

She grins at me like nothing happened. The customer is too busy playing Candy Crush on his phone to notice.

When it's my turn, I order a turkey, Colby with extra mayo on white, but smirk like a naughty Mona Lisa.

Steph glances at me while folding the meat on the bun, as I beam back. She pauses, grabs the mayo bottle and looks at me again.

"You are positively sparkling, Allison," she says with eyes squinched.

I shrug my shoulders.

Continuing, she adds, "If I didn't know any better, I'd say you just got laid."

"Steph, please don't make a big scene about it," I answer, giggling.

"I knew it! I knew it sooo bad!"

She shakes the mayo bottle up and down, squeezing it, squealing, "Oh Toby! Oh Toby baby! Oh right there!"

The mayonnaise spews up, out and all over her hand.

"Steph," I say, trying not to laugh but dying of embarrassment.

"What kind of condoms do you want on your sandwich? I mean, condiments?" she cackles.

"Stop it, now," I say, turning four shades of red in a short second.

Wrapping up the sandwich, grinning, she yells, "Hey, Allison. You sure you don't want a footlong? Oh wait! You already had one last night!"

The customer ahead of me looks up from his phone, glances at Steph, back at me, then fumbles with his wallet to pay. He swipes his credit card, noticeably flustered.

Then, the poor man rushes out the door with his meatball sandwich just as Steph starts singing, *When I Think about you I Touch Myself* as loud as she can.

I snatch my sandwich, and race out the door too.

"I want the details, girlfriend! Call me with the juicy details!" I hear her scream halfway down the block as I run back to work.

CHAPTER TWENTY-TWO

I'm on heaven's cloud for the rest of the day. But after work, I think about Kristin. I don't know if it's too early to go over and check on her. It's probably none of my business, but want them to know I'm worried about her.

I pedal over to the sad house on Castle Court. Her husband answers the door. The stroller is nowhere to be seen, thankfully.

"Hi. How's Kristin?" I ask, nervously.

"You're from the hardware store, right?"

"Yes."

"What's your name again?" he asks.

"Allison. Allison Couch."

"Like the thing you sit on in the living room?"

"Exactly like the thing you sit on in the living room."

He squints, stumbles out the door and takes a seat on one of the rattan peacock chairs.

I take a seat in the other.

I don't smoke marijuana, but he lights up a big, fat joint. Holding his breath, he passes it to me, but I decline.

He takes another tug, then puts it out. Leaning back, he closes his eyes.

"So, I take it she's not here?" I ask.

His head flops to one side and he answers, "I put her on a plane to San Diego today. There's a spa-treatment-yoga-mental health place out there that might help her. Her sister flew out there with her."

"That's probably for the best."

"She can eat all the kale she wants out in California."

"Uh, yeah. I suppose so."

His head flops to the other side.

"I hate her sister."

"Sometimes that happens with family," I say.

"Her sister is a stupid bitch."

"That happens too."

"You have no idea how stupid a bitch she is."

"No, I probably don't have any idea."

"I mean, we only live in a state with 10,000 treatment centers for anything you can imagine or make up. We've got the Mayo Clinic, for gawd's sake. But her sister insists Kristin go to the most expensive one in California."

This guy is higher than Willy Nelson in a hot air balloon over Woodstock.

"Her sister's name is Emily," he sneers.

Riling up, he continues, "Piss off, Emily. Emmie. Mimi. Ems for short. Elle but you ain't fucking French. More like enema... I'm so sick of her."

"Oh, sorry to hear that."

"Really, Emily?" he says, shaking his lighter at the cast iron pig potted with flowers. "Why don't you go pick some organic rutabagas in your butt-ugly, Frankenstein-looking Birkenstocks."

"I, huh..."

"Screw Emily and her bags of hairy kale chips and dairy-free moose nipple milk and whatever else crap she comes over with. She doesn't even look at me. Whatever."

"Mmm..."

"You wanna know what I really want, Allison Couch, the thing you sit on in the living room?"

"No. What."

His head lulls towards me and he calms down.

"If I could have my lovely wife back. Like it was before. Before the loss."

He lights up the joint again. Slowly exhaling, he adds, "Kristin is the most beautiful woman inside and out."

The smoke wraps around his face, his sorrow, his rage at life's cruel tricks.

"Before Daniel," he adds.

"I'm just so sorry, I don't know what to say."

He lays back in the chair, looking up at the clear, blue sky. He then glowers at the potted pig planter and shoves it over with his foot. Kicking it again, the pig rolls off the porch snout first, spilling the azaleas and marigolds onto the manicured lawn.

"Her smile could power up an entire town. Like, somewhere in India. If a village in India had no electricity, she could be flown over there and sit on a mountain top and shine down. She'd light it up forever. All the little villagers and their donkeys and chickens and fuckin' elephants would have all the light they need."

He adds, "Sorry, nothing against elephants. I really like elephants."

"Me too," I say.

"Their feet are like giant marshmallows. Except heavy. Heavy marshmallows. And gray."

"Yeah…"

"The only thing I hate more than Emily, is a circus. That's not right to do that to elephants."

"No, it's not. I hate circuses too."

"Have you ever wanted to grab a star out of the sky and play with it? Toss it around?"

"If I could, I would…" I answer.

"Thanks for checking on Kristin," he says. "But I don't want to talk about my baby boy. Not to you. Her. My in-laws. My parents. Her sister. Her silly friends. My co-workers. Our doctor. Not on Facebook. Or in email. Or over the phone. Or in a box. Or with a fox. Not in a house. Not with a mouse. I do not like it, Allison Couch."

"Okay. You don't have to talk about it."

He lights up his joint again, not wanting to talk about it. But between puffs, keeps talking about it.

"They all ask me, 'How's Kristin? How's Kristin doing? Poor Kristin.' You know what, Allison the thing you sit on in the living room?"

"No, what?"

"Daniel was my son too. I'm going through the same hell she is. Imagine that. So, go ahead. Go ahead and ask me how I'm doing," he spits, glaring at me.

"How are you doing?"

"Well, I guess I'm doing just fine because I get up every day and go to work so my colleagues can ask 'How's Kristin?' I wanna say, 'Crazy as hell. And I'm here at work doing a good job but holding what little I can of myself together and trying to keep from punching you in the face so my wife can push an empty-ass baby carriage around a middle-of-nowhere hick town all day."

He stumbles into the house and returns with two craft beers. After spinning the top off of one, he hands it to me, but I hand it back.

He sits back down with both bottles in his lap, and takes a long drink.

"Now she's into kale salad," he sighs, like that's something worse.

"I know you'll never get over Daniel. But I bet at some point you guys will figure out how to manage it."

Sitting up, he guzzles the rest of the beer. He hands the second, full one to me but once again I decline. In a breezy 'cheers', he waves it up and takes a sip.

I add, "Have you thought about going out to that place in California to be with Kristin, and get some help with all this for you, too?"

Nodding, he says, "Yes. Her doctor called and wants me out there. At least for a few weeks. He wants to see both of us together."

Exhaling in relief, I ask, "Do you need someone to check on your house, get the mail, turn the porch lights on or off? Anything?"

"Thanks, but no. We got timed lights and I put the mail on hold today."

"Okay."

"But we do have a pet guinea pig. Kristin thought it would be a good starter pet for Daniel. She didn't want a cat because she thought it would sneak into his crib during the night and suck his breath out. She didn't want a yellow lab until Daniel got bigger. But we do have a guinea pig."

"I could take the guinea pig home if you want. I could watch it until you get back."

He smiles for the first time. I can see now why Kristin married this man. He obviously loves her more than anything.

"Where do you live? I'll drop the thing off at your house on my way to the airport tomorrow. The cage is way too big for your bike," he says.

"470 Chestnut. And what's the guinea pig's name?"

"Florence Fiddle Bottom," he says, lighting up his joint again.

"And your first name is Zach, right?" I ask as he holds in the smoke.

"Yep. Zach. But my college buddies call me Zacman," he answers, still holding his breath.

"I'll just stick with Zach."

"Okay, Allison the thing you sit on in the living room," he says, finally letting the smoke drift from his mouth. "Thanks for coming over."

I get up and pedal home.

~~~

Early next morning, my phone rings. Maple rolls over and yawns. The screen flashes six a.m. as I tap on it to answer.

"Ally?"

"Toby?"

"Why did this guy in a business suit knock on my door, yell your name, leave a guinea pig in a cage on my porch, jump back in an Audi SUV, then speed off before I could even get down the stairs?"

I rub my eyes and sit up. Last night I must have given Toby's address by mistake.

"Oh. Her name is Florence Fiddle Bottom," I answer.

"I'm pretty sure it was a guy that left it."

"No, not the guy. The guinea pig's name is Florence Fiddle Bottom."

"Okay. Why is Florence Little Vermin on my porch?"

"That's not her name."

"What's her name again?"

"Florence Fiddle Bottom."

"Can I just call her Flo?"

"Sure. I don't think she'll mind," I answer.

"All right. Why is Flo on my porch?"

"Sorry. I told him to drop her off."

"Who?"

"Florence Fiddle Bottom."

"No. Not Flo. The guy."

"Long story. I'll be over in about ten minutes, okay?"

"All right," he chuckles and clicks off.

Maple and I run over to 470 Chestnut, which is Toby's address, not mine.

Toby opens the door with Florence Fiddle Bottom on his shoulder, nibbling his ear.

"She's cute," he says, scratching her back. "The cats are scared of her, though. They're hiding under my bed."

Maple catches sight of the guinea pig and goes bonkers. She jumps up on Toby, knocking Flo off of his shoulder. Maple catches her by her neck in mid air. She then runs to the living room, shaking the poor thing around like a tambourine.

"No!" I scream.

Toby tackles Maple, pries open her jaw and grabs Florence Fiddle Bottom. He then tosses the wet ball of fur over his shoulder towards me.

I'm too slow to catch Flo, and she ricochets off my stomach, thudding to the floor. Maple pounces again, snatches Flo by her butt and runs to the kitchen.

"OFF!" Toby yells, and Maple drops Flo. Cocking her head to one side, smiling wide, tongue lolling, Maple loves her new chew toy and only wants to play some more.

Toby grabs Florence Fiddle Bottom and sits at the kitchen table. But she is lifeless in his lap.

"It's not looking too good," he says.

"Is she dead?" I ask.

"I'm not sure." Trying to puff her up with his fingers, he adds, "Hang on, little girl."

She doesn't move.

Toby tickles her back. Her ear twitches, but that's it.

"Is there a vet in Granola?"

"Tons of them."

He glares at me and says, "I mean a vet-veterinarian. An animal doctor."

"The nearest clinic is in Grimoire. But Sheldon is a retired veterinarian."

"We've got to get Flo to Sheldon," he says, jumping up.

He shoves Flo into my hands and we rush outside, get in his truck and speed to Sheldon's house.

Sheldon and his wife, Golda, are out in the yard watering their teacup rose bushes. Sheldon drops the hose as I run towards him holding Florence Fiddle Bottom in my outstretched hands.

"Sheldon!" I yell.

"Oy veh! What you got there, Allison?" Golda asks, worried.

"Florence Fiddle Bottom," I gasp. "Maple thought she was a stuffed play toy…"

"Well, bring her inside. Let's take a look-see," Sheldon says, shutting off the hose.

In Sheldon's kitchen, he lays her on her back on a thick towel. He puts one finger to one side of her neck, then to the other side. Squinting his eyes, he turns her to the side, then her stomach, then the other side, then on her head, then on her bottom.

"Don't see no puncture wounds," he says, nodding.

"That's good," Toby says.

But Florence isn't moving. Sheldon pushes on her fat chest. Counting to three, he pushes again. He leans over and puts his mouth on Florence's snout, and puffs.

Nothing.

He pushes her chest a few more times, and puffs into her snout again.

Sheldon lifts both her front legs up, down, over her head, and down. The rest of us watch in fear and hope, praying for a sign of life.

Finally, Florence twirls one of her little front legs up in victory and starts breathing on her own.

The guinea pig CPR worked.

"I think the little critter went into traumatic cardiac arrest," Sheldon says.

He carefully moves her to the center of the towel, wrapping her up like an enchilada. Only her little nose and a few whiskers are sticking out.

"She's a little shaken up now. Or a lot, I should say. But I reckon she'll be okay," he says, wiping a piece of fur from his mouth. "Take her home. Put her back in her cage in a quiet room, and leave her alone. And for God's sake, please be more careful with her."

I'm so relieved I can barely utter a 'thank you', only smile in gratitude.

"Thanks, Sheldon. Thanks, Golda," Toby says.

~~~

We return to Toby's house as black, burly clouds bulge over Granola. It's going to be another one of those Minnesota thunderstorms that beats down for an hour, then unfolds into a bright, cloudless day.

Florence Fiddle Bottom's cage is on a desk in Toby's bedroom. I gingerly put her back in, and she curls up in the corner. Her little snout twitches as her tiny nostrils flare open and shut rhythmically.

"Where's your mom?" I ask, watching the rodent sleep.

Outside, the swelling storm rolls overhead.

"Still in Wisconsin," Toby says softly behind me.

He wraps his arms around my waist.

"What time do you need to be at work?" he asks.

His warm, wide lips rest on my throat. I'm sure he can feel my pulse race. We breathe in, then out, together.

I don't answer.

"Did you know your hair shines like brown sugar in the sun?" he says, tugging my ponytail so my head falls back onto his shoulder.

It begins to rain.

"And sometimes your eyes are hazel, and sometimes green, depending on what you wear," he whispers, pulling me closer.

A flick of lightning flashes through the window.

"And when you get nervous, you squeeze your nose."

"No, I don't."

Wheels of thunder roll overhead.

"Yes, you do," he murmurs, covering my face with his hand, then pulls his fingers over my lips, down my neck.

All the way down on me

The other moves up

I close my eyes

Turn around

He says

So I

do

CHAPTER TWENTY-THREE

"Good morning, Mr. Whitehead. Are you going to show me how to make the keys today?" I ask in the most *I just had sex with the greatest man ever* tone of voice possible.

Preoccupied, Mr. Whitehead stares at his computer screen, with one hand on the mouse, his other wrapped around his yellow mug.

"Not today, Allison. I have forty pallets stacked up in back, so Tommy's coming over to get them for firewood. Then, I've got to deal with that sidewalk issue Mr. Clancy wrote us up about a few days ago. Need to get some paperwork in order. I'm going to need you out front, if you don't mind."

"Don't mind at all, Mr. Whitehead. Will do," I answer and go start the popcorn.

After I flip over the OPEN sign, Sheldon comes through the door soon after.

"Good morning, Allison, and an exciting morning it was. I want to know how the little patient is doing. Is our Flo resting well?"

"Thanks again, Sheldon. And yes, sir. Flo is safe and recovering nicely."

"Good to hear. And by the way, how's Ethylon? Golda wants to know if she's been staying out of trouble."

Golda, Sheldon's wife, was an older classmate of Grandma's, fifty plus years ago, back when Granola was a little town on the prairie. Both Grandma and Golda talk often of their beloved teacher, Miss Bell, who they remember as 'the finest woman on earth.'

Miss Bell had moved all the way from St. Paul to teach them and the other children in Grimoire county. Rumor had it she couldn't get a job nor a husband in the big city, so that's why she bought a one way bus ticket to Granola.

Grandma said she was 'queer as a six-fingered glove', but back then you had to hide that sort of thing, and that's the real reason she moved here.

Golda's dad and Grandma's dad would often car pool the kids to school, if you would call it that.

They couldn't afford a car, so one or the other would hook up a wagon with a team of horses and head off to town. The fathers hauled the box of kids, over the rough roads in the spring, through the falling leaves in autumn and fresh snow in the winter.

Their mothers were too busy at home chasing and chopping up chickens for supper, cleaning and washing.

"Tell Golda that Grandma's doing fine," I say. "But ya know, she has her ups and downs. Some days are better than others, that's for sure."

"Don't we all," he nods.

We then watch as a wrinkled, gangly man walks in carrying a puffy, purple bag. He's wearing a baseball cap that reads *Granola Floral* and a Minnesota Twins tee shirt.

"I'm looking for a Miss Crotch," he says, scanning me up and down.

Sheldon heaves out his sunken chest, concerned, and says, "What did you say to her, sonny?"

The guy's eyes dart back and forth, then lands on me again. "Are you Miss Crotch?"

"You need to watch your mouth," Sheldon says, stepping between him and I.

"I have some flowers for her, is all. Looks like they are from Dodo," he answers nervously, reading from a little envelope taped to the bag.

I pluck off the envelope. Sure enough, that is what's written on it. Pulling out the card, I see it's from Toby.

"Thank you," I say, pointing to the counter. "You can set it there."

"You're welcome. Enjoy your flowers, Miss Crutch."

"That's not my name," I say.

"So, they aren't for you?"

"Yes, they're for me. But my last name is Couch.

"Like the thing you sit on in the living room?"

"Yes. Exactly the thing you sit on in the living room. You guys just spelled it wrong."

He squints at me and says, "Sorry about that. It was a phone order and Dorothy at the front desk is a little hard of hearing."

Pulling a five dollar bill out of the register, I hand it to him as a tip just so he'll leave.

"Thank you, Miss Crouch."

"That's not my name, either."

"Whatever you say," he says, turning to leave. He gets in his little Kia Rio, lights a cigarette, and putters away.

As I unwrap the package, the clean, earthy aroma of the fresh flowers bursts out. I carefully take out the crystal-cut vase overflowing with a dozen red roses, white sprays of Queen Anne's lace and fat, golden daisies.

Sheldon starts chuckling, nodding his head.

"Look at them beauties. They must be from Toby?"

"Yes," I sigh.

"I think you got yourself a keeper there, Allison. You better not throw him back. There's a lot of fish in the sea, but not many who send a pretty girl, pretty roses."

"Awe, thanks Sheldon. And I think you're right about Toby," I say, apple-cheeked and rosy too. "I've never received flowers before."

Pulling out a rose, I give it to him. "Here, you give this to your lovely wife, Golda."

He waves his hand no.

"I've got a better idea. I'll just stop over at the florist and pick up my own bouquet for my bride. It's been more than fifty years and she hasn't thrown me back either."

~~~

Later in the morning while I'm doing inventory, a squat woman with tightly curled, pale blonde hair waddles into the store. It's Grettie Olson, Grandma's cousin who married their second cousin and have the inbred kids.

She hates Grandma, and by default hates me too. She always pretends she doesn't know me. I pretend to not know her, either.

"Hello, welcome to Whitehead's Hardware," I say.

"Hello," she answers. Her voice sounds as if she is gargling wet bread.

Grettie slogs to the back and makes a hard right into the gardening aisle. I follow her a few minutes later.

"Can I help you find something?"

She picks up a plaster-of-Paris garden gnome.

"Do you have the spring selection of Fingerlings?" she asks, stroking the red hat of the ugly elf.

Grettie Olson smells of yeasty dumplings. Her pull-on jeans are hitched up high. Her boobs flop over the wide waistband like oblong water balloons.

I shake my head and say, "I'm sorry ma'am. What selection of what?"

"Fingerlings. The miniatures. They're from the 'Elf in the Gay Garden' line."

"I don't know what that means."

"Fingerlings," she repeats, voice raised.

"You mean like the potatoes?"

She shakes the gnome at me. Her acne pocked face is dusted with pink talc. I notice her knuckles have dimples, like a young child's.

"No. Not the potatoes. Like the sly and mischievous elves that have little tea parties in your garden. Those Fingerlings. Do you have Fingerlings?"

I still don't understand what the heck she's talking about, so answer, "Uh, no. Just these 'Made in China' crappy lookin' elves."

Her head seems to explode with hatred for me. I still don't know what exactly Grandma said or did to burn the bridge with this family years ago, but I'm glad she did, whatever it may have been.

"You're a nut job just like that crazy grandma of yours. In fact, I think she's sneaking around and kicking over my garden gnomes. Next time it happens, I'm calling Sheriff Goldberg. I don't have proof but I know damn well it's Ethylon!" she yells, turning on her clogs.

"You're welcome. And say hi to your kids, I mean your cousins, my cousins, or whatever they are," I call after her.

Jimmy comes in as she's leaving and she nearly knocks him over, rushing out the door.

"Get out of my way you hippie freak," she snaps.

"That's Mr. Hippie Freak to you, madam," he answers as she storms down the sidewalk.

"Sorry about that Jimmy," I say, then head back to the paint aisle to finish my inventory. Jimmy follows and stands at the end with his hands on his skinny hips.

"You know what, Allison?" he says, gazing into the far off distance.

"No. I don't know what," I answer. "And I don't want to hear any of your war stories today."

"Did I ever tell you about the guy in 'Nam that jumped on a grenade and saved our squad?"

"No. Just leave me alone. I'm busy," I answer, but he ignores me.

Jimmy bounces up on his toes, wild-eyed, and says, "Well, he did. The Irish kid. Kinky red hair. We called him Pubic Head but his name was Private Bailey. It happened during a firefight in the north paddy south of Bao Hai."

Mr. Whitehead runs out of the back room swinging his coffee cup, bellowing, "Knock it off, Jungle Jim. You just heard that story about Private Pubic Head from Bill at the American Legion last night."

"I was there!"

"Getting drunk at the American Legion, yes, but not over fighting in 'Nam."

"I could have been."

"But you weren't."

"But I wanted to be," he says with hot, burning eyes.

Mr. Whitehead takes a step back, rubs his forehead and says softly, "Jimmy, I know you wanted to be there. We all know that. But you went where the Army sent you. That's all that matters so stop with the bullshit thinking you should've been somewhere else."

I don't understand how these veterans feel bad about not doing enough, or feel they could have, should have, would have done more. All I know is the guilt seems to last a lifetime for these guys.

Jimmy doesn't look up.

"Thank you for your service, Jimmy. And I mean that, buddy," Mr. Whitehead adds.

"You're welcome," Jimmy mumbles.

Mr. Whitehead grabs the inventory sheet from my hand, and says, "I'll order these tomorrow. Now, if you'll excuse me, I have work to do. God bless 'murica."

"Well, I better get going, too," Jimmy says.

"Have a good day, Jimmy," I say.

He halts and twirls back around.

"You too, Allison. Hey, how's that new dog of yours?"

"Doing fine. Just fine. I named her Maple because she's sweet as can be."

"I used to have a few pits myself, but when I moved into Mrs. Halverson's basement, had to give them up. She's allergic and all. But I sure miss those block heads."

He grins, then he asks, "Do you put Crisco on her?"

"That's different."

"Crisco," he repeats.

"I know you said Crisco. But why would I do that?" I ask, confused.

He looks at me like I'm a short stack of pancakes, and answers, "It'll keep her from getting hot spots. Their fur is crazy dry, so rub a little Crisco on her back, then brush it through. Works like a charm."

"I'll give it a try."

"The blue can. The big blue can."

"We have a can of that," I reassure him.

"Glad you and Toby did that, ya know. Everyone in town is glad you did that."

Jimmy runs a nicotine-tinted finger across his thin lips and continues, "How's Toby doing?"

"Not too bad."

"What do you mean, not too bad?"

"Mostly, he's fine, but if you want to know the truth, I think he has some rough patches to work through."

"Tell him if he ever needs to talk to someone, I'm probably not the best person to talk to. But if he wants to talk anyway, I'm all ears. Okay?"

I look at Jimmy like I've never seen him before. Obviously, I'm not giving this man enough credit.

"I'll be sure to let him know. Thanks, Jimmy."

As soon as he leaves, I look at my phone. A text from Toby dings in, saying he'll stop by later. I text him back with a smiling face.

CHAPTER TWENTY-FOUR

About noon, I bike over to Taco Gong to get some lunch.

When I return to Whitehead's, my stomach drops. And it's not because of the Loco Beano burrito.

"What's going on?" I ask, stopping in the doorway.

Toby's shaking his head, leaning back against the counter, looking down. Mr. Clancy is gripping his phone, wiggling it in his nervous hand. Mr. Whitehead is standing in the middle of the main aisle between them with his arms outstretched toward both of them.

All three men are silent for a second. Then, like a mother walking in on three misbehaving children, Mr. Clancy screams, "He hit me! He hit me!" pointing at Toby.

"No. No, he didn't, Clancy. He didn't hit you," Mr. Whitehead says, holding up both hands.

"He pushed me! And you let him, Whitehead!"

Toby doesn't move.

Mr. Whitehead's eyes crackle like broken glass. He says, trying to sound calm, "Mr. Clancy just called 911. Now, we have to stand here until Sheriff Goldberg shows up, so we can work this out."

"Work what out?" I ask, not sure I want the answer.

"You know why I called 911? I was being assaulted!" Mr. Clancy yells, pointing his finger towards Toby.

"No, you were not," Mr. Whitehead answers.

"He shoved me!"

"He moved you out of the way because you purposely bumped into him and started talking nonsense racist garbage," Mr. Whitehead says.

"But he vigorously shoved me!"

"I want to vigorously shove you every time you walk through my damn door, Clancy. So shut your big mouth," Mr. Whitehead retorts.

"I know he's got a gun because I know all the permits issued in this county. This is what happens. All kinds of people like him think they can move to town."

"What the hell does that even mean?" Mr. Whitehead asks, staring at Clancy.

"You know damn well what I mean."

"All I know is you weren't being assaulted," Mr. Whitehead answers. "Toby moved you out of his way because you were egging him on."

Toby remains quiet. He doesn't look at me, just at some far off distance on the floor.

Mr. Clancy thrusts his phone toward Toby, sputtering, "Guess what, hero? The police are coming. You can tell all your war stories to them."

"Please, Mr. Clancy, stop it," I say, walking forward. "Don't talk to him like that."

Toby doesn't react, but his whole body seethes, bubbling like a thick boiling stew.

Mr. Whitehead looks at them, then me, desperate, then says, "Let's just take a deep breath and calm down."

Toby clinches his arms around his stomach, hugging himself, trying to keep his anger inside.

We all hear Sheriff Goldberg's squad car pulling up to the store.

"How do you like being arrested, boy?" Mr. Clancy says, poking a chubby finger into his chest. "Or maybe your kind is used to that."

Toby pushes him roughly away and he stumbles back, knocking over a paint display.

Sheriff Goldberg rushes in the door with his hand on his holster, and asks, "What the hell is going on in here?"

"Watch out! He's got a gun!" Mr. Clancy hollers, pointing at Toby. "He assaulted me and now he's gonna shoot me!"

"No, he didn't and no, he's not," Mr. Whitehead yells.

Sheriff Goldberg steps between them and nearly spits,, "Both of you be quiet." Then he turns to Toby and asks, "Now son, where's your weapon?"

"Right side, sir."

"Will you do me a favor and put it on the counter? Until we get this sorted out?"

He doesn't move.

Sheriff Goldberg takes a deep breath, and asks, "You having a bad day?"

Toby doesn't answer, but his face softens.

"We all have some bad days now and then. Some are better than others, that's for sure," Goldberg says.

Toby takes out his gun and lays it on the counter.

The sheriff exhales, walks over and takes the pistol. He then adds, "Thank you. Now, if I was you, I'd go over to the American Legion, grab a burger, and hang out with those old geezers. There's no better therapy than talking with some old geezers that can put things in perspective. They might not be black, but they're your brothers in arms. Most have been through it all and lived to talk about it."

"Yes, sir," he mumbles.

"But I'm going to keep your weapon for a few days. You didn't do anything wrong, but I think it's best for now. I want you to cool down a bit."

"Yes, sir."

"You understand?

"Yes, sir."

Sheriff Goldberg then shifts and glares at Mr. Clancy. I've never seen the sheriff so angry before. He says in a low, hard voice, "Now, you listen here. I'm the only person authorized to be a bully in this town. Me. Not you. And I could make you have a very bad day. I could run you over like a hundred ton locomotive. Do you understand that?"

Mr. Clancy purses his lips, and looks away.

Toby rubs a hand slowly over his face, turns, and simply walks out the door. He doesn't want to talk to me, Mr. Clancy, Mr. Whitehead, Sheriff Goldberg, nobody, no more. He only wants to leave.

I become tongue tied. Speechless. Immobile.

I let him go.

Maybe he just needs to be alone for a bit.

As soon as I see him get in his truck and pull away, I realize I should not have let him go. I should have jumped on his back, tackled him, tied him up, something.

I have a sick feeling he ain't going to the American Legion for a beer and a Vikings game. But I let him go.

After everyone leaves, I send Toby a text, but get no reply. Twenty minutes later, still no answer.

Suddenly, Steph screeches into the parking lot out front and rips through the door in a wide-eyed panic.

"O M G! I think it's Toby's truck! O M G!" she yells.

"What?" is all I manage to say.

"On my way home from Grimoire! Come on!"

I jump into her car, and know she's blabbering a mile a minute but I have no idea what she's saying.

Not far out of town on the road to Grimoire, there's already several highway patrol cars, Sheriff Goldberg's squad, a firetruck and an ambulance.

I run toward the scene but wonder why someone is yelling in my ears. I realize the scream is coming from me.

I'm looking through a kaleidoscope of crinkled blue metal and shattered glass.

Someone pulls me back as I watch in still frames. Snap. Snap. Snap, as the paramedics lift the stretcher filled with Toby, still, lifeless, out of his crushed truck.

I can't believe this. Why didn't I stop him from leaving.

Puke rises up my throat. Which makes me stop screaming. I lunge toward the ambulance, but told no. no. not yet. no. you can't. let them go. you'll get in the way. stand back. it will be okay.

The wail of the sirens, lights flashing hysterically. My mind simply collapses. Can't think. My eyes, blood shot. I'm unable to process one. thing. more. An invisible and horrible fist hits me. The world goes dark.

Thank God it was all a dream. A terrible nightmare.

I must've fallen asleep on the counter after lunch. Or maybe I got food poisoning from Taco Gong, which is why I feel so nauseous.

All I need to do is stand up, go home, take Maple to the field and wait. Wait for Toby to come sit by me under the tree. This is all I need to do. This is all I want to do.

But I hear Grandma singing.

"Monkeys go to heaven in little row boats. Bunnies go to heaven in yellow rain coats. Cats go to heaven in high heeled shoes, but dogs go to heaven weeping the blues…"

I open my eyes. I'm home on the couch, and lift up to my elbows. Grandma's holding my socked feet in her lap. She stops singing, and smiles softly at me.

Bob is crouched in the arm chair, eyebrows crunched so tightly together they touch. Maple snuffles her soft, wet nose into my side.

Sitting on the floor in front of me, Steph is chewing her gum in long smacks. Laying her hand on my arm, she says, "Girlfriend. I'm so sorry about what happened to Toby."

It really did happen.

"I need to see him," I mumble.

"He's banged up bad, but will be okay. There's nothing we can do right now, so go back to sleep," Grandma says lucidly. Her age-spotted hands squeeze my toes.

"You fainted," Bob says.

"How did I get here?" I mutter.

"Steph brought you home. I gave you some of my pills to calm you down," Grandma answers. Her beautifully old, crazy face shines with all the love she has for me.

"Mr. Whitehead brought over some lefse and roast beef sandwiches, because whenever something bad happens, Norwegians always bring food," Steph says.

"Sheriff Goldberg said he'd give us a call later to let us know how Toby's doing. But he advised against going to the hospital right away. You wouldn't be able to see him anyway," Bob says. "We can get you there tomorrow."

Grandma gives me a glass of water and says, "Go back to sleep, Allison. It will help you with the worries."

I roll over, stick my face into the worn cushions as Grandma's pills take over. I want to be led somewhere that makes sense. I wish I still believed in Jesus so I could bow like a dog and pray for Toby.

I dissolve back to sleep.

CHAPTER TWENTY-FIVE

"Are you awake?" Bob calls from the kitchen. "Someone's at the door. Will you answer it, please."

I'm on the couch, curled up like a twisted tumor, brain aching, thoughts pulsing. The knocking becomes louder. From my head. Or the door. It's hard to tell.

"Allison, wake up," Bob says. "It might be some news about Toby."

As if slapped in the face, I remember now. Rushing towards the front door, I yank it open. Sheriff Goldberg takes a step back, both hands on his hips.

"Good morning, Allison," he says.

He looks grim but gives me a reassuring nod.

"How is he?" I ask, shielding my eyes from the crystal-clear morning.

"I need to come in for a minute," he says softly.

I step aside, and he wipes his big, black boots off on the rug in the entryway.

Grandma's shuffling around in her thick slippers, making coffee and clanging the cups.

"Ya'll better sit the heck down and tell us what's going on, Gabe," she says.

The good Sheriff takes a seat at the dining room table, grabs a napkin and twists it tightly until it's a thin mess.

I sit down too. Bob joins us.

"You want some coffee, Gabe?" he asks.

"No, thank you," he answers, throwing the mangled napkin aside.

"Horse shit. Drink this," Grandma says, slamming down a half cup of hot coffee in front of him. She pulls a bottle of Baileys out of the curio cabinet and fills the rest of his cup. Then, does the same to hers.

Both Bob and I are too upset to even protest. Sheriff Goldberg doesn't drink Grandma's jacked-up coffee, but lingers above the wafting aroma.

"Toby's at the St. Cloud VA hospital. He's going to be okay, but is in intensive care," he says. "Long story short, I went over to his mother's house to inform her of the accident. She jumped in my squad, and we drove to St. Cloud and she stayed most of the night. She just got home a few hours ago. I'm not sure if he can take visitors yet, but I bet he'd like to see you, Allison, when he can."

I nod.

"The state patrol took over the investigation."

"What's there to investigate?" Grandma asks.

"His blood alcohol level was over the legal limit. He had been drinking when this all happened, but I didn't realize it when he left the store. We aren't going to talk to him just yet, not until he is more stabilized."

Sheriff Goldberg is sitting here heartbroken, trying to maintain a professional demeanor.

"It's odd," he says. "There were no skid marks on the road. It doesn't appear he was trying to avoid a deer or something. More like he ran straight off the road into the damn ditch on purpose, allegedly, of course. So tell me, what did you see happen before I came into the store?"

I tell him the truth.

"I didn't see what led up to the fight, sir. But when I came in after lunch, Mr. Clancy got in his face, saying all this insulting stuff. He poked Toby with his greasy fingers. No one likes to be poked. So, he pushed Clancy away."

"And people wonder why I sneak over and shit on Clancy's lawn," Grandma mutters.

"Did you know Toby had been drinking?"

"No, I didn't. But I could tell he was upset," I answer, wanting to cry but my eyes are too dry.

Goldberg adds, "I'm very sorry...I should have...I'm sorry this happened. In my town."

He slowly gets up and I walk him to the door.

I follow him to the porch.

"You said Mr. Clancy was going to get in trouble about all the fraud and tax stuff. You said so. He shouldn't have been in the hardware store starting trouble with him in the first place," I quietly plead.

On the steps, Goldberg turns around, clears his throat and says, "Yes, Allison. I did say that about Clancy. And he probably will be charged. However, building a solid case takes time. But that's an other issue."

I don't say anything, so he adds, "Take care, dear. You go visit Toby today. I'm sure he'd like to see you."

"...thanks..." I whisper, and click the door shut.

I run into the bathroom, brush the furry coat off my teeth and slap my face with cold water. Taking a deep breath, my head begins to clear.

I need to talk to Mrs. Davenport. Maple chugs after me as I pedal over to Toby's house.

I walk quietly up to the porch and tap on her door.

Cats purr like tiny motor boats on the other side. Maple jaunts up the steps and cautiously sits beside me. But when she hears the cats, she barrels off the porch, bolting full speed home with her tail between her legs.

I knock again.

Nothing.

I knock louder.

Still nothing.

It feels like mosquitos are buzzing through my veins. I start banging on the door with my fist, then hit my head against it for good measure.

"Hang on," someone calls from inside.

Finally.

"Mrs. Davenport, hello?" I say through the door.

"Who's there?" a voice asks.

"Me," I answer, calming down.

"Who's me?"

"It's me, Allison Couch," I answer.

There is some shuffling, meowing and shooing until the door finally opens.

Mrs. Davenport is wearing an Easter egg yellow, velour robe wrapped tightly around her plump body. Her curly, black hair is flattened to one side. I obviously just woke her. With eyebrows up, she rubs her forehead, then pinches her eyes shut.

"Sorry, Mrs. Davenport. It's early. I just want to know how Toby is doing. And how you're doing."

Standing to the side of the door, she opens it wider, motioning for me to come in. The cats reappear, floating around her thick, bare legs.

I step inside and she leads me to the formal dining room. The scent of orange furniture polish and beloved, old books fills the room. There are books everywhere. High piles. Stacks. On the shelves. On the table. On the floor and on the chairs.

"I'm going to start the coffee. Would you like a cup, hon?" she asks.

"Sure," I answer, and she carefully removes a stack of books off a chair. I sit at the gorgeous, dark oak table centered with a bright red pot of white cyclamen.

Mrs. Davenport pads into the kitchen. A few minutes later, a rich drift of French roast floats out. She brings two porcelain cups of coffee to the table and sits down.

Her nails are short but fingers long and elegant like Toby's. She licks her generous lips, and they glisten. It's obvious where Toby gets his good looks.

"I just got home a few hours ago from the hospital," she says, her eyes fracked bloodshot pink. The skin around them are melted deep brown.

"Sorry about what happened," I blurt. "I just stopped over to see if maybe you need anything but I can't drive you anywhere I don't have my license maybe someday Toby has been teaching me he's so nice and puts up with all of me maybe someday I love him so much I can't stand it how is he now will it be okay?"

I start bawling. Mrs. Davenport puts her hand on mine, pushing a box of tissue towards me with the other.

"I've already been through a box of these, but have plenty more, hon," she says gently, smiling. I hardly know her but in this moment her eyes wrap me in warm compassion. I can't imagine what she's going through, yet here she is trying to make me feel better.

I dab my eyes and blow my nose.

"Toby thinks the world of you. All he talks about is you whenever he does decide to talk," she says.

"Oh gawd," I answer. "I'd bet my entire life on him."

She grabs a tissue also, lips tight, and answers, "I would, too, sweetie."

Mrs. Davenport stirs her coffee, glancing up at me, and continues, "I can't tell you enough how proud I am of my son." Then, shaking her head, she adds, "He used to be a chatterbox. I couldn't get him to shut up sometimes. But Afghanistan sure did a number on him."

I sigh. The coffee is cool enough to sip. She shuts her eyes while taking a slow drink and says, "He's had a hard time. After he was injured, he spent months at Walter Reed hospital. He recovered and went back to Fort Campbell to finish up his enlistment. He told me he was doing well. But he obviously wasn't. I just didn't know."

I'm sure he hid a lot of things from her.

She continues, "The first week or so after he got home he seemed fine, but I could tell he wasn't wrapped too tight. Spent all his time in his room. I had to send him on errands around town just to get him out of the house. I'm sure getting out of the army after eight years of that exciting lifestyle, all his buddies, traveling the world, all that adrenaline, the war, and to end up in little Granola, gave him time to think too much. But it was his decision to move here. He wanted to come here. I thought it would be good for him. Low key, low stress, not a lot of people or problems."

"How badly is he hurt now?"

"I was there at the hospital all night, and will go see him again later today. He's going to be fine, they say. Broke some ribs and a leg."

I hold my breath.

She adds, "He'll have some legal issues, but I don't care. He's alive and that's all I, we, need to focus on. Praise the good Lord Jesus Christ have mercy."

"Did they say how long he'll be in the hospital?"

"They have no idea. He's in intensive care, and will need more care after that. His VA doctors that have seen him before want to keep him there longer. To get him sobered up and get him some mental health help," she says. "There's an in-patient program for that."

"That would be good for him. I noticed him drinking at weird times of the day. I'm sorry for not making a bigger deal out of it. I probably should have said something to you earlier," I say.

"I should have mentioned something to you, also."

Mrs. Davenport pushes up and walks over to the majestic hutch in the living room. She pulls open a drawer, and takes out a box of Marlboro silvers. Lighting one, I watch the gentle puffs float in the air. The white swirls circle around her gracefully. The ribbons of smoke glide over and comfort me somehow.

She slowly nods and says, "That boy survives all that business in Afghanistan only to come home to hurt himself. Don't make sense."

Puffing out a cloud, she flicks the ashes into the pot until her cigarette is done. The blooms on the gentle flowers look down, petals back, gracefully sad as well.

Mrs. Davenport walks to the kitchen, turns on the faucet, then chucks the wet butt into the garbage can.

"Please don't tell Toby I still smoke," she adds, sitting back down at the table, properly folding her hands.

"I didn't see a thing, Mrs. Davenport," I say quietly.

"He keeps wanting me to meet your grand mother."

"People tend to find her, uh, interesting," I answer, reaching over to put my hands on hers, like I do on Grandma's.

She silently starts to pray. I can feel her desperate love for her son rushing up through my fingers. I don't believe in Jesus anymore, but, pray with her also, just in case.

She remains quiet, eyes closed, so I get up, slip on my shoes, and pedal back home.

CHAPTER TWENTY-SIX

"Bob! Will you take me to the Department of Motor Vehicles station in Grimoire so I can get my license today?" I yell, running through the front door.

Bob clicks off the TV, grinning, eyes twinkling.

"Why, Allison? So you can get your license and drive to St. Cloud?" he asks.

"To see Toby," Grandma pipes in, sitting at the dining room table, nervously knitting her Godzilla scarf.

"Yep. I need to," I answer.

"You better go and tell him to get well soon," she says. "And tell him not to worry about Clancy. I'll take care of that asshole. I have my ways, you know."

"Absolutely, Allison," Bob says, turning down *Jeopardy*. "I'd be more than happy to help you get your license."

"What time do they open today?" I ask.

"We can get you there by nine sharp and be the first in line," he answers.

"Well, I hope you don't run over that fake rubber kid like you did before," Grandma says. "You need to get that license so you can go see Toby."

I call Mr. Whitehead.

He tells me he's keeping the store closed today anyway. "We all need a day off after yesterday's excitement. You go do what you need to do. I'll be down at the American Legion, so if you need me for anything, that's where I'll be."

"Thanks, Mr. Whitehead."

"Good luck, Allison. I know you can get your license. And give my best to Toby."

I hang up and nod towards Bob.

He boosts himself off the couch and says, "Come on then, let's get going."

Grandma stands up, shoves her knitting needles at me and says, "Just tell old Helen at the DMV she still owes me for that time I saved her life from that crazy Cambodian lady with the three-legged cat that attacked her over at Oily Dick's bar. Helen owes me big time for that and needs to pass you on the driving test!"

"I'll use that as a plan B, Grandma," I answer, as Bob, Maple and I head out the door.

~~~

I'm parked in front of the motor vehicle building, waiting anxiously in the Buick Regal for my test to begin.

"Buckle up for safety," Miss Helen says as she stuffs herself into the car.

"Good morning," I answer. Maple sticks her blocky head on the front seat and licks Miss Helen's shoulder.

"Why is this dog in the car?" she asks, holding up her clipboard to protect herself from the slobber.

"She wanted to come with, is all," I answer. I then tell Maple to lay down and knock off the slurping, so she does.

"Is it a pit bull? It looks like a pit bull."

"Nope. She's a purebred, pedigreed bull-doodle. I paid a thousand bucks to AKC breeders in Fargo. You can only find fancy bull-doodles in fancy cities like Fargo, ya know, because they're so rare."

Miss Helen glares at Maple and lays her clipboard on her chubby knees.

"Name?" she asks with a huff.

"Maple."

"Maple what?"

"She doesn't have a last name. Just Maple."

Peering over her glasses, she says quite loudly, "I'm not asking about your over-priced, purebred ugly mutt. I'm asking what is *your* name."

"Oh."

"Name?"

"Allison."

"Allison what?"

"Couch," I answer.

"Like the thing you sit on in the living room?"

"No, ma'am. Not *like* Couch, but *exactly* Couch."

"Age?"

"Twenty-six."

There's a silence.

"Twenty-six," she repeats.

"Yes."

"And you're only now getting around to getting your license? Hmph."

"No, ma'am. I actually got around to it last month but you failed me."

Nodding, she says, "Oh. I remember you now."

She taps her pen while removing her bifocals, and adds, "Yes. You did indeed fail."

I roll my eyes as Miss Helen continues, "Well, then, Ms. Couch, like the thing you sit on in the living room. I hope you practiced so you don't fail again. Like you failed before. You don't want to waste my time and yours and fail twice in a row. This test is ninety-five bucks a pop. No refunds if you fail. Like you failed the first time."

"Yes, I understand that."

"You were a fail."

"Yes. I was," I say.

"A big fail."

"You can remind me again if you want, just in case you think I forgot."

She gasps, suddenly staring at me in shock and awe.

"Are you Ethylon's grand daughter?"

"Yes."

"Last time she was here she put the pedal to the metal straight through the DMV building."

"Uh, yeah, I heard about that, ma'am," I say, antsy to start my own driving test.

"She tried to bribe me with fifty dollars if I would pass her anyway. But, I couldn't because everyone was running out of the building screaming and crying. And then Sheriff Goldberg came, then the news reporter came ..."

I nod my head, not sure how to respond.

"So, how's Ethylon doing these days?" she adds, softening down, perking up, almost sounding friendly.

"Doing well, ma'am. Doing well," I answer.

"Does she still drink boiler makers?" she asks, starting to snicker into her clipboard.

"Umm, I'm don't know what those are."

"You don't want to know what they are but she could do three of those at the beginning of the night and still be the last one dancing when the lights came on!"

"I'm sure she could," I answer, staring through the windshield at the ominous driving route ahead of me.

I add, "Whatever they are…"

"She had a hard time keeping her clothes on. She used her brassiere like a slingshot one night, hit this guy in the face with a full can of Schlitz malt liquor," she says, laughing. "Broke his front tooth right out of his head."

"That sounds like Grandma."

"I heard she stopped drinking. But Mr. Clancy. You know Mr. Clancy, the county building inspector? He says she poops on his lawn. Is that true?" she asks.

I adjust the rear view mirror and answer, "Grandma told me you still owe her a favor. Something about a three-legged Cambodian cat and oily dicks."

Maple lets out a sigh behind me.

Miss Helen abruptly stops laughing, sits up, and clicks on her seat belt. She brings the clipboard back to her lap, regaining her composure.

Wiping the tears from her eyes, she says, "Okay, Miss Couch. We are about to begin the test. Please pull ahead. At the stop sign, you will turn right. From there I will continue to give you instructions. Is that understood?"

"Yes, ma'am," I answer, thankful we are starting this. I push my foot down slightly on the gas pedal and move the car forward. Here we go again.

~~~

I pass with flying colors.

They take my fingerprints and I pose for the mugshot photo. After I sign my name on the little computerized pad, the clerk shoves a thin, onion-yellow piece of paper across the counter without looking at me.

"Here's your receipt," he says. "You'll get your actual license in the mail in four to eight weeks if you're lucky. Maybe twelve or fourteen. Hopefully more like ten weeks, but might be as long as sixteen. Anyway, you'll get it at some point. In the meantime, keep this with you until then. This is your valid license until you get your official plastic card."

He then screams, "Next!" even though there is no one else in line.

"Thank you," I answer. I carefully fold the paper so it fits perfectly in my wallet, and run out the door. Bob is sitting outside on a stone bench, drinking a pop, surrounded by food wrappers.

"Well?" he asks, standing up, crumbs from a vending machine raspberry danish sprinkle down his solid belly.

"Bob! I did it! I got my license!" I squeal, handing him the keys and give him a big hug. Maple jumps around my legs, wanting a hug too, of course. She has no idea why I'm so happy, but if I'm happy, she is.

Bob gives me back the keys.

"These are yours, lovely lady. You take the dang keys. You drive us back to Granola."

Grandma is out by the side of the garage, watering her morning glories when we arrive home.

I roll carefully into the driveway and toot the horn. Grandma throws down the hose, flinging her arms wide open. She knows I passed the test.

I forget to put the car in park as I jump out, so it rolls back down the driveway. Bob yanks the emergency brake handle up as Maple yelps from the back seat.

"I got it!" I say, running into her skinny arms. It feels good to hug Grandma. She leans back a bit and smiles, "I knew you could do it. I knew you could get it all along. I'm proud as peaches of you, Allison. Always have been, always will be. You're a survivor like me."

I put my head down on her boney shoulder and keep hugging her.

"Sure enough she did it," Bob says, getting out of the car with Maple jumping behind.

"Well, then you better get back on the road to St. Cloud and go see Toby," she says, pushing me away.

"You know how to get there? Do you have UPS on that fancy phone of yours?" Bob asks.

"GPS? Yes, I do. I'm sure I'll find it just fine," I answer.

"Bring me back some cheese curds from the *Keep on Truckin' Oasis* just outside of St. Cloud. Get me the spicy buffalo ones. Tell Clyde the owner you're my grand daughter and he'll give you a few bags and a free tank of gas," Grandma says. "He still owes me for a couple of hand jobs from back in the day."

"I don't want to hear about that, Ethylon," Bob says.

He pulls a twenty out of his wallet, presses it into my palm, and says, "Here's some gas money. First tank will be my treat." He pulls out another ten and adds, "And this is for just-in-case. Spicy buffalo cheese curds and such."

"Thanks, Bob."

"Drive safe and say 'hi' to Toby for me," he says.

"Will do. Thanks again."

Maple leaps back into the car beside me.

"Sorry, girl," I say, petting her thick head. "You have to stay home. I'll tell Toby you're thinking about him, okay?"

She seems to understand and jumps out.

Before I go, I text Steph the good news about the license. She texts back a big CONGRATS, STOP BY WHEN YOU GET HOME, SAY HI TO YOUR BOYFRIEND!

I plug in the key. The dashboard lights up, and the engine grumbles.

Grandma and Bob, with Maple beside them, stand in the yard until I back out again. They wave until I turn the corner and drive out of sight.

CHAPTER TWENTY-SEVEN

Leaving Granola completely on my own for the first time in my life, I roll the window down once I get on the interstate, wondering why I haven't done this years ago.

I turn on the radio, and the only station I pick up is Garrison Keillor talking about loons and lutefisk and lakes. After twenty million years on air, you'd think at some point he'd find something else to talk about. But he never does, so I flip the radio off.

Once I told Mr. Whitehead we should pay for a billboard or something along the interstate, to get more travelers as customers to come to the store. He emphatically said, 'Hell no. I hate billboards. Ugliest things I ever seen. Got these fifty foot high Norwegian pines and you gonna put up a billboard? Nothing is worthy enough to cut down God's pine trees and put up some damn advertisement,' he answered.

I'm glad he didn't listen to me back then. Instead, I listen to the rushing, summer air and brawny pines swishing by along my way.

~~~

I make it to the VA hospital in St. Cloud.

It's a square monument of stone and concrete. A soft-green glows from the hundreds of square windows. Prim trees and pruned bushes, in orderly formations, are neatly encircled by red mulch.

There's a slow processional of both old and young men in wheelchairs, being pushed by worried family members, weaving in and out of the revolving door. Most everyone else has either a cane, cast or walker.

I pull into a parking spot, hitting the car in front of me. Almost relieved, I at least now have something else to worry about other than Toby. I quick leave a note and stick it under their windshield wiper with my phone number, apologizing.

Inside, the floors shine with industrial wax. The long, wide halls whiff of bleach and lemon sanitizer. The people range from fat, tattooed bikers to elderly trim gentlemen in golf polos. Clustered outside office doorways, looking through paperwork, they glance at me, nodding.

It doesn't take long to locate the intensive care unit.

"Sorry. The doctor ordered very limited visitors for Mr. Davenport. He can only have members of his immediate family at this time," says the pretty, freckled nurse from behind the high counter.

"Yes, I know that."

"Are you a family member?" she grimaces.

"I'm his sister," I answer with a straight face.

"He's black."

"He's adopted."

"His mother's black."

"She's adopted too."

The nurse slaps her hand to her forehead, stands up and leans over the ledge. Under her breath, she says, "Look. If you're his girlfriend, just say you're his girlfriend. Mmm 'kay?"

"I'm his girlfriend."

The nurse sits back down and gives me a big smile. "Alrighty then. So what I can do now is give Mrs. Davenport a call to verify and get her permission. If she approves of you, I can let you in."

"Thank you, ma'am."

"And your name is?"

"Allison."

"Allison what?"

"Allison Couch."

"Like the thing you sit on in the living room?"

I take a deep breath and answer, "Yes. Exactly like the thing you sit on in the living room."

Her eyebrows shoot up. Giggling, she says, "Oh my gawd, that is too cute. His last name is Davenport, ya know, like the thing you sit on in the living room."

"Yes, ma'am. I know that."

The nurse picks up the phone. In about thirty seconds, she hangs up and bustles out from behind the desk. She swipes her security card on the heavy doors. There's a loud click, and they fly open.

I clip behind her, my heart clomping like a galloping horse. When we reach his room, she opens the door, steps aside, and motions for me to enter.

~~~

My love for Toby overwhelms my entire body.

It's hard to breathe, my heart panics. I want to press my hands on him like a televangelist, or shaman, or clary sage witch, and heal him.

He turns his head from the yakking CNN anchor on TV towards me. His broad chest heaves up, then down. His stomach is wrapped thickly in white bandage, and he has two tubes disappearing underneath the gauze. Several machines beep and blink next to his bed.

He smiles weakly.

One of his eyes is swollen nearly shut and he has fresh stitches from the side of his forehead into his hair. His left leg is in a fresh cast.

"Hi, Ally."

He's the only person that has ever called me Ally.

I pull up a chair as close to his bed as possible. He has a tube going into his wrist too, so I carefully lay my hand on his outstretched palm.

"Sorry," he says.

"Sorry," I answer.

I'm not sure what he's sorry about.

"Don't be sorry," I say, and my hand molds into his.

"Don't you be either," he answers, and limply holds my hand back.

I realize I've been waiting to meet him all my life.

Without looking, I found someone who makes me the most beautiful and smartest woman in the world. I want to be with him, all my pieces. All the time. And he can throw all of his on me, and I will not sift nor sort them, just let them tumble on the table, and let them be.

I tug on my nose, now nervous, wanting to say the right thing to him, to make it all better, to make the heavens open and angels sing.

"Do you like beans in your chili?" I ask, because I have no idea what to say.

He immediately answers, "Yes. But I also like noodles in my chili. Beans are fine, but have you ever tried it with those little hollow noodles?"

The room brightens.

"You mean elbow macaroni?" I ask.

"Yes, those," he says.

"No. I tried chili with rice in it though, that was good."

"Rice would be good in chili, as long as there is cheddar cheese on top. And sour cream."

"And Fritos," I add.

"Of course, Fritos. Not a little, but a lot."

He takes a labored breath and continues, "I make a mean chili. I'll put some 'peenyoz' from Farmer Chuck in there, you just wait."

"You make me some when you get out of here."

A young, harried nurse rushes in, wearing panda printed scrubs and pink rubber clogs.

Toby sits up a bit and opens up his other hand, hungry for his pills. She pours the plastic cup into his palm.

After he swallows them, she takes his temperature, checks the machines and types in a note on a laptop. She then pinches around on the IV tube, turns up something, then fluffs up his pillow.

"You're doing great, Mr. Davenport. Your mission now is to sleep and not move too much," she says. "Roger dodger over and out?"

"Affirmative," he replies, grinning.

The nurse flicks up the remote and clicks off the TV. She holds up a hand, flashing two fingers at me and mouths, 'two minutes please,' before bustling out.

Toby melts back into the bed, releasing my hand.

"Hey," he asks, serenely. "How'd you get here?"

"Drove."

"Did you get your license?"

"Yep."

"About damn time. We've got a lot a places to go."

"I bet my life we do…"

His eyelids flutter down.

I sit quietly, smiling at him, until he drifts off to sleep.

THE FINAL CHAPTER

Toby and I are celebrating his two years of sobriety today.

At the hospital, it was discovered through an initial blood draw that he was nearly twice the legal alcohol limit when he ran off the road. When he was stabilized, he was transferred to the addiction and mental health program at the VA. He ended up with a DWI, but the judge was easy on him as long as he completed treatment.

I drove to St. Cloud every Saturday to see him. Sometimes by myself, sometimes with the traveling fun show of Jimmy, Bob and Steph.

But without Grandma.

She died a few weeks after I got my license. In her sleep. When Bob, Maple and I opened the door to her room that morning, wondering why she hadn't come down for breakfast, she truly did look like an angel at rest.

Grandma believed in Jesus, so is up in heaven raising hell, I'm sure of it. She left me the house and a very secure financial future. I loved, love and will always love her so much I want to crack into tiny pieces.

Yet, it was bittersweet, because I also felt some relief. With her passing, and me having to let go of her, I felt a certain freedom. I was finally able to move on and reach forward. Toby embraced me back with open arms.

He spent nearly five months in St. Cloud before returning home to Granola. That was the second happiest day of my life.

The first happiest day was our wedding day last year.

Steph was the maid of honor and Kristin, Maggie Root and three of Toby's cousins were my bride's maids.

Maple was the ring bearer, even though she ran around the church, shaking the little pillow with the ring on it for about five minutes. Toby had to lure her to the alter with a communion wafer to get the ring back.

Both Bob and Mr. Whitehead walked me down the aisle. Jimmy was an usher, and he didn't do anything stupid, because Sheriff Goldberg was the other usher.

Mrs. Davenport and his entire family sang choir, then kept singing through the night at karaoke until five a.m.

A dozen cute, beefy guys who were in the Army with Toby came to town for the wedding.

Let's just say Steph, as well as all the other girls in Grimoire county, had a pretty good time that week. I'm not saying anything more about that.

What happens in Granola, stays in Granola.

Except Emily, Kristin's sister.

The day after our wedding, she eloped to Las Vegas with Theodore, a retired infantry captain who's left leg was blown off in Iraq.

When they came back a week later, they bought a hobby farm in southern Minnesota and are now raising alpacas. Toby, Maple and I go visit them once a month.

Goldberg was right about Mr. Clancy. The federal investigators had their case against him locked down tight.

About three months into Toby's treatment stay, they showed up at Clancy's house with a warrant for his arrest. They hauled him down to Minneapolis to face some serious charges of fraud and theft by swindle.

Clancy was dirtier than anyone in our naive little town could imagine. With no real choice, he had to accept a plea bargain. He was sent to do time for seven years, but will get out in half of that. Half is better than none, I guess.

Clancy's wife divorced him, sold their house and moved to some religious commune in Idaho. She now sells macrame plant hangers on Etsy.

Devin is a whipped dog with his tail between his legs. Caught up in all his father's drama, I almost feel sorry for that guy. But not too much.

Bob still comes over every night to watch game shows and usually ends up sleeping on the couch.

He took it hard after Grandma died. Real hard. But we hold up together. Toby, Maple and I need him as much as he needs us. I just can't imagine life without Bob on the couch. Either can Maple.

Toby has bad days too, sure, but I still have a few also. When they happen, we stay up all night talking with our arms wrapped around each other. Sometimes, though, without saying a word, we'll just let each other be.

Mrs. Davenport fusses about me eating too much fast food, or Toby getting Bs when he should be getting A grades in school. Just like the mother I never had but always wanted, she begins her list of advice with, 'Allison, now this is none of my business, but ya'll need to...'

For example, she'll say, "This is none of my business but ya'll need to read bedtime stories to my grand babies.' She brings over books by Toni Morrison, Marlon James and James Baldwin, you know, light reading like that.

And just like Grandma, she wants 'tons of grand babies!' I don't know about a 'ton' of babies. I do have a bun in the oven now, so we'll just start with one. But we haven't told her yet, because she'd probably send over a U-Haul full of books.

Kristin is lovely and very fat. I never knew she had such a great sense of humor. She can't stand kale chips anymore and only goes for barbecue ripple Lay's with homemade sour cream-bacon-cheddar-chive-ranch dip.

Her husband Zach can't keep his hands off the dip. Or her. She now pushes a double designer stroller around, full of Chloe and Zoe, their adorable, curly-haired twin girls.

Every Wednesday, Kristin and the twins come over while Toby and Zach go to their AA meeting in Grimoire. Bob, me and Kristin sit on the couch, order pizza and watch game shows.

Maple and the babies roll on the floor and have the best time ever. Her glorious pit bull instinct of being a 'nanny' dog shines through.

Kristin is making elaborate plans to turn Grandma's room into a gender neutral nursery, and has the color scheme all contrasted and coordinated.

She wants to knock out a wall and hire a contractor to turn it into a big bay window. She said that circus animals are 'so ten years ago and endangered animals are in.'

Rich mothers in the new developments around town are calling her because they want her to design their nurseries too.

Florence Fiddle Bottom, by the way, is doing fine.

Chad, Steph's Taco Gong boyfriend, managed to pass the drug test for the Army and joined soon afterwards.

He's down in Georgia learning how to jump out of airplanes. Toby's proud of him but Steph is the proudest.

A few months ago, she packed up her kids in the red Chevy Gran Prix, drove down there and married him. Although she never made it to nursing school, she doesn't care. She's happier than when the McRib comes back.

Mr. Whitehead retired last year and I bought the store.

On the last day he worked, he showed me how to make the keys. With great pride, he cranked up the screeching machine and taught me everything. The key he had me duplicate was his own key to the store.

However, whenever I get a key request, I call him to ask for help instead. He'll drop everything and shuffle over as fast as he can. Nothing brightens his day more than shaving out a key.

To help me at Whitehead's Hardware, since I spend a lot of time back in the office, I hired Melanie.

She's a misfit teen lesbian who barely made it out of high school. With neon blue hair and a pierced nose, she's a fireball of energy and ideas. Showing up early, leaving late, she is honest as a Minnesota summer day is long.

But she always asks me to show her how to make the keys. And everyday, I answer as nicely as I can, 'No, not today, Melanie. Maybe tomorrow.'

She nods her head, signs her time card, puts on the red apron, goes up front to make the popcorn and deal with Jimmy and whoever else walks in.

Jimmy, by the way, won $50,000 from a scratch off lottery ticket. But he blew it all on truck stop hookers and cocaine. He was broke again six months later.

What more can be said.

That's life, in Granola, Minnesota.

THE END

IN GRATITUDE

Mary Doyle, thank you for being gentle with my cringeworthy drafts and questions. You've believed in me from day one and I'll appreciate that to the end.

LeAnne Howe, thank you for getting my style of writing. Your amazing support truly changed everything.

Anitra Budd, thank you once again for your sharp advice and encouragement. Your help is incomparable.

Beth Caruso, thank you for your honesty. I'm blessed to have you by my side as we continue life's great adventure that began so long ago and so far away.

Alun Seymour, I'm fortunate to have 'met' you. Your insistence for accurate details is invaluable. I admire your passion for a good, believable story. Cheers.

Sandy Esson-Grogor, thank you my deer fiend. Your my favorite spelling and grammer nerd.

Ayden and Ariel, thank you for your patience and staying out of my hair when I said I was busy. I love you both more than anything in the world.

THE LOFT LITERARY CENTER
&
THE MCKNIGHT FOUNDATION

Thank you for your generous fellowship.

www.loft.org

www.mcknight.org

VETERANS WRITING PROJECT

Thank you for your support and mentorship.

www.veteranswriting.org

ABOUT THE AUTHOR

Susanne retired from the US Army Reserve, having served as a photojournalist in Bosnia, Cuba, Panama and twice in Kuwait. She also trained as a drill sergeant.

She is a former Peace Corps Volunteer, Thailand, and also worked in Israel and North Yorkshire, England.

She holds a English degree from the University of Minnesota and is the recipient of the 2015 McKnight Artist Fellowship in Creative Prose.

Her website is: www.aspleywrites.com

YOUR NEW BEST FRIEND IS WAITING

Please consider adopting your next dog.
In Minnesota, a good place to start is:
www.secondhandhounds.org